Michelle Davies was born in Middlesex, raised in Buckinghamshire and now lives in north London.

Before turning her hand to crime, Michelle was a journalist writing for women's magazines, including *Marie Claire*, *YOU* and *Stylist*. Her last staff job before going freelance was as Editor-at-Large at *Grazia* and she was previously Features Editor at *Heat*. She began her career straight from school at eighteen, working as a trainee reporter on her home-town newspaper, the *Bucks Free Press*. In between writing her novels she now mentors upcoming crime fiction authors.

Also by Michelle Davies

Shadow of a Doubt

DC MAGGIE NEVILLE SERIES

Gone Astray
Wrong Place
False Witness
Dead Guilty

THE
DEATH
OF ME

MICHELLE DAVIES

ORION

An Orion paperback
First published in Great Britain in 2021 by Orion Fiction,
an imprint of The Orion Publishing Group Ltd,
Carmelite House, 50 Victoria Embankment,
London EC4Y 0DZ

An Hachette UK Company

1 3 5 7 9 10 8 6 4 2

A CIP catalogue record for this book is
available from the British Library.

ISBN (Mass Market Paperback) 978 1 4091 9346 3
ISBN (eBook) 978 1 4091 9347 0

Typeset by Input Data Services Ltd, Somerset

Printed and bound in Great Britain by Clays Ltd, Elcograf S.p.A.

www.orionbooks.co.uk

To Mary and Joe

Prologue

I've never liked swimming in the sea. Even the slightest tang of salt water on my lips makes me gag. Such was my loathing of it as a child that on holiday I would never venture further than the shallows, primed to run back up the beach the moment I feared the sea was getting too rough and might splash me. As an adult I never willingly go near it.

This I am reminded of when I am shoved forward into the next breaking wave and it hits me full in the face. I retch as my mouth is doused and water reaches my throat. Coughing furiously to expel it, I battle between wanting to keep my lips tightly sealed and knowing I have to keep sucking down deep breaths for as long as I can, for as long as I remain above the surface.

The waves are at my waist now and the further we've waded from the shoreline the more urgent they've become. The rising current pulls at the folds of my dress while the trainers he forbade me to discard on the beach now encase my feet like cement. Every step forward is a physical strain but he doesn't care – he is impatient and testy, pushing and shoving me onwards until dry land is far beyond my reach.

We shuffle onwards until the water laps my shoulders. It's here he finally unties my wrists. I beg him to let me go back, to think about what he's doing, but he's much taller than me so he's not out of his depth yet, and because of that he wants to keep going. I'm shivering with terror as much as from cold and I'm trying desperately not to cry, knowing I need to preserve every ounce of energy I have left if I'm going to survive this. And I need to survive for Daniel. I want to howl when I think about how I've let my son down. I could've stopped all this after what happened at the awards. I should've heeded the warning. But I didn't, I kept going in my pursuit of the story and this is where it has brought me, up to my neck in freezing cold sea off the Devon coast, about to be drowned.

I take another step forward but this time my foot doesn't connect with the bottom. It's a shelf break and the sudden drop knocks the wind out of me as I plunge below the surface. I want to scream that I'm not ready, that I haven't taken a big enough breath, but the water has already closed over my head and then I feel his hand upon my crown, pushing me deeper still. I claw at his skin, raking it with my nails so sharply I must be drawing blood, but he has a fistful of my hair now and I'm writhing back and forth but it's not getting me anywhere, so I grab his wrist with both hands and pull as hard as I can so he loses his footing and plunges beneath the waves with me and it works, he's loosened his grip.

But I can't fathom which way is up now. The current is pulling me back and forth like I'm a rag doll and I'm trying to kick, I'm trying to get back to the surface, to fresh air . . .

Come on, Natalie, kick.

I break the surface, gasping, but the next wave pummels into me and I'm under again. I keep trying to swim upwards but I'm so tired already and my eyes are stinging and I know I can't scream or call for help because I mustn't let any water in.

Kick, Natalie, kick.

Then he's next to me. I can't see him in the murky darkness

2

but I know he's there. He's grabbing at me and I'm trying to swim away but he's too strong . . .

OhmygodallIwanttodoisbreathein.

My lungs are burning now and I feel dizzy and sick and my arms are heavy and everything hurts, everything really hurts . . .

Kick Natalie, kick.

I'msinking . . .

lungsburning . . .

thepain . . .

Kick, Natalie, kick.

needair . . .

haveto . . .

breathein . . .

So I do.

Chapter One

Four weeks earlier

TUESDAY, 4TH JUNE

I've been staring at the sums on the spreadsheet for the past hour and they don't add up whichever way I look at them. Even including potential income for articles I've pitched to editors but haven't actually been commissioned to write yet makes no difference: the outgoing column of my finances still exceeds the incoming by an eye-watering amount. I fiddle with the figures a bit more, trying to trick my brain into believing I am better off than I am, but the spreadsheet refuses to bend the truth: I am broke, in debt and it's getting worse.

With a tremulous sigh I snap my laptop lid shut, wishing that out of sight really did mean out of mind. Instead, my cash flow imbalance is a constant, hovering presence, like a fly that can't be swatted, a direct consequence of being a self-employed writer in an industry that apparently values creativity over actually paying people on time or half decently. But covering the music scene for national newspapers and magazines on an ad hoc basis has positives that far outweigh the negatives, the most important being I set my own hours and can work flexibly around my son's schooling on the days I have him.

I leave my laptop on the table in the reception room and

retrieve my mobile from its charger in the kitchen. There's a pressing call I need to make, but it's indicative of how much I'm dreading it that I call my landlord first to tell her my rent is going to be late again. On answering she listens politely to my grovel-soaked explanation, then sighs when I finish by saying, 'Please don't tell Mum and Dad', which admittedly is a strange thing to say to your landlord when you're a thirty-seven-year-old woman who has lived independently of her parents for almost two decades, but in this instance my landlord is also my godmother, Gayle.

It was to her and not my parents that I turned when my marriage fell apart eighteen months ago. They viewed the divorce as my fault and sided with my ex, Spencer, whereas Gayle, a friend of Mum's from school, simply consoled and counselled me and kept me supplied with gin. She also, on hearing I was having to leave the marital home, invited me to stay at the Maida Vale mansion flat she bought in the sixties with her late husband, Charlie, when property in this exclusive part of London cost less than a week's holiday in Spain would set you back today. The apartment sat empty apart from the odd weekend when Gayle would leave her main residence in our home county of Suffolk to shop on Bond Street and she said I'd be doing her a favour by keeping an eye on it.

'Of course I won't tell them, Natalie,' she says, 'but if they knew you were struggling I'm sure they'd help.'

'I don't want to worry them.'

'In that case, don't think about paying me anything this month. It doesn't matter,' says Gayle.

'It matters to me,' I reply hotly. Gayle was disinclined to charge me any rent at all when I first moved in, but I didn't want to fall into the trap of not paying anything and then thinking I was better off than I am. So we agreed on an amount that is nominal when compared to what it would really cost to rent

6

in Maida Vale, one of the wealthiest areas in London. 'I'm due a payment from *The Times* on Friday. I'll transfer what I owe as soon as it's in my account,' I add.

'You know I don't care about the money, Natalie. My concern is that you're struggling and that will impact on you getting Daniel back.'

Mention of my ongoing custody battle prompts my stomach to flip-flop. On my spreadsheet there is a column entitled 'legal costs' and it's the most depressing of all. I am spending thousands I don't have on fighting my intractable ex for equal custody, funded at first by a loan, but now creeping onto credit cards. The battle has become protracted and costly because I'm trying to persuade the family court that my letting Daniel stay with Spencer when I moved out wasn't the abandonment he claims it to be.

'It won't. My solicitor is doing a great job,' I say. It is a whopper of a lie, but I cannot bring myself to admit to Gayle that my solicitor has paused working on my case until I can settle what I already owe him. She would be rightly horrified if she knew. But I'll find a way to pay, I always do.

'I'm glad to hear that,' she replies. 'You must keep me updated while Andrew and I are away.'

Andrew is what Gayle calls her companion and next week they are flying to Kenya for a month's vacation. He's nearly twenty years younger than my godmother and wants to marry her but at seventy-one she says she feels too long in the tooth for a third shimmy up the aisle. She reckons Charlie and his brief successor, Leon, who she married in regretful haste in the early days of widowhood when grief stopped her seeing straight, have between them provided as much matrimony as any woman needs in her lifetime. She's a great role model.

'In the meantime, why don't I lend you some money to tide you over while we're away?'

My cheeks burn with shame that she's felt compelled to offer. 'Thanks, but I already owe you enough.'

'Natalie—'

'Sorry, I've got to dash. Someone's sent me an email with a commission and I'd better reply to it. Have a great trip and I'll see you when you're back.'

I hang up before she can respond, feeling wretched that I fibbed so I could get off the phone. There's no email waiting in my inbox I need to reply to, no commission I should hurriedly accept. My synced-up phone would've beeped with a notification if there were.

Ironically, music was never my passion growing up. I was a journalism studies post-grad desperate to get a foot in any door, so I applied for, and bluffed my way into, a junior writer's role on a weekly music magazine called *The Frequency*. The magazine has since folded, along with half a dozen music titles like it, so now I freelance for publications here and abroad supplying interviews, reviews and features. It turns out I'm very good at it too, which is why my name is always high on the list for the best gigs and events and why I'm on first-name terms with a raft of music stars and record company executives. The kudos that comes with famous people knowing who you are is extremely potent and seductive and that's why it's easy to justify rejecting the stability a staff job would give me. Then I remind myself that yesterday I pitched a feature idea to one publication that a few years ago might have earned me £500, only for the commissioning editor to email back offering £75 for 1,200 words. 'Budgets are tight,' she wrote. You don't say.

I plug my phone back into its charger and make a cup of tea. It's mid-afternoon and I've got a few hours to kill before I head out to a showcase for a new female singer whose record company insists is this year's/month's/week's Next Big Thing. I've heard a sample of her songs, and while she'll never be my thing, I'm not going to turn down an interview I can sell on or an evening of free alcohol.

Tea made, I open the floor-to-ceiling French doors leading from the reception room onto a secluded private patio, a perk of being on the ground floor. I once looked up how much other apartments in the block have sold for and should Gayle ever sell this one she would walk away with around two million. Even when I get my share from the sale of the house in Clapham that Spencer and I bought together, where he and Daniel still live, I'll never be able to afford anything as lovely.

It's warm outside and I let the mellowness of the mid-June day wash over me as I set my mug down on the wrought-iron patio table. I love how tranquil it is out here. To the right of the patio there is a gate that opens onto a beautifully maintained communal garden, its dense hedgerows buffering noise from the surrounding streets. Sometimes it's so quiet it's easy to forget I'm in the capital, where nearly nine million people live cacophonously cheek to jowl, and not somewhere in the countryside.

I fetch my laptop from indoors and settle down to work. Ignoring my finances spreadsheet, I open another one entitled 'commissions' that helps me keep track of all the ideas I pitch. I'm fortunate compared to the vast majority of freelancers in that papers and magazines will approach me to write for them because of my specialism, but I still send ideas in on spec because I don't take the work for granted. Right now, however, there is a depressing lack of ticks in the column marked 'responded', so I spend the next half an hour chasing up commissioning editors, only to receive 'out of office' replies from half of those I email, the causal effect of it being the onset of summer and the start of the great annual getaway.

I fire off a couple more emails then open my internet browser and click on the first tab on the right. An amateurishly designed page titled 'Below the Line' pops up and a smile spreads across my face. This is my guilty pleasure, an American gossip site that peddles the most ridiculously salacious and invented titbits about celebrities that would never make it past UK defamation or libel laws to publication. The way the site works, and what I like about it most, is that it posts a story dropping clues about an unnamed celebrity and subscribers have to guess who it is. I do far better at this than I ever would a round of *Pointless*.

The first couple of posts are too obvious to tax my brain but then a heading halfway down the page jumps out at me.

Is one of music's greatest mysteries about to be solved?

We're told that producers in London have been snapping up songs by a mystery songwriter and that some of the tracks have gone on to be solid top ten hits and one was even award-nominated last year. But no one knows the songwriter's name and the only point of contact is via a lawyer. Why the cloak and dagger? It turns out the lyricist in question was a massive star until he did a headline-grabbing retreat from the spotlight – but his disappearing act was FAKED and he's really been in hiding. It's debatable whether the stars he's turned hit-maker for are going to be happy when they find out about his resurrection though – when he left the scene his reputation was dead in the water.

My forehead creases as I ponder the possibilities. Who the hell could it be? Then I scroll down to see what guesses have been posted beneath it and my jaw drops.

AF123: My money's on Isaac Naylor. 'Dead in the water' is a dead giveaway!

SoulSista: Isaac Naylor. Has to be. I've heard loads of people say he faked his suicide, so this proves it.

TaDa: How mad would you be if you were the rest of the band and he'd pretended to be dead all this time????

SteviesMicks: Forget the band, what about his family? I remember seeing pix of his baby brother sobbing at his funeral. Bloody heartbreaking.

BanalBob: Isaac Naylor was a GOD. Even if this were true, which I don't believe for a second, he'd never write songs for shit pop stars. He was too cool for that.

I am incredulous. Isaac Naylor was the lead singer of The Ospreys, the most successful British alt-rock band to rival Coldplay. Record-breaking stadium tours, four consecutive number one albums and the kind of fame that meant even your granny had heard of them. Then it all came crashing down about eight years ago, on the opening night of the band's latest tour. A teenage fan was found dead in Naylor's hotel room in Glasgow with a heroin needle still lodged in the crook of her arm. Naylor, who'd not been long out of rehab after years of highly publicised drug addiction, was arrested on suspicion of causing her death, but two weeks later, while out on police bail, drowned himself off the coast in Devon.

I re-read the post and shake my head in wonderment. The suggestion that he faked his suicide is bizarre. How could he have done it? Where would he have been hiding all this time? Naylor was one of the most famous men on the planet – how could he just vanish and never be seen again? It's impossible.

As my mind throws up more questions, I check the timestamp on the blind item and see it was posted only half an hour ago. With a chuckle I screen-grab it and email it to my best friend Bronwyn, who loves industry gossip as much as I do because she's the manager of a recording studio in south London and knows everyone who's anyone. It's how we bonded: I was invited to the studio to watch a band record and she and I got chatting between takes and she told me a brilliant bit of gossip about a girl band member and her manager and that was that, we were friends. In the ten years we've known each other Bronwyn has become the second most important person in my life after Daniel, the one friend in London who appreciates how insane my hours can be because hers are similar and who doesn't judge me for them. My best friends from home and the school gate mums I hang out with, lovely as they are, don't understand why I don't apply for a position with regular hours, as though it were that simple. It's only Bronwyn's unequivocal support that has kept me sane during my wretched divorce.

Within five minutes of me pinging her the screenshot, Bronwyn's on the phone, as I knew she would be, and I laugh as I answer the call.

'I know, right? Can you imagine if it was true! It would be the comeback of all time,' I say.

'Natalie, where did you see this? I need to know, now.'

Bronwyn's serious tone quells my laughter. This is not the response I was expecting.

'Um, it's on that American gossip site I've told you about.'

'Right. What's it called again?'

I regale her with the name then I hear her repeat it as though she's talking to someone in the background, except her voice is muffled like she's holding her hand over her phone. I can't hear what the person says in reply; I can't even tell if they're male or female. Then Bronwyn's voice rings clearly back on the line.

'Is that the only place you've seen it?' she asks.

'Hang on,' I say. I do a quick internet search using the key words 'Isaac Naylor', 'mystery songwriter' and 'lawyer' but only the blind item is returned. 'It doesn't look like it's been picked up yet, but it was only posted half an hour ago,' I say. 'You know it's bollocks, right? It's made up.'

Again Bronwyn repeats what I say to whoever is in the room with her.

'Who's that you're talking to?' I ask her.

'No one,' she replies quickly. A pause follows. 'Just don't tell anyone else about this, OK,' she says sternly. 'And definitely don't forward the screen-grab to anyone else, Nat.'

'What?' I laugh, bemused by how snippy she's being. 'Why ever not?'

'Because I'm asking you not to,' she says. 'Look, I have to go, I'll call you later.'

'Bronwyn—'

'I mean it, Nat. Don't tell anyone else about this.'

Chapter Two

Daily Mirror

16 July 2009

Take that, Robbie!

The Ospreys shatter Robbie Williams' Knebworth record with half MILLION-crowd tally

By Showbiz Writer Nik Tweedle

The Ospreys have confirmed their status as the biggest band in the world after shattering the attendance record for gigs played at the historic UK music venue Knebworth House. The Brit heartthrobs, led by Isaac Naylor, performed to crowds of 125,000 on four consecutive nights, beating Robbie Williams' previous record of 125,000 on three consecutive nights in 2003. The half million total has now earned them a place in the *Guinness World Records*, after almost four million fans worldwide applied for tickets to attend.

The incredible four-night run ended last night with The Ospreys inviting some of the biggest legends in music to perform on stage with them, including Madonna, who stole the show with a rocked-up duet of her own song, 'Get Into The Groove', with Naylor, and The Who's Roger Daltrey, who said afterwards that 125,000 Ospreys' fans belting 'My Generation' back at him would go down as 'one of the best moments of my career and that's saying something considering how many I've already racked up'.

For The Ospreys, their Knebworth triumph is the latest in a long line of successes, including simultaneous number one albums both sides of the Atlantic. But if they were hoping Knebworth would detract from Naylor's well-documented issues with drugs and alcohol they were disappointed – while the gigs went off without a technical hitch, his performance was patchy at times and on Wednesday night he almost stumbled off the edge of the stage, clearly drunk. He also announced on stage each night that the band's lauded manager, Derrick Cordingly, had been begging him to go to rehab again, inspiring a crowd-wide sing-a-long of the Amy Winehouse hit of the same name.

Speaking backstage at the gig, where 500 VIP guests including Liam Gallagher, who famously played Knebworth in 1996 with Oasis, availed themselves of complimentary champagne and vodka, Cordingly brushed off Naylor's on-stage comments. 'Isaac's his own man and a grown one at that, it's not for me to order him what to do,' he told the *Mirror*. 'Let's not take away from what's been a phenomenal four nights for the band, breaking all Knebworth records. This is why The Ospreys are the biggest band in the world right now.'

It was Cordingly who had the idea for the band to beat Robbie Williams' record and it took him almost eighteen months of negotiation and planning to pull it off. Unlike other gigs at Knebworth where the artists have profited, The Ospreys are giving 80 per cent of the proceeds to ten different charities and the other 20 per cent is being split between the 3,000 backstage staff needed to put the gigs on, netting each one of them an estimated bonus of up to £2,500. When announcing they wouldn't make a penny from the gig, Naylor and his band mates Danny Albright, Archie Samuels and Robert 'Renner' Jones said in a statement, 'We've got more money than we know what to do with now, it's only right we share the wealth.'

The Hertfordshire venue has played host to many of the greats before The Ospreys made it theirs, with Led Zeppelin kicking things off in 1979. It was also where Freddie Mercury performed his last concert with Queen before his untimely death in 1991.

Chapter Three

Among those who gave evidence at Isaac Naylor's inquest was a tides expert who said the current on the particular stretch of Devon coast where he drowned could easily have taken his body far out to sea, rending it unrecoverable, and may have been precisely why he chose to die there. It was also the early hours of New Year's Day, meaning far less chance of someone walking by and spotting him. I shudder as I read through the account of the expert's testimony in an online article: how desperate must Isaac have been to deliberately walk himself into the water and force himself below the waves. I wonder if he was inebriated before he did so.

I close down the article and open the next one. Despite the blind item being a load of rot, I've fallen down a rabbit hole of reading up on Isaac's suicide, where it happened and how, as I kill time before I go out. The facts of what led him to take his own life I am well versed in already: I covered the story of his drug-induced downfall for *The Frequency* and have written about The Ospreys a few times as they continue on without him. But I've never given much thought to the details of how Isaac killed himself, other than to consider it was a pretty cowardly thing to do, denying as it did the parents of the poor girl found dead in his hotel room any chance of justice.

He drowned himself off a stretch of Devon coastline he had never visited before. His brother, Toby, confirmed it at his inquest: there were no childhood holidays anywhere nearby that might have inspired a longing to return, no sojourns in adulthood either. But it is an area known for strong tides. Was that something he could've looked up online? Did the police check his internet history after he skipped bail? I'm wondering this idly to myself when I notice it's nearly six p.m. and I should be getting ready for the showcase. But I can't quite tear myself away from my laptop yet.

I do a bit more digging and, fantastical as it sounds, I discover there are actually plenty of people out there who would swallow the blind item's ridiculous notion that he's still alive and is staging a clandestine comeback. Ardent Ospreys' fans who can't bear to think of him dead and pop culture conspiracy theorists who like to perpetuate the scenario that he's spent the last eight years living in a wooden hut on Bora Bora with Elvis and Marilyn Monroe as near neighbours. That makes me laugh: imagine the street parties.

Pushing thoughts of Isaac Naylor from my mind, I take my laptop and mug inside and go into the bedroom to change into the outfit I've already laid out for tonight's event, a flowing mid-length Zara dress that every woman I know seems to have bought, judging from their Instagram feeds, and which looks better on the vast majority of them than it does on me because I'm too short and too curvy to make it hang nicely. But I don't care, because I love its emerald green shade, it compliments my auburn hair, and I like how comfy I feel swishing about in it. Besides, if I let myself be concerned about how my very un-model-like self looked in clothes I'd never leave the house.

I'm just trying to get my blunt fringe to sit straight, silently cursing my hairstylist for talking me into having it cut, when I receive a text. With a flicker of delight when I see it's from Neil

Caffrey, a venerated publicist who made his mark working with The Beatles for a brief time in the sixties and who continues to represent some of the biggest names in music. For our first meeting, not long after I started at *The Frequency*, he took me to The Ivy and over a long boozy lunch regaled me with stories of the most outrageous rock star behaviour imaginable that I couldn't print in a million years. We've worked together many times since and I count him not only as one of my best contacts but also a dear friend.

NAT, ARE YOU ANYWHERE NEAR SOHO? I'M GOING TO THE GROUCHO, COME JOIN! NX

I would love nothing more than to meet him at the private members' club in Dean Street, as it has been the scene of many a great night out for us, but I think of its bar prices and grimace. Part of the reason I am in debt is from trying to maintain a work persona that requires wining and dining my contacts at the best restaurants and shouting them expensive cocktails in bars with clandestine entrances only those in the know are aware of. It's an anomaly that my livelihood depends on splurging and I have to counter the extravagance by living off pasta the rest of the time.

I'm about to decline when another message pings on my phone.

DRINKS ARE ON MY EXPENSES ACCOUNT! NX

I grin. Like I said, he's a dear friend.

It's only when I'm out the door and on the way to the Tube station that I remember the other phone call I was meant to make this afternoon and my insides constrict as I dial Spencer's number. Trying to maintain a cordial relationship with my estranged husband for our son's sake is exhausting and complicated and isn't getting any easier with the passage of time.

To outsiders it appeared our marriage ended abruptly, but the truth was we were in a rough patch and had been for months, a gradual, snapping-at-each-other build-up of resentment that afflicts many couples juggling busy careers with parenthood. Who did the most housework, whose turn was it to drive to football practice, which of us was the most tired, rinse and repeat. We should've sought help in the form of counselling but how many couples like to admit they're not getting along? We now live in a culture where people are compelled to present only their best side to the world and no couple wants to be the ones in their social circle who are the least happy. But the pressure of keeping the veneer crack-free proved too much and one evening, in the midst of another row, after Spencer asked what it was I wanted from him because nothing seemed to make me happy, I blurted out I wasn't sure I was in love with him any more.

No words spoken do I regret more than those. I didn't mean I didn't love him, I just meant we'd lost that giddy feeling which grips every new couple at the beginning of a relationship, when everything is fresh and exciting, and I was sad the buzz had eroded. That's what I was trying to articulate but I failed miserably, because Spencer took it to mean I was done with him and the damage I inflicted with my clumsy phrasing was evidently irreparable. He withdrew from me almost immediately and within three months called it quits for good, much to my devastation.

'What do you want?' is how he answers my call. I don't even warrant a hello these days.

'I need to talk to you about Daniel's birthday,' I say, already feeling on the back foot.

'Now what's wrong?' he sighs. 'I've already changed the day of the party because the timing didn't work.'

He's being disingenuous. Currently Daniel stays at mine every other weekend and overnight on Wednesdays and it just so happens that this year his birthday falls on a Sunday when he's with me. Spencer declared the party would have to take place the weekend before instead, but Daniel got upset and begged that it be on his actual birthday and that's why it was moved. Not to suit me, to suit our son. I appreciate Spencer's not happy, but it's not as though I've said he can't attend – it's being held at a trampoline centre – unlike last year when it fell on his weekend and I didn't receive an invite.

'It's not about that,' I say. 'I can't pay you for my share of it yet. I'm waiting to get paid again.'

To give Spencer his due, he does give me leeway when it comes to money. My solicitor advised I should continue contributing to the mortgage and bills on our family home to maintain my claim upon it until it's sold, and Spencer doesn't baulk if I'm a bit late because an invoice hasn't gone through, as he knows I'm at the mercy of accounts departments and their dinosaur-era payment processes. It was the same throughout our marriage: me rarely being paid on time and him covering my half of everything until I was. His gainful employment as a commercial architect allowed me to pursue my freelance career and I miss the financial buffer it provided.

'We don't need to pay the balance until the day of the party,' he says, 'so don't worry about it.'

'I'll have it by then,' I say gratefully. 'How's Daniel? Is he having a good week?'

'He's fine. He might call you later if he's not too tired. He's got basketball after school.'

The casual way he says Daniel *might* phone me stings. I never thought I'd end up in the position of not seeing my child every day and it kills me that I don't.

'I'd love to speak to him later but I've got a showcase tonight,' I say apologetically.

Again, Spencer's reaction is actually one of understanding because he knows that nocturnal hours are part and parcel of my work and it was actually at a gig that we met. But the lifestyle he so admired at the beginning lost its allure over the years, especially after Daniel was born and I went back to work after maternity leave and left him holding the baby in the evenings. Me doing the day shift with Daniel, writing up articles between naps, and Spencer doing the evenings might have saved us childcare costs but it cost us our marriage in so many ways. We were passing ships, team-taggers, and it's little wonder the rot set in.

'Tell him I'll message him and we can FaceTime in the morning before school,' I say.

'He'll be at breakfast club tomorrow. I've got an early meeting. Sorry.'

Spencer doesn't sound sorry and now I'm annoyed. If we split custody equally Daniel wouldn't have to go to breakfast club – we could arrange it so I could take him to school. Before I moved out I did all the school runs, medical appointments, ferrying to clubs and hosting play dates.

'It's OK,' I say, even though it isn't. But experience has taught me that losing my temper won't get me anywhere. 'I'll pick him up from school tomorrow as usual. Tell him I love him.'

There's no reply though, just a click to signal he's gone.

Chapter Four

The members' bar at The Groucho is an assault on the senses. Teal-blue walls, chairs upholstered in the most vivid shades of yellow, purple and red and lurid artworks lining the walls. It's already filling up for the evening, or maybe it never emptied from lunchtime. On entering I spot an actress who won a BAFTA a few years ago snuggled on a couch with a man who most definitely isn't her equally famous actor husband. People are studiously ignoring them though, because The Groucho has an unwritten rule that what goes on inside, stays inside. The club bears witness to much, yet very little leaks out and what does is almost certainly via non-members signed in as guests who don't know any better.

Neil is occupying a corner table. He's on his mobile as I approach and waves with his free hand for me to sit down. As I shrug off my coat, he mouths 'Tessie' at me and I guess he's speaking to one of his clients, an eighties-era singer called Tessie Flick who's enjoying a comeback after the rapper Dave sampled one of her hits.

'They've guaranteed the cover, darling. It's a sure thing, I promise you,' he continues. 'Yes, you will have your own hair and make-up: Gina and Mark are booked and confirmed. So please stop fretting. What you say goes on this shoot – they need this cover more than you do.' He pauses to listen, then smiles. 'Happy now? Good. I'll see you at the studio tomorrow. Car's booked for nine.' He hangs up, leans over and air kisses my cheeks. 'Bloody divas.'

He says it in the tired manner of someone worn down by his client's demands, but I know Neil and I know this reaction is purely for show. The truth is he thrives on the dramatics that come with dealing with celebrities and he takes all the hissy fits, tantrums and ridiculous requests and channels them back into dealing with journalists like me. Not by being a diva himself, but with a zeal for getting the job done. It's why, despite being eligible for a senior bus pass several years ago, he's still at the top of his profession, revered by his clients and feared by editors.

'Which cover?' I ask.

'I can't possibly say, my sweet. Not until it's in the bag.'

'It sounds like a done deal.'

'You know as well as I do to never count your chickens until the magazine is on the newsstand,' he says.

'They're not going to pull one of your clients from a cover, Neil,' I laugh.

'Oh no, I'm not worried about that. They wouldn't dare. I'm more concerned with Ms Flick behaving herself on set and letting the poor sod of a photographer do his job. Talking of which, if I've got an early start to chaperone her, we should get stuck in now.' He grabs the drinks menu off the low, round table set between our chairs. 'Shall we get some fizz, my sweet?'

I'll never say no to champagne, especially when someone else is paying. 'That would be lovely, thank you.'

We discreetly discuss the BAFTA winner and her mystery man as the waiter takes our order then brings a chilled bottle of Perrier-Jouët to our table. Neil says he has it on good authority her marriage is one of those sham couplings that celebrities enter into for profile-boosting purposes. 'Their mutual agent put them together,' he whispers as the waiter opens the bottle, fills our glasses and pretends not to listen. 'Six months and the split announcement will come, mark my words.'

My mouth tingles as I take a sip and instantly I feel the tension ease from my shoulders. The first blast of bubbles from a glass of champagne will always be one of my favourite sensations and is another reason I'm always destined to be broke. When you develop a thirst for expensive tastes it's hard to go without.

Neil suddenly reaches over and grasps my hand. 'Now, tell me how you are,' he says, 'and don't pretend everything's OK, because I can tell from your face that it's not.'

I hadn't realised I was carrying my woes so obviously. I thought my make-up did a good job of masking how I am, a carefully painted portrait of faux happiness – but apparently not. To my horror, tears prick my eyes.

'I'm not OK, but I will be,' I manage to reply.

'Is the ex still playing hardball?' Neil asks, draining his glass of champagne and refilling it. He nudges my arm. 'Drink up, slow coach.'

Neil was one of the first people I told about Spencer and I splitting up. I hadn't intended to, it just came tumbling out on a night like tonight, after many drinks had been consumed. He, like my parents and Bronwyn, Gayle, and most of my other friends, expressed disbelief we were getting divorced over something taken out of context and Neil had repeatedly asked if I was sure there was no way back from it. At that point I'd have crawled over broken glass to save my marriage, but Spencer shut down every attempt I made. It took me six months after I moved out to finally accept there was no going back.

'We've been given another court date,' I reply, holding my glass out to be topped up. 'I'm hoping this time the judge will grant shared custody.'

As I say it, an all-too familiar panic flutters inside my chest. The hearing is in ten weeks and unless I can get some more money together to clear my bill with my solicitor I'll have to represent myself against Spencer's legal team and I dread to think what will happen then. His side has done a very effective job so far of painting me as a career-obsessed woman who missed her son's bedtimes because she was out partying with musicians, and despite my protestations that it is my job to attend gigs and events, the judge sided with them at the last hearing and ordered a continuation of the arrangement which gives Spencer main custody and me visitation rights. Unless I can pull a rabbit out of the hat at the next hearing, Daniel might end up staying permanently with his dad and I'll have to continue parenting him from the sidelines until he's eighteen.

It was never my intention to leave my son behind, and the memory of the day I was forced to festers like a raw, gaping wound. Spencer had refused to move out, despite him wanting to end the marriage, and our living situation became so toxic I decided to take Daniel to stay with my parents until I got back on my feet. I tried to explain to Daniel why we had to leave, telling him 'Mummy and Daddy will get on better if you and I live somewhere else for a bit', but he became so bewildered and upset that he welded himself to Spencer like a barnacle to a rock. I realised it was too much for him to process and so, after shedding many tears, I agreed he should stay in the family home with Spencer while we sorted out our separation and divorce. What I wasn't anticipating is that eighteen months on he would still be there, and that Spencer would thwart my bid for equal custody rights. He claims it's because he doesn't want to disrupt Daniel's life now, that our current arrangement suits our son and his schooling, and that my absence has not impacted his emotional state, which hurt like hell to hear, but I am certain Spencer is doing it to spite me, just because. A couple of divorced friends did warn me even the most amicable splits can turn nasty, but I never thought we would end up being one of those warring couples playing out their hatred of one another in court. If I'd known what was going to happen, I would never have left Daniel behind.

'But I didn't come to talk about my shitty life,' I say, pasting on a grin I can tell Neil is not convinced by. I grope for something to say that will alleviate the mood, and remember the blind item. Bronwyn didn't want me to tell anyone else, but where's the harm? It's only gossip.

'I read the most brilliant rumour online today,' I say.

Neil perks up. 'Oh do tell.'

'It was a blind item saying Isaac Naylor faked his suicide.'

'Ah, divine boy, always reminded me of a young Bowie. Those rumours are nothing new though. What's the theory this time?'

Something makes me hesitate. I don't like withholding from Neil, but I know his reaction to the bit about Isaac being the mystery songwriter would match mine and the entire industry would know about it by the end of the evening and even though I think it's nonsense, Bronwyn's warning still rings loudly in my ears.

'Just that, really,' I say, gulping down a huge mouthful of champagne to cover my unease. 'He didn't drown like everyone thinks.'

'Well, as I say, that rumour's old hat, it's been circulating

27

for years,' Neil remarks. 'People don't want to accept he killed himself because it was such an immense waste of talent.'

I arch an eyebrow. 'Try telling that to Emily Jenkins' family.'

'Oh, don't misunderstand me; it was a tragedy beyond the pale. Their only daughter found dead in a rock star's bed like some washed-up groupie when she was anything but.'

Neil is right about that. Emily was only two months past turning seventeen when the lethal dose of heroin flooded her veins and killed her. The pathologist who carried out the post-mortem confirmed there were no traces of historic needle marks anywhere else on her body, so it was almost certainly her first time injecting drugs and she would very likely have needed someone to administer the heroin or at the very least show her what to do. That someone being Isaac, who was found sobbing in the bed next to her claiming he had no idea how she got there or how she died. One small saving grace for her parents: the pathologist ruled out signs of sexual activity.

'What's always interested me about his suicide is what the band said afterwards,' Neil muses.

'Meaning?'

'In the months before he died Isaac had been to rehab and was sober for the first time in years. Everyone knew he was in a good place. Yet after he died the other three claimed they'd been on the verge of sacking him for errant behaviour and their lawyer had even drawn up the paperwork.'

'He relapsed behind closed doors and the others had been covering for him,' I protest. 'They were hardly the first band to do that either.'

Neil leans towards me and lowers his voice. 'I happen to know someone who was with Isaac the morning before it happened, someone who worked with him. We've talked about it often since then and he swears Isaac was as clean as a whistle that day. He even went to the police to tell them as much, but they weren't interested. They took his details but never bothered to follow it up.'

'He doesn't think Isaac relapsed?'

'He doesn't just think it, my sweet. He's sure of it.'

Chapter Five

Neil has my full attention now. 'How can he be certain?' I ask. 'Was he with Isaac that evening after the gig?'

'You'd have to ask him that,' says Neil impishly. 'I think I've probably said enough.'

I don't want to let the matter drop though.

'There are plenty of people who think Isaac's still alive,' I venture.

'Music fans do love their conspiracy theories. You know the one about Paul McCartney dying in a car accident in 1966 and being replaced in The Beatles by a look- and sound-alike? That's my personal favourite,' Neil chuckles, then falls serious again. 'What you should be asking is *why* Isaac might've faked his death.'

'That's obvious – he thought he was going to prison for killing Emily and he wanted an out.'

'Ah, but with a good defence lawyer he might have been exonerated. You know the police didn't find any of his fingerprints on any of the drug paraphernalia found in his hotel room, including the syringe still lodged in the girl's arm?'

I shake my head. I don't remember hearing that while covering the story for *The Frequency*, nor has it cropped up in any of the reports I've read online today, but I'm not surprised Neil knows. He has an encyclopaedic knowledge when it comes to music and an enviably sharp memory for detail.

'It was explained away as him having wiped everything clean in a panic to save his own skin. Yet Isaac was adamant he hadn't touched a thing. He woke up, saw the girl's body and rang reception to ask them to call for an ambulance.'

'How do you know this?' I ask wonderingly.

'The transcript from his police interview was leaked online after his death. I'm sure you can find it somewhere if you look.'

I'm shocked. 'You're saying Isaac knew they hadn't found his fingerprints?'

'Oh yes,' says Neil, draining his glass. 'As I said, with the right lawyer he might've swayed a jury in his favour.'

My head is spinning. Isaac claimed to have no idea how Emily ended up in his bed, let alone how she came to have taken drugs. He even issued a statement after he was bailed saying he planned to clear his name. Now it turns out he knew there was no physical evidence linking him to the syringe and drugs that killed her.

'What if he really didn't inject her,' I say, 'but thought the situation seemed so hopeless that's why he killed himself?'

'Then the next question you have to ask yourself is who did.'

'Who did what?'

'Pumped poor Emily Jenkins full of drugs. The police always maintained she couldn't have done it unaided.'

I stare at him for a moment as the realisation of what he's saying hits home. 'You mean if it wasn't Isaac someone else must've killed her?'

'Yes, and got away with it. At least that's what my friend reckons. He's always said there was more to what happened that night. He's never believed Isaac was guilty of her death, not for a single second.'

'I don't suppose I can get his number?' I ask hopefully. 'I'd love to chat to him about it.'

Neil thinks for a moment. 'Let me run it past him. He's never spoken publicly about it and might be a bit funny about a journalist approaching him out of the blue. But I'm happy to vouch for you.'

'Thanks, I'd appreciate it.'

He takes another sip of champagne. 'It would certainly be a good story to revisit right now, as next month is the anniversary of when The Ospreys signed their first deal. I expect Derrick Cordingly will be doing the PR rounds to mark the occasion,' he adds snippily.

Derrick Cordingly is the manager who steered The Ospreys to global superstardom and is to them what Brian Epstein was to The Beatles, Malcolm McLaren to the Sex Pistols. Without Cordingly there would be no Ospreys and he's rightly as famous and as wealthy as they are. He does milk it though, with a staggering amount of interviews and personal appearances in the guise of promoting the band.

'You're not a fan?' I smile.

'I don't suffer egos gladly, but I can't deny the man knows what he's doing. Everyone said The Ospreys were done after Isaac died, in the same way Nirvana couldn't go on without Kurt Cobain. Cordingly not only kept them going, he's pushed them to even greater success. It's rather incredible what he's done.' Neil's eyes twinkle as he leans forward and I just know that what he's about to say will probably be outrageous – and it is.

'Call me callous if you want,' he whispers, 'but Isaac Naylor's suicide ended up being the best thing that ever happened to them.'

Chapter Six

NME.COM

'It hurts to hear Isaac's voice'

The Ospreys explain why the late Isaac Naylor has been removed from their forthcoming greatest hits EP

By Steve Marshall

First uploaded 3 March 2017

To mark the release of The Ospreys' greatest hits next week, drummer Robert 'Renner' Jones, manager Derrick Cordingly and the band's long-time stylist Cicely Harris were guests on Lola Maurice's award-winning Downbeat podcast last night. In part 1 of the recording they discuss the lasting impact of Isaac Naylor's suicide and the band's controversial decision to re-record their earliest tracks for the triple The Best Of . . . EP, replacing Naylor's vocals with current front man Jem Spencer's. Below is a partial transcript. Click **here** to listen to the audio extract.

Lola: I'd like to talk about Isaac for a bit. When you think of him now, what comes to mind?

Cicely: There wasn't a nicer guy in music than him. [Renner protests in background] Sorry, Renner, but you know what I mean. Isaac would give you his last fiver, the shirt off his back, the keys to his house. There wasn't anything he wouldn't do for people.

Renner: Yeah, on a good day Isaac was the best person to be around. The best.

Derrick: I agree, but sadly the good days were just too few and far between. [pauses] Look, if we're getting into this now, I think we should take a moment to remember Emily Jenkins as well. It would be wrong not to. I don't want her family to think we're sitting here banging on about Isaac as though she doesn't matter. But we miss him, of course we do. He was the beating heart of the band and it's taken a lot of adjustment to continue without him.

Lola: There was a lot of speculation at the time the band would split. What kept you going?

Renner: There have been many times when I thought we shouldn't carry on if Isaac wasn't out front. But then we found Jem and it clicked again.

Lola: A lot of fans aren't happy you've re-recorded Isaac's vocals for the EP though.

Derrick: It was my suggestion and the boys thought long and hard about whether to do it. Jem had to be convinced as well. He feared a backlash, even though he's been a member of the band for nearly six years now—

Renner: [interrupts] Do you know how hard it is for us to listen to Isaac singing? Even now when I hear his voice it's like I've been punched in the head. It's fine when Jem's doing them live, but playing back those tracks with Isaac . . . it's just too fucking hard. So we decided to re-record them with Jem so we could enjoy listening to them again ourselves. We're sorry if some fans are upset, but the early stuff with Isaac on is still available.

Lola: Any comeback from Isaac's family?

Cicely: Well his parents were already dead when he died, so there was only his brother, Toby. I haven't spoken to him in years, have you, Renner?

Renner: No, which is a shame. Toby was like our unofficial fifth member. He'd hang out with us at school while we rehearsed, then snuck into our first gigs in pubs while he was still underage. When things took off, Isaac made sure he always had a role on the crew as his assistant. But after . . . [pause] well, it was tough. Toby was devastated, we were devastated, things just drifted. I regret that now, we should've looked out for him more. If you're listening Toby, give me a call!

Derrick: I want to make it clear we're not airbrushing Isaac from the band's history by re-recording these tracks. We would never do that; without Isaac there would be no Ospreys. But nor is it fair to Jem that his contribution is overlooked. Think of what the boys have achieved since he joined: four Grammy wins, another couple of Brits, a global tour that broke box office records. Re-recording those early tracks for The Best Of . . . EP is also our way of saying thank you to him. Jem saved The Ospreys, no question.

Cicely: Yeah, it took a lot for him to step into Isaac's shoes and then he got hammered for not looking the part, because his hair wasn't blond enough and his eyes weren't blue enough. Jem deserves to be recognised as his own man. He earned this.

Lola: Such a rags to riches tale too: him on the road crew, then Danny hearing him playing a guitar on the tour bus one day and realising he had talent.

Renner: It blew us away how good he was. At the time we'd just come back from the two-year hiatus we took after Isaac died and Danny had taken over the lead vocals but he didn't like it. He's not a natural front man, he'll admit that himself. But after hearing Jem sing and play it was a no brainer. We all saw he could be as good as Isaac was.

Derrick: We've never entirely reconciled ourselves to the loss of Isaac, or the tragic circumstances that led to him taking his own life, but even the fans upset with us about the EP will have to admit that it all came good in the end.

Chapter Seven

I never made it to the showcase. Neil insisted on buying a second bottle of champagne, then a third. I managed to escape not long after midnight, just as a tray of vodka shots had been ordered, after he was distracted by the arrival at our table of another of his clients, a national radio DJ, and her entourage. All that booze on an empty stomach saw me stagger my way through Soho to Oxford Street, where somehow I managed to catch the number 98 night bus back to Maida Vale in one piece. I even managed not to lose an item from my person – something of a miracle, as I'm on my third phone in a year and in the eighteen months I've been staying at Gayle's flat I've had to change the locks twice because I mislaid my keys.

My head pounds to the beat of a clanging hangover as I rise up from the mattress and reach for my phone, which I'd left beside the bed as I fell into it last night. I check the time, see it's only eight o'clock, let out a groan and fall back onto the pillow. One of the benefits of setting my own hours as a free-lancer is that apart from every other Thursday when Daniel stays over and I need to get him back to Clapham for school, I'm in no rush to get up in the morning. So why does my brain always shake my body awake after a night out when I need to recover? It's a punishment, I'm convinced, for maintaining the same drinking habits I developed when I moved to London in my early twenties, when I could stay up partying until five in the morning, have two hours' kip and then stroll into the office as though I'd had a full night's sleep. Pregnancy and the creep towards forty might have lowered my tolerance to alcohol to the point where it's no longer as fun to drink, but unfortunately my consumption hasn't reduced with it.

I'm just closing my eyes in an attempt to force myself back to sleep when suddenly I remember last night's conversation with Neil about Isaac Naylor and they fly open again. What he told me was incredible. Propping myself up on my elbows, I reach for the notebook and pen I always keep beside my bed in case inspiration ever strikes and laboriously write down everything I can remember of our chat, including the lack of fingerprint evidence and the friend of Neil's who thinks he's innocent and what all of it might mean in the light of the blind item suggesting Isaac never drowned at sea as presumed, and that he's staging some kind of surreptitious comeback as the mystery songwriter. Pieced together like that, it translates into the kind of exclusive that could elevate my career to a stratospheric level, involving the kind of long-form investigative journalism that wins awards and lands spin-off book deals, podcasts and Netflix true crime stories. I could earn enough money to win custody of Daniel and start afresh, free of debt.

I allow myself a few moments to daydream of infinite riches until reality brings me crashing back to earth with a jolt: how could anyone possibly prove any of it? I read my notes back and further doubt sets in: if Isaac was innocent of any wrong-doing and someone else was responsible, that means he was set up – but who would do that, and why? Also, there was no fathomable reason for Isaac to skip police bail and fake his death if he knew the evidence against him was questionable. He had the money and means to secure the best legal representation in the world to fight any charges brought against him. The man was a superstar, for crying out loud. With a sigh of defeat I toss my notebook onto the bed and throw back the covers. I really should know better than to believe gossip I read on trashy websites and to let Neil fill my head with champagne-fuelled fantasies.

After a shower and some painkillers for my headache, I park myself at the narrow breakfast bar in the kitchen with my laptop and the strongest coffee my stomach can tolerate. My first action of the day is to email an apology to the PR who organised the showcase last night, saying I got caught up doing another interview in The Groucho. That way if she had any spies in there last night I won't get caught out for lying. She replies instantly to say this afternoon the talent will be at a recording studio in Camberwell and she can get me some time with her there. It's the studio where Bronwyn works, so buoyed by both the PR's positive response and the prospect of seeing my best friend, I email a thank you and suggest I get there at noon, so I can do the interview before the afternoon recording session starts and then I'll be on time to collect Daniel from school. The PR agrees.

Closing down her email, an image of Daniel fills my mind. There isn't a particular time of day that I miss him more – I just miss him constantly. I hope he realises that. I think he does. When we're together I try not to mention how sad I am when we're apart, and how much I miss him, so as not to upset him – instead I focus on savouring every moment. So maybe he thinks I'm OK about not living with him. But I'm not. I'm really not. I still get teary-eyed when I drop him off. Never while Daniel's present, but once the door has been shut between us, parting us again until the next time.

As I'm making another coffee an email arrives from a contact at Sony asking if I'm free to ghost some sleeve notes for an established singer. They want me to draft an essay in the singer's words about the recording process and throw in a few thank yous. The fee won't make much of a dent in my overdraft but it's still one I'm grateful to accept, so I email back to say yes and ask my contact to clarify the deadline.

Mollified by caffeine and the commission, my thoughts drift back to my conversation with Neil last night, and to Emily Jenkins. I cannot imagine the horror of losing your child: if anything happened to Daniel I don't know if I'd survive it. I wonder if Emily's parents ever go online and see the rumours and supposition about Isaac's suicide. I hope they don't.

Without thinking, I click on the bookmarked link to the gossip site and start to scroll down to where I saw the blind item, curious to see if anyone else has commented on it. At first I think I must've missed it, but when I reach the bottom of the page and return again to the top I realise it's not there.

I check again and I'm right: the post has vanished.

Chapter Eight

The nineties' trend for musicians building home studios in their mansions and the internet making it possible for band members to record together while on separate continents means quite a few of London's formerly iconic studios have been lost over the years, snapped up by property developers and turned into flats. But a few, such as The Premises in Hackney and Hot Money Studios in South Bermondsey, still attract the major stars of the day through their doors, as does The Soundbank in Camberwell, outside which I find myself standing now.

I'm almost an hour early but I'm hoping I can grab a coffee with Bronwyn before the PR sweeps me away for my interview. It's been a couple of weeks since we've seen each other because Bronwyn's been busy with work and she and her wife Lucy also have two small children, one aged three, the other eighteen months, so she has her hands full at home too.

The front door to the studios is locked to the outside world but I'm buzzed into reception after I announce my name via the intercom. I sign in at the front desk then ask the receptionist if Bronwyn's about.

'Did I hear my name?'

I turn to see my friend coming down the staircase at the side of reception and smile. Bronwyn's one of the tallest women

I've ever met, at least six feet in her socks and she always wears heels. If you didn't know her I'm not sure you'd guess she worked in the louche world of rock 'n' roll: her sharp brunette bob, crisp shirts and tailored trousers seem more apt for a City office setting. I always feel positively dishevelled standing next to her, and very short.

On reaching the bottom step she envelops me in a hug. 'You're here for Jo-Jo Jones aren't you? Lizzie said you were coming by.'

Lizzie is the PR and Jo-Jo the alliterated pop star she's promoting.

'Yes, but I've got time for a coffee if you can escape?'

She tilts her head. 'Let's go next door.'

The studio has a cafe attached to it, also called The Soundbank. We order lattes then take a seat in the window overlooking the street.

'How are the kids?' I ask.

'Wolfie's decided the only form of clothing he's prepared to wear at the moment is his pyjamas,' she says, referring to her three-year-old. 'Won't take them off ever and wants to wear them to nursery. I've told Lucy to let him but she thinks we're indulging him if we agree, and so the battle continues,' she sighs. 'Harrison's great too. Babbling away non-stop now.'

Harrison is also my godson. Both boys were conceived by IVF using a sperm donor, with Lucy being the carrier.

'How's Daniel?' Bronwyn asks.

'Great,' I say, my voice artificially bright, because I don't actually know how he is today. Or how he was yesterday. But Bronwyn understands and flashes me a sympathetic smile. 'I'm going to pick him up after this and then he's staying at mine tonight,' I add.

'Send him my love. We need to organise another Sunday lunch. I know Wolfie would love to see him.'

'That would be great.'

We chat a bit more about the children, then I bring up our odd phone conversation yesterday.

'Who were you with when I sent you that Isaac Naylor story?'

'Just one of the guys in the studio.'

She says it nonchalantly, but my eyes are drawn to the red flush warming the hollow of her throat. Bronwyn's skin always reddens when she's feeling stressed and right now it's glowing.

'Why didn't you want me to send the screen-grab to anyone else?' I ask.

'Because it's too ridiculous for words.'

Her response surprises me. She's not normally this po-faced about celebrity hearsay.

'You didn't say that about the actor and the donkey story,' I scoff. 'Come on, Bron – Isaac Naylor faking his death and then making a comeback as the mystery songwriter is brilliant gossip. Weirdly, though, the item's been removed from the site now. I checked this morning and it's disappeared. That never happens. I've seen the most outrageous stuff written about people on that site, including the one about the donkey, and no one ever seems to complain.'

I raise my cup to knock back the dregs of my coffee but stop when I see Bronwyn staring at me pensively, the redness marking her throat now blossoming like an ink stain across her chin.

'What's wrong?' I ask.

'You need to stop going on about it.'

'Why? It's just a ridiculous rumour according to you—'

The redness spreads to Bronwyn's cheeks and I stop talking, transfixed by her having such a corporeal reaction to our conversation. Then it hits me. 'Hang on, is there some truth in it?' I gasp. 'Do you know about the mystery songwriter?'

'Keep your voice down,' Bronwyn hisses, her eyes darting to the table next to us, where a man is tapping out a message on his phone.

But I cannot contain my excitement. 'Oh my god, Bron, it is such a good story. The papers would love it. What else do you know about him?'

'Natalie, pipe down, everyone can hear you,' Bronwyn implores, her face now scarlet.

'I will if you tell me what you know.'

She hesitates then exhales. 'OK, but you can't tell anyone you got it from me. If people find out I've spoken to a journalist about this, even if you are my best friend, I could lose my job.'

'I won't. You have my word.' Bronwyn knows she can trust it too – I've never reported any gossip she's told me previously about The Soundbank and the stars that record there.

She beckons me closer and I lean in so our noses are practically touching.

'There *is* a songwriter fairly new to the scene who's a bit of an enigma and can only be contacted via his lawyer.'

'That's exactly what the blind item said,' I hiss back.

'I know.'

'Is it Isaac Naylor?' I ask her eagerly.

'Of course not, he's dead.' Bronwyn rolls her eyes but her expression is pinched and the redness that was beginning to retreat back down her neck flares again.

'They never found his body,' I point out.

'It's nothing to do with him or The Ospreys. This guy, no one knows who he is, but we've had a couple of artists record his tracks here.' Bronwyn whispers the name of a former boy band member who released a critically acclaimed solo album in March. My jaw drops even further.

'Seriously? How ironic that the reviews banged on about his lyrical genius.'

'So did the BRITs committee who voted him Best Male Newcomer last year,' says Bronwyn wryly.

'But surely the mystery songwriter was credited on the album in some way?'

'Apparently not.'

'Did the person you were with yesterday tell you that?' I ask. She rolls her eyes again. 'No, they didn't.'

'Why won't you tell me who they are?'

'Why does it matter?' she frowns.

'Well, you seem so intent on me keeping my mouth shut about the mystery songwriter I'm wondering whether if the same applies to them.'

Bronwyn bites down hard on her lip, catching her teeth on her carefully applied lipstick.

'Well?' I prompt.

'They won't say anything.'

I think for a moment then lean in even closer. 'Bron, all I need is the lawyer's name. I promise I won't tell anyone it came from you. I just want to look up who else he represents, to see if I can work out the songwriter's identity that way.'

I know my best friend well enough to know when she's wavering.

'Please?' I plead. 'It's such a good story.'

With a sigh, Bronwyn reaches for her phone and begins stabbing at the screen. 'Let me call Felix Thompson's office.'

Felix Thompson is one of the most sought-after producers in the business. I listen intently as her call is picked up.

'Hey Jess, it's Bronwyn from The Soundbank. Yeah, I'm good, thanks. You? Good. Listen, I haven't got long, but you know that songwriter Felix was talking about last time you guys were in, the one he couldn't get hold of? Do you have the contact details for their lawyer? Someone else needs to get in touch with him.'

She says it so breezily that it does not appear to rouse any suspicion or concern from Felix's assistant and a few seconds later Bronwyn is reciting aloud the lawyer's name and address as Aidan Rowlock, 17 Rushton Avenue, Kentish Town. Immediately I reach for my own phone to look him up. To my surprise, nothing comes up. I scroll down pages of results but there is no law firm anywhere in Kentish Town by that name.

I interrupt Bronwyn in a whisper and ask her to re-check the details with Jess and it turns out his first name has an unusual spelling: A-d-e-n. As they continue to chat, their conversation veering onto the subject of an upgrade of the mixing desk in the main studio and when it might happen, I search again with the correct spelling but still nothing comes up. Then I check just the road and the postcode and both are correct – Rushton Avenue does exist. 'Aden Rowlock', however, is still coming up blank. My frown deepens as I try again, this time searching through all the social media platforms for any mention of him, but I don't find any.

I lean back in my chair, flummoxed. Why is the mystery songwriter's only point of contact a lawyer who appears not to exist?

Chapter Nine

My instinct is to rush to Kentish Town and check out the address in person, but the interview with Jo-Jo Jones and collecting Daniel from school have to take precedence. By the time Daniel and I are sitting on the top deck of the number 137 to Marble Arch, where we will then change onto the number 98 to Maida Vale, I've pushed it to the back of my mind.

Being with my son is like having balm applied to a wound that stings – I feel sheer relief to be sitting next to him again, his little face upturned to mine as he regales me with what he's done at school today. As I do every time we're reunited, my gaze rakes his face for signs that he might love me a little less than he did the last time we were together. It's a constant fear that being apart is eroding the affection he has for me but, thankfully, I can see he's as happy to be with me as I am to be with him.

'We learned how to play rounders in PE today but it's not as good as football. I don't like the bat, I'd rather kick the ball,' he tells me, while simultaneously stuffing in the crisps that I bought him as a snack. I know I shouldn't resort to treats every time I see him, but it's hard enough parenting from a distance without trying to enforce healthy eating. So I let Spencer worry about that and I always get in Daniel's favourite foods for when he's with me. It will change when I have him half the week.

It's not until we are back at Gayle's apartment and Daniel is playing outside in the communal garden that I think about Aden Rowlock again. Opening my laptop I decided to focus on 17 Rushton Avenue. I know it's an actual address – but for what, if not a solicitor's firm? A search of the electoral roll throws up a few names as current dwellers but none of them is his.

I'm about to do a search of Companies House when Daniel sprints through the open French doors. My mood lifts at the sight of him. His light brown fringe is pasted to his forehead with sweat and his cheeks are flushed from running. I push my laptop to one side and smile.

'Hey, are you hungry? I'm about to start tea,' I say.

His answer is to burst into tears. 'A man just shouted at me, Mummy.'

I get to my feet. 'What, outside?'

He nods miserably, his cheeks getting wetter by the second.

'Was it one of the neighbours?' I ask, peering through the French doors. I can't see anyone milling about but some of the older residents can be really huffy about children using the communal gardens, even though they have every right to if their families live in the block. Daniel might not live here all the time but he too is entitled to roam outside whenever he wants.

Daniel jiggles on the spot, tears pouring down his face, and I stare at him, surprised. I don't know if I've ever seen him so agitated. He's normally such a laidback child, never one to get worked up about things, and I think that's largely why he's weathered the storm of his dad and me separating. He's been upset, naturally, but he also seems to possess an innate pragmatism that helps him deal with the rough stuff in life. He gets that from me, whereas Spencer's far more emotional. Put it this way, if Spencer had said to me what I said to him during the row that killed our marriage, we wouldn't be divorcing. I would've shrugged it off as a comment hurled in the heat of the moment that was designed to hurt and which did its job very effectively. It wouldn't have blown up into the life-shattering episode it became.

'He said I was a horrible naughty boy.'

'What were you doing?'

'Just kicking my ball.'

'On the grass?'

'It went in the flowers. I didn't mean it to, but that's when he shouted at me.'

That's when I realise my beautiful boy is scared. I rush over and pull him into a hug and he trembles against me. 'It's OK, you're safe indoors now.' I wait a beat, then say next time he should keep well away from the flowers. 'You might've damaged them and that's why the man got upset—' I'm about to add the neighbour shouldn't have shouted at him like that and that he should have come and spoken to me, but Daniel doesn't give me a chance.

'That's not fair!' he yells, pulling away from me. 'I didn't do anything wrong, Mummy. I didn't hurt the flowers.' His little chest heaves as he tries to catch his breath. 'I want to go home.'

'Daniel—'

'I want to go home now.' He stamps his foot angrily, something he hasn't done since his toddler years. 'I don't like it here and I don't want to stay. I want Daddy.'

His words pierce my heart and it takes some effort not to show how upset I am to hear him say them. But I can't, because I don't want to emotionally manipulate him in any way. Shakily exhaling, I suggest that we have some tea and he can watch some telly and hopefully he'll feel better after that.

'I don't want tea,' he howls, 'I want to go home!'

His body begins to judder as he sobs harder and I feel so wretched that I find myself saying it's fine, I can take him back to Clapham, but first he has to eat something. At that his crying begins to slow, and I am engulfed by the hurt of seeing him perk up at the thought of leaving.

'Really?'

'Yes,' I nod, pasting on my brightest smile as I blink furiously to banish unshed tears. 'I'll make us some pasta and afterwards I'll take you home.'

Chapter Ten

Woman & Home, December issue, 2019

HOLD THE FRONT PAGE!

What's it like being at the centre of a news story that's making headlines worldwide? Rose Burton interviews three women who unwittingly found themselves caught up in some of Britain's biggest scandals.

Margot Turner, 42, is a nurse from Exeter and the witness who found Isaac Naylor's belongings on Moor Sands beach in Devon after the singer committed suicide on New Year's Day 2012.

'I still don't know if I'd have paid attention to the pile of clothes had my dog, Molly, not started rooting through them. You get all sorts of rubbish left on beaches but it was only when I got closer that I could see the clothes had been neatly folded and there was a smaller pile of items next to them that included a wallet, passport and a watch. But it was the envelopes that really raised the alarm bells. There were two of them and they appeared newly sealed and addressed, but with no stamps or sorting office hallmarks. One was made out to three men who

I know now were Isaac's band mates, the other to his brother, Toby. It was seeing those letters that made me think I should call the police. I'll never forget how shaky the handwriting was: it was like a spider dipped in ink had crawled across the front of them.

'The emergency operator asked me to read the name out on the passport and when I said it was Isaac Naylor he actually swore! It turns out he was a huge fan of The Ospreys and was very upset. He asked me over and over to check the shoreline again, in case Isaac had only just entered the water and I could help him. But it was six in the morning and dark still and I couldn't see a thing.

'I think Isaac chose the early hours of New Year's Day because he thought there would be nobody about. The only reason I was there so early was because I was newly single and after spending the evening before moping indoors on my own I thought the fresh air would do me good.

'Obviously by that point everyone knew a fan had been found dead from a drugs overdose in Isaac's hotel room and the police were saying he was to blame. I do think it's a tragedy for the girl's family that he never answered for what he did, but as a healthcare professional who has had experience of working with patients with mental health issues I also understand how desperate he must've been after he was arrested if he thought suicide was the only way out.

'I never expected any of the attention I received after being a witness at Isaac's inquest. Even though his body was never found, they still went ahead with the hearing so he could eventually be legally declared dead. I had fans coming to my house and knocking on my door to berate me for not saving him. It was horribly intrusive and upsetting – there was clearly nothing I could've done, because he was nowhere to be seen by the time I got to the beach. That's why it took me a while to agree to do this interview, because I didn't want to rake it all up and have people bother me again. But it's years ago now and hopefully everyone's moved on since then.'

Chapter Eleven

Dropping Daniel off in Clapham is horrendous on two fronts. First, it kills me to give up my precious time with him, knowing I won't see him again until next week, second is Spencer's reaction to it. He is tediously predictable in his response to me bringing Daniel back early — I can't look after his son properly, Daniel needs to be with him, I should stop fighting him for shared custody, etc. — but that doesn't make it any easier to listen to. On and on he goes, until I lose my temper and start shouting back and he shuts the door in my face and that's another black mark against me.

With no Daniel to tuck in I am at a loose end now and feeling agitated with it. I need to do something to clear my head and reduce the simmering anger provoked by Spencer's onslaught. Also, if I allow myself to dwell on the fact my son would rather be with his dad than me I'll go to pieces.

Ruling out a return to the apartment where there is more risk of that happening, I head to the Tube station and on the way my thoughts finally refocus on the mystery songwriter. I know I said to Bronwyn I wanted his lawyer's address for research purposes only, but, really, where's the harm in me seeing for myself where he's based? The Northern Line that runs through Clapham Common station also goes to Kentish

Town – I could be there in half an hour. Mind made up, I stride purposefully towards the station and the further I walk from my former marital home the calmer I feel.

Rushton Avenue turns out to be a residential street with no shops or businesses anywhere along it. That's not to say a solicitor can't work out of his or her own home, but standing outside number seventeen and taking in the state of it, I'd be surprised if Aden Rowlock is. 'Down-at-heel' is the politest phrase I'd use to describe the three-storey house, which, judging by the multiple buttons on the entry system, is an HMO split into bedsits. I climb the rubbish-strewn steps to the grubby front door and check the labels next to the buttons on the entry system. Only a couple are filled in with names and Aden Rowlock isn't one of them. I hesitate for a moment, because it wasn't my intention to speak to him. But I need confirmation this is the right address, because my first impression really does suggest otherwise.

I press my finger on the button next to the name 'Soumy'. Somewhere deep inside the property I hear a buzzer sound. I give it a few seconds then try again, holding my finger down on the button for longer. This time the speaker part of the entry system crackles to life.

'Yes?'

I've already decided I'm not going to announce myself as a journalist. Mine is a widely hated profession that inspires mistrust and I don't want to reveal my hand until I'm ready.

'Sorry to bother you,' I say loudly into the speaker, 'but I'm looking for Aden Rowlock.'

'Who?'

'Aden Rowlock. Apparently he works in this building.'

'Don't know him.'

I try another buzzer but I get the same response: no Aden

Rowlock. There are ten buzzers in all and my shoulders sag as I hit the ninth, expecting the same answer again.

'I'm after Aden Rowlock. Is he there?' I ask.

There's a long pause.

'Who wants to know?' replies a heavily accented male voice.

'My name is Natalie. I was told this is his address.'

A second pause, but shorter.

'He's not here right now. Goodbye.'

'Wait! You're saying I have got the right place for him?'

'Aden is not here.'

'Do you know when he'll be back?'

The speaker falls silent, but moments later I detect the noisy tread of footsteps coming down bare wooden stairs. Through the opaque glass panels of the front door I see a figure moving swiftly along the hallway, then the door swings open and a man appears. He is foreign in appearance, dark haired, short and slight in stature, and if I had to hazard a guess I'd say he was in his mid-thirties.

'What do you want with Aden?'

I parry the question with one of my own. 'Do you know him?'

His face contorts and I can tell he doesn't want to answer me. 'Who are you?' he asks.

'I'm Natalie. I need some urgent legal advice and a friend of mine recommended Aden,' I fib. 'They gave me this address.'

'Aden is not here.'

'Do you know him?' I ask again. 'Is this where he works?'

This time he nods.

Gazing over his shoulder into the hallway with its peeling, mildewed walls and dirt-embedded floorboards, I wonder what kind of circumstances have forced Aden Rowlock to run his legal practice in a place like this. My curiosity sky high, I make the snap decision to forgo simply confirming his address. Now

I want to speak to him. 'Can I go and leave a message in his office?' I ask.

'No. Aden cannot help you.'

Now it's my turn to frown. 'I'd rather hear that from him. Can I give you my number so he can call me?'

The man shakes his head. 'No.'

Precisely as I'm about to argue the toss, another man comes down the stairs and into the hallway. Much younger but with similar features, he stops by a small, battered console table covered in takeaway menus. 'Hey Bibek,' he calls to the man I've been trying to talk to, 'where are the letters today? I wait for one.'

Bibek glares and shouts something back in a language I don't recognise. The younger man reels back, patently shocked. He tries to respond but Bibek shouts him down again and he scuttles back up the stairs empty-handed. I say nothing as Bibek turns to face me.

'Go,' he says. 'Go away.'

I'm not easily dissuaded, and certainly not when I sense someone knows more than they are letting on.

'If Aden is a friend of yours you need to tell him to call me. It's in his best interests.' With that I fish my business card out of my bag and hand it over. Bibek's frown deepens as he takes in the words printed upon it.

'You are a journalist?'

'Yes. I write about music and I'm hoping to speak to Aden for a story I'm working on. I was at The Soundbank studio earlier and I heard all about his new songwriter client.' Guiltily I bat away the sound of Bronwyn's disappointed voice reminding me of my promise not to drop her in it. It won't come back on her, I tell myself. I'll make sure of it.

Bibek shrugs. 'I don't know what you speak of.'

It's on the tip of my tongue to launch into an explanation,

but instead I blurt out, 'Do you know who Isaac Naylor is?' I don't know what's made me say it, other than to provoke a reaction.

And it does. Bibek fights valiantly to remain impassive but his eyes are a giveaway: on hearing me say Isaac's name they widen, although I can't tell whether it's with surprise, alarm or confusion.

'Isaac Naylor was a musician who died,' I add.

Bibek nods. 'Yes, he was very famous.'

'He was. Then he killed himself.'

'That was a while ago.'

'It was.' I stare up at him, waiting for him to speak again, but he remains annoyingly tight-lipped.

'OK, I'm going,' I sigh. 'Please ask Aden to call me. I'm not digging for dirt, I just want a quick chat.'

'He will have nothing to say,' Bibek intones.

'Like I said, I want to hear that from him.'

I'm down the steps and on the pavement when Bibek calls after me.

'I wasn't here when it happened.'

'When what happened?'

'The drowning of the rock star,' he says with a shrug. 'I wasn't living here then.'

I nod, then walk away, bemused. Why would it matter to me if he were?

Chapter Twelve

SUNDAY, 9TH

Naively, I assumed my inquiries about the mystery songwriter would compel Aden Rowlock to hastily respond, but four days tick by and all I hear is radio silence. Every time my phone rings my heart leaps, thinking it might be him calling me back, and every time I'm disappointed. I've decided if I don't hear anything by Tuesday I'm going back to doorstep him again—

There's a screech of brakes as the black cab I'm in narrowly avoids ploughing into the car in front, which has come to a halt. The momentum plunges me forward in my seat and I have to grab the door handle to stop myself sliding in an ungainly fashion to the floor.

'Sorry, it's a bit stop-start along here,' the cab driver apologises over his shoulder.

I nod my understanding as I push myself back into the seat and readjust my dress, which has shifted awkwardly up around my hips. My invitation to attend a music awards this evening required me to dig out the only dressy dress I own, a black, fitted, mid-length number with cap sleeves that's a high street rip-off of a designer version. Now, sweating profusely in the back of the taxi bearing me to the venue, the hair I spent ages straightening defiantly reforming into waves around my damp neck, I'm wishing I'd stuck to something less formal and definitely less clingy.

Tonight's awards have been organised by Motif, a UK-based digital music streaming service that launched a few years ago to rival Spotify, and they're being held at Alexandra Palace, north London's grandest landmark. While the Motifs are nowhere near as vast as the BRITs, as prestigious as the Novellos or as anarchic as the NMEs, nevertheless the industry will be out in force tonight – including, according to the PR of the drink sponsor who invited me to be a guest at their table and who rattled off the list of who's going as though I might need persuading to accept, The Ospreys.

Although I've written about the band before, I've never actually interviewed them. The Ospreys enjoy the kind of fame that means they don't need to do press to promote their latest release; their records sell themselves. Every now and then they might agree to a sit-down, but it's usually with a big-name columnist with befitting status. However, it's an unwritten rule at these events that journalists can approach the attendees once the awards are over for a quick sound bite, as long as they don't pester them while they're trying to enjoy themselves. All I want to do is see if the band has heard of Aden Rowlock, or even know him. That's all I plan to ask; I certainly won't be mentioning Isaac or the blind item. I just think their reaction could be telling.

I stare out of the window as the streets of north London trickle by. We've already passed through Archway and are now trundling up the hill past the Whittington Hospital to cut through Crouch End. It's a familiar route for me: lots of bands play Alexandra Palace so I've been to many gigs there. Thankfully the drinks sponsor has paid for the cab in advance, as I wouldn't be able to afford the £55 fare from Maida Vale myself. I've had three text messages already this week from my bank asking me to call to arrange an 'account review' in my local branch. I know the messages are automated but I still feel sick to the pit of my stomach when they pop up. I don't know what will happen if I don't comply, but right now I cannot face going through my finances with a stranger who I know will judge me for the mess I'm in.

Ten minutes later my cab has joined a queue of vehicles stretching up the approach road to the venue and after a few more minutes of stop-start the driver lets me out. I shoot along the red carpet that's been laid out for attendees, knowing I'm of no interest to either the fans behind the barriers or the photographers jostling for shots. Just outside the main entrance I pass the press pen and see two freelancers I know who couldn't get a ticket for inside. I return their waves sheepishly: being offered a seat at a table at one of these events is a privilege I know not to take for granted.

Inside, Alexandra Palace is even busier. I'm ushered through the Palm Court entrance into a cavernous, glass-ceilinged space decorated with evergreen foliage and a tiled floor that echoes with the click-clack of high heels, mine included. Here, people are milling about in no discernible order, a waiting pen before we'll be ordered into the main arena where dinner will be served and the ceremony will take place. I accept a glass of champagne offered to me by a waiter bearing a trayful and head deeper into the crowd towards a large easel displaying tonight's seating plan. I want to see where my table is and whether it's anywhere near The Ospreys'.

Before I reach it, however, a hand grabs my upper arm and aggressively pulls me back. Shocked, I turn to find Bronwyn gripping my arm and glaring down at me. She looks stunning in a navy jumpsuit, but her expression tells me a compliment would be wasted right now – I can see she's livid about something.

She drops her hand from my arm and leans down to hiss in my face.

'What the hell did you say to that lawyer, Nat? You said you wanted to know who he was, not harass him.'

It takes my brain a second to catch up. She's talking about Aden Rowlock.

'I haven't spoken to him yet,' I splutter. Her expression hardens: she doesn't believe me. 'I'm telling the truth. I did go round to the address but he wasn't in so I left my card with one of the other occupants asking him to call me but so far he hasn't. I haven't harassed him either, I only went the once.'

'You must've have done something to upset him,' Bronwyn snaps, 'because after you went round to see him he fired off a legal letter going ape-shit that his client relationships have been compromised by someone giving out his address to a journalist. Which I gave to you in good faith, Nat.'

'I know you did, but I swear I did nothing out of order.' That's not true, I suddenly remember. I told Bibek it was at The Soundbank that I'd heard about Rowlock's new client. I feel a pang of guilt that my blurting it out might have got Bronwyn into trouble, but I daren't say anything, I know how cross she'll be. 'Maybe yours is the only studio where his client's songs are being recorded at the moment?' I offer lamely.

Bronwyn bristles. 'It's not the point though. I could lose my job over this. He quoted GDPR.'

'But it was the person in Felix Thompson's office who gave you the address. The fault lies with them.'

'Jess didn't know I was giving it to you though,' says Bronwyn sternly. 'I never said why I needed it.'

'Isn't it a bit precious of a solicitor to complain about his address being given out though? How does that compromise him and his clients?'

Bronwyn is in no mood to debate the whys and wherefores.

'I don't care what he's upset about, just that he is. I was stupid to have helped you out.' I can see she's near to tears now and guilt rears up inside me. 'If I get sacked for this I'll never get another job as a studio manager. No one will trust me, my reputation will be mud.'

'That won't happen,' I assure her, feeling wretched that I've put her in this position. A thought then occurs. 'Did the letter mention me by name?'

'No, it just said a journalist—'

A loudspeaker announcement telling us to take our seats at our tables cuts her off. People start to flow past us and I'm almost sent flying as a man shoulder-barges into me. Bronwyn grabs me by the arm to steady me, but her grip hurts and she increases the pressure as she thrusts her face into mine. In all the years we've been friends we've barely had a cross word, but the way she's glaring at me now makes my insides curdle and I want to kick myself for not being more careful when I spoke to Bibek; I was so swept up in the moment that I never thought to consider Rowlock might retaliate formally.

'You better had make sure it's not traced back to me, Nat,' says Bronwyn, her voice quivering. 'If I lose my job over this it's your fault.'

Chapter Thirteen

Bronwyn stalks off before I can muster a reply. I think about going after her, but the crowd begins to swell around me and instead I allow myself to be swept along with it into the main room where the awards are taking place.

On taking my seat for dinner I have to force myself to engage in conversation with the person I'm seated next to, someone high up in the drinks company, when really I want to slump back in my chair and process what just happened. I hate that I've upset Bronwyn and I want to make amends, but it will have to wait until the awards are finished. I do send a text saying 'I know you're angry and I'm sorry. Can we meet up after?' but she doesn't reply.

Clearly I've struck a nerve going to see Aden Rowlock but I stand by what I said to Bronwyn: why is a solicitor getting so worked up about his address being given to a journalist? Surely solicitors want to be found, to attract more clients if nothing else? Then I remember how I found no record of Rowlock's practice online and how shabby his premises were. Something's clearly odd with the way he operates, unless its deliberate subterfuge to detract from the kind of work he does?

However, the last thing I want is for Bronwyn to get into trouble because of me and I have to hope word doesn't get back to Felix Thompson that Rowlock is upset, so his assistant who gave us his address can't put two and two together and realise she inadvertently gave it to Bronwyn to pass to me. But, again, I keep coming back to the same thing: why would any solicitor be bothered about people knowing their business address unless they had something to hide?

Or, I think, *someone*.

Rowlock's complaint would make sense if Isaac Naylor happens to be the client he wants to protect. Excitement swells inside me. The more I look into this story, the more it's starting to appear as though there's a grain of truth in the blind item, that Isaac Naylor isn't dead and he's writing songs and Rowlock must be desperately trying to micromanage the situation until the time comes for him to step back into the limelight. That's why me going round there rattled him into sending the letter—

The drinks company hotshot nudges my elbow, jolting me out of my reverie. 'This is the category we've sponsored,' he crows.

'Excellent,' I pretend to enthuse, reaching for the awards programme that was left beside my place setting. The category is Best Band Download of the Year – and among the eight nominees are The Ospreys. Immediately I scan the room to see where they are seated, my heart jittery in my chest. The hotshot asks me who I'm looking for but I ignore him.

The sudden swoop of a spotlight across the venue makes it easier for me. It's picking out the nominees one by one so a camera crew navigating the tables can project live footage of them onto the large screen at the side of the stage. When the presenter of the category – a well-known comedian – reads out 'The Ospreys', I follow the spotlight and watch as it falls on the smiling faces of Isaac Naylor's former band-mates.

They're sitting five tables away.

A hush falls over the room as the comedian rips open the envelope he's holding. 'The award goes to . . .'

He reads out the name of another band to deafening applause but The Ospreys are not bothered to have lost. They shrug their shoulders and reach for the bottles of champagne generously littering their table. Their manager Derrick Cordingly, a face as familiarly famous as all theirs, fails to hide his disappointment though, grimacing at the stage, where the winners are now delivering their acceptance speech. I watch as he leans over the table to say something to the band then rises to his feet. Sensing my chance, I excuse myself from my table, saying I need to use the bathroom, and trail him to the outer room, where he bumps into someone he clearly knows well, judging by the jovial way they greet each other. The two of them then head outside.

The view from Alexandra Palace is spectacular, the entire London skyline visible to the eye, but I pay no heed to it as I casually stroll over to the balustrade where Derrick and the other man have lit up cigarettes and are chatting as they smoke. Journalists aren't meant to approach any talent until after the awards are over, but there's nothing in the unwritten rules that says we can't chat to a manager outside the venue during a fag break. I'm not a smoker but will partake for the sake of a conversation opener and I keep a packet of cigarettes in my bag for moments exactly like this.

'Excuse me, could I borrow a light?' I ask, holding up the cigarette I've just taken out of my clutch bag.

'Sure,' says the other man, taking his lighter from his pocket and flicking the flame to life.

'Thanks,' I say, leaning forward to use it. Then, not giving them the chance to re-start their conversation, I turn to Derrick and hold out my hand. 'Hi. I don't think we've met before. I'm Natalie Glass. I was a writer on *The Frequency* and now I freelance for the nationals.'

'Right. Yes, I've read your stuff. It's good to put a face to the name,' he smiles, shaking my hand. He introduces his companion as Tony Croft, from the band's record label. 'You having a good night?' Derrick asks.

'I am, yes.' An idea suddenly clicks into place. 'I'm glad I ran into you, because I'm working on a piece about The Ospreys and I'd love to get your take on it.' Not strictly accurate, but he doesn't need to know that yet.

'What's the angle?' he asks, eyes narrowing.

I scrabble for a convincing hook. 'Um, it's about how they've managed to thrive despite a key member dying, when other huge bands like Nirvana and Led Zeppelin weren't able to. I thought I could tie it in with the anniversary of them signing their first deal next month.'

Both Derrick and Tony nod approvingly, because every manager and label want their bands to be compared favourably with the greats. I offer up a silent thank you to Neil for telling me about the anniversary.

'I was going to ring Sherry to see if I could get some time on the phone with you. I'd love to hear your take on what helped The Ospreys survive the tragedy.'

Sherry Caputo is the band's publicist. Derrick's gaze flickers to Tony, then lands back on me.

'As long as it doesn't dwell too much on Isaac's suicide,' he surprises me by saying. 'I know there's still public interest, but it's not nice having it raked over time and time again.'

He looks genuinely pained and I'm reminded it wasn't just the band members themselves who suffered Isaac's loss. Derrick was the person who discovered them, nurtured them and made them famous. What happened must have devastated him too.

'Call Sherry to set up a time, tell her I said it's fine,' he adds.

'Thank you, I shall.'

I wonder how he'd react if I told him about the blind item. I won't though, because he might not react well to me repeating gossip. But I do have a related question that I carefully put to him.

'I'm also trying to track down a couple of other people from that time to interview. Do you know how I can get in touch with Aden Rowlock?' I say it matter-of-factly, as though I am sure Derrick will have heard of him, yet both men frown.

'I don't recognise the name,' says Tony.

'Me neither,' says Derrick. 'Who is he?'

I can feel my face flushing and hope I can pull off the lie convincingly. 'I was told he worked for the label and was a friend of Isaac's.'

Me saying Isaac's name has a palpable effect on Derrick. His face falls and for a moment he looks forlorn again. Fearing I've pushed it enough, I stub out my cigarette and make a move to leave.

'Never mind,' I say. 'Thanks for the light, I'll call Sherry tomorrow.'

Derrick's expression evens out and he smiles. 'Don't rush off on my account. It's just hard, you know. Talking about him. Even after all this time.' He stares out over the balustrade, the illuminated cityscape twinkling back at him. 'It changed us all, losing Isaac. I don't know if I'll ever forgive myself for not saving him.'

Tony shifts awkwardly on the spot and looks to me to say something; I'm guessing he's not used to Derrick opening up like this in the course of their usual dealings. But for once I am lost for words, knowing I could offer sympathy, but fearing it might ring hollow, an empty platitude for someone I never knew. Fortunately for both of us Derrick snaps to.

'What was that name again?' he asks me.

'Aden Rowlock.' I spell it out and Derrick looks intrigued.

'That's an unusual spelling. Isn't it usually A-i-d-a-n? Still doesn't ring a bell though.' He reaches into the breast pocket of his suit and pulls out a plain white card with just his name and a phone number printed on it. He hands it to me. 'This is my personal mobile number. I'm choosy about who I give it to so don't go sharing it. Call me tomorrow and we'll talk then.'

'You don't want me to go through Sherry?'

'No, this way's fine.'

I thank him and shake both their hands. I walk away, heading back into the venue, when Derrick calls out to me.

'Good luck finding your mystery man.'

I turn away quickly so he can't see my startled expression. He has no idea how close to the mark he is.

Chapter Fourteen

Everyone at my table is drunk by the time I return to it. An undeniable benefit of being with one of the drink sponsors is that the waiters are under orders to make sure our glasses are constantly replenished, and as I sit down mine is immediately filled to the brim with wine. Thrilled to have seemingly scored an interview with Derrick Cordingly, one of the most successful managers in modern music, I knock back a large mouthful, then another. The sponsor bigwig sees what I'm doing and grins.

'That's more like it. I was starting to think you were one of those rare journalists who didn't like a drink!'

Barely an hour and a bottle of wine to myself later, I'm well on my way to being drunk as well. The last few awards of the evening have thrown up surprises – the best album wasn't Adele's latest as widely predicted – and as we reach the penultimate category, Best Female Act, the mood of the room is buoyant. The bigwig and I are deep in a discussion about long-term record deals becoming obsolete when a waiter taps me on the shoulder and hands me a folded piece of paper. Puzzled, I flip it open and see it's a scrawled message in Bronwyn's handwriting.

The waiter whispers in my ear. 'She asked me to take you to where she is.'

I nod and rise from my seat, grabbing my clutch bag from the table.

'Work emergency,' I tell the bigwig. 'I'll be back in a sec.'

'Make sure you are,' he grins sloppily, raising his glass at me. 'When the awards are over, that's when the real partying starts.'

I follow in the waiter's slipstream, my stomach churning with nervous anticipation as we wend our way through the tables. I'm pleased Bronwyn wants to talk, but a bit surprised she didn't come and find me herself or simply text. The terseness of the note and its angry caps do not bode well.

Instead of leading me through the doors back into the Palm Court though, the waiter takes me to the side of the room where there are glass-panelled exits spaced at intervals that he and his fellow servers have been coming in and out of all evening.

'Back here is out of bounds to guests,' he says, pushing the swing door open, 'but if anyone asks, Harry gave you permission.'

I probably should ask who Harry is but I don't because I'm too busy trying to keep my balance. Now I'm standing, the effects of the wine I necked far too speedily have become glaringly acute; I'm lightheaded, my limbs feel woolly and I'm unsteady on my high heels. I grip my clutch bag tighter under my arm as though that might somehow balance me. It doesn't.

The area behind the door is noisy and chaotic, with waiters carting empty bottles of booze in and full bottles out. I read once that at the BRITs there are typically 550 front-of-house waiting staff and 60 chefs working 2,300 man-hours to produce three courses for 400 guests. These awards are probably two-thirds the size, but that's still a lot of personnel. Thankfully everyone's too busy for me to have to invoke the Harry line as my excuse for being there, but I am relieved when the waiter steers me away from the hubbub to a section of the room at the far end that is cordoned off by heavy-duty floor-to-ceiling black curtains.

'She's through there,' he says, and flits off.

I look for the gap in the curtains, pulling at the material until I find it. Then, cautiously, I poke my head through. The curtains are concealing a small space rendered darker than the rest of the catering area because of the shielding effect of the curtains and because there is no light source directly above. There are three screens positioned to one side and I get the impression it's some kind of temporary dressing room for someone. I blink to adjust my vision to the low light. 'Bron?' I call out.

There's movement to the right of me, so I step fully into the space, expecting Bronwyn to be there. But when I turn round it's not her I'm confronted by but a man twice my size dressed entirely in black. Before I can say anything he raises his fist and hits me so hard in the left cheek I go flying backwards into the screens. The pain is indescribable but as I sprawl on the floor I'm too shocked to even cry. Then, to my horror, he advances towards me again, huge hands still curled into fists. Whimpering, I turn my face away, fearful of another blow landing, but he doesn't hit me. Instead, he leans down until he is close enough for me to smell mint chewing gum on his breath.

'Leave the fucking story alone or this'll be nothing compared to what comes next.'

Chapter Fifteen

With that my attacker flees. I wait until I'm sure he's gone, then awkwardly raise myself up from the floor. I am in agony, the whole side of my face throbbing so viciously I think I might pass out. I realise I must look a state because when I stagger out from behind the curtains a waiter – not the one who led me to the ambush, but another one – swears loudly before rushing over to me.

'Are you OK?' he asks. 'What happened to your face?'

With terrifying clarity I realise I cannot tell the truth. The man who assaulted me could be hiding nearby, watching and listening. 'I fell over,' I say. 'Too much wine.'

The waiter peers at my cheek. 'You should go to hospital to get it checked out. It looks nasty.'

I go to nod but even the slightest movement hurts so much I want to howl. 'Is there a way out here?' I ask him.

He ushers me across the room to a fire door marked 'emergency exit only' and pushes down hard on the metal bar to pop it open. 'I think there's a taxi rank set up near the car park,' he says.

By now my cheek has swelled to such an extent that my eye is closing up and the excruciating pain means I can only mumble my thanks as I stagger through the doorway. Rounding the corner of the venue I see a bank of black taxis waiting idly, the soft glow of their orange for-hire lights illuminating my path. The drinks company PR already said I can reclaim the cost of my cab home from them, so I pile gratefully into the back of the first one in the queue and give him my address.

'Not being funny, love, but are you sure you don't want A & E?' the driver asks.

I gingerly raise my fingers to my cheek. The swelling feels enormous now. Tears fill my eyes.

'No. I'd rather go home first.'

'You sure?'

'Please,' I implore.

With obvious reluctance he nods and starts the engine.

The last thing I want is to go to hospital where I'll be asked awkward questions about how I came to be injured. What would I say? 'I thought I was meeting my best friend but instead a shaven-headed thug in a sharp suit sprang out of the darkness to attack me.' No, it would raise more questions than I can answer. I need to talk to Bronwyn before I talk to anyone else. Does she know him? If so, how? Why did she write the note to lead me to him? With a pang of alarm, I wonder for a second if she knew what was going to happen, but dismiss the thought just as quickly. This is the woman who cradled me when I would break down on her shoulder in the throes of my divorce, who made sure I still ate when I couldn't stomach food and who sat up with me all night keeping watch over me when I got so drunk to counter my stress I collapsed in a booze coma. There is no way Bronwyn would knowingly have put me in harm's way. Whoever my attacker was he must've tricked or forced her into writing that note. That latter, horrifying thought propels me into calling her, but she doesn't pick up. I send a follow-up text, begging her to ring back, but don't say why. I'm too scared the wrong person might see the message.

As we head down the hill away from Alexandra Palace I ask myself what kind of man attacks without provocation at an awards ceremony attended by more than 2,000 potential witnesses and the answer is obvious: one who's paid to. He knew what he was doing by luring me backstage and how to get around being seen. He also knew how to pull a punch, hitting me hard enough to hurt me but not so hard he'd knock me out cold and risk me being found by someone who might have called the police. Right now I don't feel lucky in any regard, the pain so intense I feel like my head might explode, but I know I should be grateful I am not more severely injured.

I replay what he said to me and conclude the story he warned me to back away from has to be the mystery songwriter, because it's the only one I'm working on and it's already proving contentious. But would Aden Rowlock, the only person I know with a vested interest, really go so far as to arrange an assault to warn me off it? Admittedly it wouldn't have been that hard for him to organise: I've been posting about attending the awards for the past few days on social media, so I pretty much drew him a map to where I could be ambushed. But why send a letter to The Soundbank, but a hired thug to beat me up? Threatening me with legal action would be far more effective because I really can't afford to be sued right now. Except, I think to myself, Rowlock doesn't know that and, if he is behind what just happened, might have thought he needed to push his warning to me that bit further and has banked on me keeping quiet about it.

My head starts to swim so I lean back against the seat and close my eyes. By the time I reopen them we've reached Swiss Cottage at the bottom of Fitzjohn's Avenue. Sitting up, I feel again as though I might pass out from the pain, so I haul myself forward and rap on the Perspex divider that separates me from the driver.

'I need to find a chemist that's open. Would you mind stopping?' I ask.

The driver has a gruff voice but a kind tone.

'Makes no odds to me if we stop, but are you sure you don't want to go to hospital to get it checked out, love? We just passed the Royal Free – I could easily swing round and go back.'

'No, a chemist is fine.'

I slump back in the seat and close my eyes again. Five minutes later the taxi draws to a halt.

'Here's a 24-hour one,' the driver calls to me.

We've pulled up in front of a row of shops that includes an artisan bakery and a vet's surgery. The only frontage that's illuminated at this hour, though, is the chemist's.

'Will you wait?' I ask the taxi driver.

'Of course I will. I've got a daughter and I wouldn't want her being left somewhere at night after she's been walloped in the face.'

'I wasn't hit, I fell.' I don't know why I'm lying to him, but right now I'm too paranoid to admit the truth. What if my attacker is tracking me home on Rowlock's orders?

The driver regards me for a moment then nods. 'Whatever you say, love.' Then, to my surprise, he turns the meter off. 'Get what you need from the chemist and the rest of the way home is on me.'

His kindness starts me off crying and I stumble into the chemist with tears streaking down my face. The pharmacist pays little heed to them, however, and instead comes out from behind his counter to examine my cheek close up.

'It could be just badly bruised or you might have fractured your cheekbone. You should go to hospital and have it X-rayed to be sure,' he says.

'Even if it is fractured, what can they do though?' I ask. 'It's not like they can put my face in plaster.'

'No, but they might need to operate if it's a particularly bad fracture and needs pinning. Is your vision blurred at all?'

'Um, hard to tell – I was drinking before I fell over. Everything was blurry.'

The pharmacist isn't amused by my feeble attempt at humour. 'Is your vision blurred?' he repeats unsmilingly.

'No, it's not. Sorry, I didn't mean to be flippant. I just want some painkillers and to go home to bed,' I say.

'The strongest I can give you without a prescription is codeine. If it's as painful in the morning go to A & E then. But if you experience decreased eye movement or eye pain or if your eye suddenly appears sunken, call for an ambulance.'

The thought of my eye sinking into my face is terrifying. 'I'll do that,' I promise, meaning it.

Fifteen minutes later I'm finally home. I let myself into the flat and steel myself to look in the mirror Gayle has hanging in the hallway. The shock of seeing my cheek bruised and mis-shapen makes me tremble and once I start I can't stop. I go into the kitchen and head straight to the freezer for the bottle of vodka I keep in there, and for a bag of peas, which I wrap in a tea towel to hold against the swelling. The vodka I drink neat from the bottle, held to my lips by an unsteady hand.

I keep a stack of Post-its on the breakfast bar for shopping lists and use one now to make a note of my attacker's description: at least 6ft 4 tall, shaved hair, blue or possibly green eyes, definitely not brown – the light might not have been great in the cordoned-off area but I did get a close look when he loomed over me – and he was wearing a dark grey suit with a shirt and tie in the same shade. Hands like Christmas hams. No wedding ring or any other kind, thank god. He did enough damage just with his fingers curled.

I take another swig of vodka, only this time it's to wash down two of the codeine tablets I got from the chemist. Then I put the bottle back in the freezer. I know my limits. I want to be able to sleep through the pain, but still wake up in the morning. Then I triple-check the French doors are locked and go round the rest of the apartment making certain every window is shut and secure before dead-bolting the front door. Then, still feeling unsafe, I call Bronwyn's number again. She doesn't pick up, but this time I leave a voicemail message.

'We need to talk. Someone gave me a note at dinner saying you were looking for me, but when I went to find you someone else was waiting. I think it was to do with what we spoke about earlier,' I say cautiously. 'Can you give me a call as soon as you get this? Don't worry about the time, just call me.'

Then I send a text to her wife, Lucy, saying Bronwyn isn't answering her phone and ask if she's home safely because I couldn't find her once the awards had finished. I know Lucy won't mind the late message because she's a night owl who usually goes to bed after midnight and is often up after that trying to resettle Harrison. She texts straight back to say Bronwyn got home fine and she hoped I had a good evening.

Relieved Bronwyn's OK, I clamber into bed. My body is no longer shaking and as the vodka and codeine kicks in and the pain in my face begins to ease and I start the slide into drowsiness, I reach a conclusion: Aden Rowlock's client *has* to be Isaac Naylor. If it were any other star making a comeback under the guise of the mystery songwriter, the story being leaked wouldn't be problematic: a good PR could spin it to the songwriter's advantage, hailing their climb back to the top a success story. But Isaac attempting a comeback is far more fraught, with endless complications and consequences. Not only would he face a storm of criticism for evading justice and devastating millions of fans by faking his suicide, he could actually still face charges over Emily Jenkins' death if the police decided to reopen the case in the light of his reappearance. No wonder Rowlock is prepared to do whatever it takes to stop me reporting what I know before they are ready to reveal the truth. I've thrown a spanner in what must be a meticulously thought-out plan.

Almost asleep now, I tell myself that I should probably heed the warning about walking away – the agonising state of my face tells me I should. Yet if I'm inching closer to exposing Isaac as the mystery songwriter, as I believe I now am, I'd be crazy to stop. Isaac's return from the dead could make my career. I just need to be more careful – and to prove unequivocally the blind item is true.

Chapter Sixteen

Daily Mirror

3 January 2012

NO ENCORE FOR NAYLOR: SEARCH FOR ROCK STAR'S BODY CALLED OFF

Coastguard fails to recover Isaac Naylor's body after he drowns himself following arrest for fan's death

By Chief Reporter Michael Jones

The Ospreys' lead singer Isaac Naylor is presumed dead after committing suicide while being investigated for the suspicious death of a teenage fan.

Platinum album-selling Naylor, 29, was arrested three weeks ago when the body of 17-year-old Emily Jenkins was discovered in his hotel room after the band played a gig at Glasgow's Hampden Road stadium on 10 December. She died from a suspected heroin overdose and police launched an investigation into Naylor's involvement, believing he injected her with the drugs.

Naylor was bailed after his arrest, but when he failed to turn up at a police station in north London on 21 December, as per his bail conditions, he was reported missing by his manager, Derrick Cordingly.

Despite a nationwide police hunt there was no sign of the singer's whereabouts until eleven days later, when a woman walking her dog on Moor Sands beach in Devon on New Year's Day morning found his belongings. The police believe he drowned himself, but a two-day search by the coastguard was called off late last night after it failed to recover his body.

According to a police source, the belongings recovered on the beach were Naylor's clothes, passport, wallet and two letters, one addressed to his three band-mates and the other to his brother, Toby, 26.

'The letters point to Naylor killing himself,' the source told the *Daily Mirror*. 'It's a terrible outcome for the family of Emily Jenkins, who were desperate for answers about what happened to her.'

Emily, from Scotstoun, was found dead in Naylor's room at the Regency Country Park Hotel on the outskirts of Glasgow. Witnesses have told investigating officers that Emily was introduced to Naylor at The Ospreys' gig after securing a VIP backstage pass, then returned with him to his hotel. The last sighting of her was accompanying Naylor into his £630-a-night suite.

The teenager's body was reportedly discovered with a syringe needle still puncturing her skin. When Naylor failed to report for bail, her distraught parents, Heather and Richard, appealed for him to give himself up to the authorities. They maintain their daughter was 'a sensible, intelligent girl who never got into trouble and had never taken drugs before' and they believe she must have been forcibly injected. When news of his apparent suicide broke last night, they issued a further statement saying they were devastated to have been denied justice for their daughter.

'We take no pleasure in learning that Isaac Naylor is presumed dead. We had hoped he would come forward with the truth about what happened to Emily so we could begin the long, terrible process of grieving for her. Now we've been robbed of that and also of any hope of getting justice for her,' they said.

Naylor's three band-mates Danny Albright, Archie Samuels and Robert 'Renner' Jones said they were 'heartbroken and numb with shock' at the death of their friend, who they'd known since boyhood.

'The past two weeks have been incredibly trying for the band as they've pleaded with Isaac to come forward and answer for what he did,' said Ospreys' publicist, Sherry Caputo. 'This is the outcome of their nightmares and they have asked that the media respects their privacy as they come to terms with the loss of their dear friend and colleague.'

Hundreds of distraught fans gathered outside Naylor's north London home to pay their respects last night, lighting candles and singing Ospreys' songs, sparking criticism from his neighbours. One disgruntled resident, who didn't want to be named, said they hoped the police would move the fans on, adding, 'After what he did to that girl in Scotland he doesn't deserve their adulation and crass attempts at mourning.'

Naylor grew up in Jarrow, Tyne-and-Wear. His father, John, died in 2008 and his mother passed away when he was a child. The younger brother who survives him, Toby, has yet to comment.

An inquest into Naylor's death has been opened and adjourned and a full hearing will take place at a later date.

Appetite for destruction: the full shocking story of Isaac Naylor's downfall and death, pp.4–5.

Chapter Seventeen

MONDAY, 10TH

There's a brief moment when I come to when I forget what happened last night and wonder why my cheek feels so sore. Then I remember and panic propels me out of bed and into the bathroom to check if the pharmacist's dire warning about my eye sinking into my face has come true. I'm relieved to see it hasn't, but the entire eye socket is now puffy and bruised to match the vivid shade of blueberry colouring my cheek. My face doesn't hurt half as much as it did last night though, and as I gingerly explore the surface of it with my fingertips, the more certain I become that there is no fracture.

I am no less shaken by what happened though, and last night's resolve to pursue the story no matter what is wavering now I am fully conscious and can see the damage my attacker's fist wreaked. What might happen to me if I do keep digging? It's a sobering thought and why, I decide, as I go into the kitchen to make myself a coffee, I won't be door-knocking Aden Rowlock again any time soon. I need to give him the widest berth until I'm able to confront him with proof of what I know.

It's only when I've finished my coffee and popped a couple more painkillers that it strikes me last night's attack makes *me* a part of the story now. Editors would clamour for my first-person exclusive of how I was attacked backstage at the awards for my silence. But I can't write it yet, as that would mean revealing the blind item before I've had the chance to stand it up. I'd need to explain the basis for the attack and instinct tells me it's far too soon to share it. In a similar vein I don't want to report the assault to the police either. If I give them Rowlock's name and why I suspect him being behind it, the story will be out of my hands for good.

Holding on to that thought, I head into the reception room to begin work. It's early, a few minutes shy of eight. Instead of using the spare room as I usually do, today I'm going to work on the sofa with my laptop on the coffee table in front of me. It's not the most comfortable position in which to work, but it affords me a clear view of the French doors and the patio and communal gardens beyond them. I have no idea if my assailant knows where I live and the thought that he might is frightening, but if he or someone else decides to pay me an unsolicited visit via the back way I'll see them coming sitting here. I'm not concerned about the front because visitors have to be buzzed through the main door into the building and then there are two long corridors to traverse before they even get to this apartment, the front door of which is still dead-bolted and staying so.

First I check my emails, only to find a stinging rejection from a commissioning editor of a female-centric website I've never written for before. I'd pitched them a couple of ideas a few weeks ago, but the commissioning editor has finally responded saying 'they fall short of our expected standard'. I wouldn't mind, but from what I can see most of the website's content is regurgitated press releases. Also in my inbox is the latest statement for one of my four credit cards. My chest tightens and a wave of dread washes over me. I can't bear to look at it, already knowing how bad it is, but I do have enough to cover the minimum payment when it's due.

I sit quietly for a few minutes to steady my breathing until the tightness in my chest eases. All my debt could be swept away in a single payment if only Spencer would hurry up and put the house on the market. He keeps saying he will, but there's always something that gets in the way, like work or the holidays or a newspaper report that houses prices are going to crash that sends him into an irrational spin. My solicitor tells me I can apply for a financial order to force the sale but I don't want to go down that route yet because I'm fearful it will incite him even further. But it has to happen soon, because I cannot continue living hand to mouth like this, the push-pull act I have to perform with my finances every month to ensure all my payments are met wearing me down.

It's the fear of accumulating more debt that refocuses my mind back on the Isaac story. While the rational side of my brain thinks I am crazy to contemplate continuing after last night, that no story is worth the risk of physical harm, the other side, the side that knows how skint I am right down to the last penny, tells me I can't afford to let it go even if I wanted to. The potential reward of nailing this exclusive is simply too great: I could make some serious money off the back of it, enough to put up a far more robust legal case for equal custody of Daniel than I'm managing at the moment. And it's that, the thought of being in a better financial position to fight for my son, which quells any rational argument. Plus, on a side note, there's also my ego. Who wouldn't want to be the journalist who confirms Isaac Naylor is back from the dead? Imagine the plaudits. My resolve strengthening once more, I close down my inbox and open a search engine.

All the background I've researched since reading the blind item centred on what happened in the immediate aftermath of

Isaac committing suicide. Yet I realise now that is the wrong approach: I should be looking at what happened *long* afterwards, for clues as to where he ended up – in other words, supposed sightings of him in the eight years since he allegedly died. And I know just the place to start looking.

MusicJabber is an online fan forum dedicated to sharing opinions about the UK music industry. It's tightly moderated, so comments that veer into nastiness or defamation are immediately removed and the poster blocked. No three strikes rule either: one vicious slur and you're gone. Instead, posters are defined by their passion for music and debates are spiritedly but fairly argued. I regard MusicJabber as the thinking fan's forum and it's a welcome anomaly in this age of trolling and takedowns.

I type 'Isaac Naylor' into the search box and am gifted hundreds of entries in response. So I search again, typing 'Isaac Naylor + sightings', and this time the results are far fewer. However, in geographical terms, they couldn't be more spread out: according to posters, Naylor's been spotted everywhere from Mexico City and Cape Town to Monaco and Tenerife. Meanwhile, those who claim to have spotted him and swear blind it was him say he's either much fatter or much skinnier (which would be quite remarkable as he was already twig-thin when he disappeared) or in one case as muscle-bound as a weightlifter. He also has long hair, no hair, facial hair or the hair he does have is bottle blond (as it was when he was last seen), black, mouse-brown or grade 1 grey. In short, Isaac Naylor looks like someone on a sliding scale between Boris Johnson and Dwayne Johnson.

I keep scrolling until a particular post jumps off the page at me. It's dated three years ago and was written by someone with the username Indigo Tango.

My brother swears he spoke to Naylor in Kathmandu when he was travelling through Nepal four years ago. There's a buzzing music scene there and one evening my brother goes to a bar to hear a Nepalese guitar duo play, on the recommendation of someone at the hostel he was staying in. When my brother gets there he's the only foreigner at the gig – everyone else is local. It's in this tiny backstreet bar, off the beaten track. Anyway, towards the end of the gig this white dude gets up on stage and starts jamming with them. My brother said he was really good, like, amazing. He goes near the stage for a closer look and is stunned when he sees the guy is a dead ringer for the lead singer of The Ospreys. My brother was a fan. But he thinks it can't be him, because Naylor is dead. My brother waits until the gig's over then sees the dude at the bar and goes over. He hears someone call him 'Jack', so still he thinks it can't be Naylor. But he can't believe the resemblance, so when the dude packs up his guitar and goes to leave, my brother calls out 'Hey, Isaac, can I buy you a drink?' He says the dude goes as white as a sheet and legs it out of there so fast that by the time my brother's followed him outside he's long gone. My brother goes back into the bar to ask about 'Jack' but the locals refuse to talk to him – like, they totally clam up. But the dude's reaction and the way everyone in the bar went weird afterwards convinced my brother it was definitely Naylor. He thinks the locals knew who he was and were covering for him.

I re-read the post three times. It's by far the most convincing of all the sightings mentioned and as hiding places go Nepal seems plausible enough. I know the country is a stop on the infamous 'hippie trail' between London and Goa first made popular in the sixties and seventies, so the transient nature of its backpacking visitors could have made it easy for Naylor to blend in on his arrival. But how could he have got all the way there from the UK without being spotted? He was arrested and bailed after Emily's body was discovered, with strict conditions that he had to report to a police station every two days. When he failed to turn up and the police realised he'd absconded, alerts were issued to airports and ports. Not to mention the saturation media coverage which meant the entire nation was aware of who he was, what he was accused of doing and what he looked like. Christ, even my grandmother knew who Isaac Naylor was back then. No, the inarguable fact is that, until his belongings were found on that beach, Isaac Naylor was the most hunted person in Britain. If he did manage to flee the country to travel to Nepal, it's inconceivable that he did it unaided.

So who helped him?

Chapter Eighteen

I start making notes in the leather-bound notebook I use when I am researching features. In a fit of paranoia I head the page 'Doris Day', so if anyone happens to glance at it they'll have no idea what I'm really working on. Pretty soon I've filled three pages.

It boils down to this: who would Isaac Naylor have turned to for help after being arrested on suspicion of causing Emily's death, other than his band-mates and manager? They're ruled out by virtue of the fact they are still mourning his death, like-wise his brother, Toby. So who else would Isaac have trusted enough to say 'I'm in deep shit, I need you to get me out of here?' and be sure they wouldn't go to the authorities and report him? Who would've had the means to spirit him out of the country when every police force was looking for him? It had to be someone he trusted with his life – and someone who believed he was innocent. It could've been someone from the record company, someone who worked with the band, a friend from home – anyone, in other words. I make a note to go back through old interviews of Isaac's for any mention of close friends who might fit the bill.

Then I perform a search for the transcript of Isaac's police interview, which Neil told me about. But while I can find references to it, I can't find the actual transcript itself. Frustrated, I wonder if the police in Glasgow will help me and so I email the press office at Police Scotland to see if I can make an inroad towards getting hold of a copy.

Next I turn my attention to Emily. It was assumed she and Isaac had never met before the night of the Hampden Park gig, but what if that's wrong? Yet pretty quickly I establish that Emily's foray into the seedier side of the music scene was tragically her first and last.

It was almost eighteen hours after the last sighting of her that Emily's body was found. That information was made public during the procurator fiscal's inquiry into her death, the reports of which I'm now reading online. Emily, who lived in the affluent Scotstoun district of Glasgow with her parents and younger sister, had saved up her own money from her Saturday job at H&M to buy a ticket for The Ospreys' gig at Hampden Park. She was going alone because none of her friends were fans enough to want to spend £100 on a ticket themselves and while her parents were a bit concerned about her going solo, they also trusted the teenager to get there and back with no hassle. Emily was a responsible child who never got into any bother either at school or outside of it. If she ever drank she must've done so within limits because her parents had never caught her drunk and they were adamant she was too sensible to dabble with drugs when Glasgow was rife with examples of what happened when you did.

But what her parents didn't know was that Emily had arranged to meet someone at the stadium, a girl she'd met online. Emily told friends on Facebook on the day of the gig that this person had wangled her a backstage pass because she knew the band. Yet the girl was never traced.

I pause reading then, and sit back. How can the police and procurator fiscal have drawn a blank with the person who provided the backstage pass? If she was a friend of the band, as Emily's Facebook comments intimated, surely she should've been interviewed for what she knew about Emily and Isaac meeting. I start scrolling again, keen to find any mention of why this girl was never traced, but it seems, inexplicably, that the trail went cold and no one felt she was worth pursuing. I wonder if that was because, according to a witness account given by a band crew member, Emily had watched the gig alone, standing apart from the few other fans also granted a VIP viewpoint at the side of the stage. Did the police therefore assume the girl simply handed over the pass to Emily at the start of the gig and that was the end of their acquaintance?

The next sighting of Emily was a couple of hours after the gig had finished and the bottleneck on King's Park Avenue caused by fans leaving had dispersed, when she was seen climbing into the rear seat of a blacked-out SUV with Naylor. The next anyone saw of her after that was when a hysterical Isaac called for help after waking up alongside her dead body.

Surely someone saw them arrive at the hotel together though? I find the explanation in a report by the *Glasgow Herald*: the hotel The Ospreys were staying at had a discreet underground entrance with a VIP lift that bypassed reception – no prying CCTV to record their movements, in other words.

Eventually I come across accounts given by Emily's parents. They make for heartbreaking reading: the mounting worry when she didn't return home that evening – they insisted it was unlike her to stay over somewhere without seeking permission first – then the knock at the door every parent dreads when they've reported their child missing. Then, after weeks of lurid headlines about their family life and what led their clever, sensible daughter to die in a rock star's hotel bed with heroin coursing through her system, her mum's gut-wrenching outburst at Isaac's inquest, when she screamed at Toby Naylor while he gave evidence that her family had been robbed of justice when his brother killed himself and she hoped Isaac rotted in hell.

Reading that inspires me to add another question to the list I've already made: why would Isaac risk returning to the UK now, knowing those calls for justice hadn't lessened with the passing of time? Presuming he would be tried in Scotland because Emily's death had occurred in Glasgow, Scottish law states a person who injects another with heroin and unintentionally kills them could be charged with involuntary culpable homicide, which carries a maximum sentence of ten years.

I'm making a note to check the statute of limitations in a case like Emily's when a buzzer sounds in the hallway to alert me that someone's rung my apartment number outside. I'm not expecting any visitors or deliveries, so it is with much trepidation that I push the intercom button and answer. My focus interrupted, I feel jumpy once more.

'Got a delivery for Natalie Glass,' says a male voice, before rattling off the name of a local florist.

Someone's sent me flowers? That's got to be a mistake. But before I can reply, a gentle female voice cuts in, which I recognise as belonging to an elderly tenant called Elizabeth, who resides in an apartment a few doors down from mine.

'Are those for Natalie at number three?' I hear her ask. 'I can give them to her on my way past her door, save her coming out.'

Silence follows until I hear the soft rap of ageing knuckles on wood. My phone clutched in my hand, poised to dial 999 if I have to, I open my front door to be confronted by a vast arrangement of white flowers, but that's not what causes me to be taken aback. It's Elizabeth who does that, because when she hands the flowers to me I can see she's tearful.

'I'm so sorry for your loss, I had no idea,' she says. 'What a terrible thing for you to experience, I can't imagine how you must be feeling. If there's anything I can do—'

A rush of blood to my ears drowns her out, because now I can see for myself what's prompted her distress. There is a small card sheathed in plastic that's attached to the arrangement and the message is plain to read.

Dear Natalie, please accept our sincerest condolences on the tragic loss of your son. No more story time for him. RIP.

Chapter Nineteen

My scream ricochets along the corridor. I snatch the flowers from Elizabeth's grasp, throw them to the ground then stamp on them. My neighbour recoils from me, shuffling backwards, hand clamped to her mouth to smother her alarm. The flowers are soon a pulpy, broken mess and I kick what's left of them away from the door, back down the corridor from where she carried them. My chest heaving with sheer terror, I call Spencer.

'Is Daniel alive?' I shriek at him.

Spencer's outside, I can hear traffic noise. 'What? Say that again?' he asks.

'Is Daniel alive?'

'Alive? I've just watched him go into class with his teacher.'

'Are you sure?'

'What the hell? Of course I'm sure. Natalie, what's going on? You sound hysterical—'

I hang up then turn to Elizabeth. 'My son's not dead.'

She lowers her hand. 'You mean . . .'

'Someone sent me those flowers as a sick joke.'

Her outraged expression reassures me that my destroying the arrangement wasn't an overreaction.

'Oh, that's awful, Natalie. Who would do such a terrible thing?'

'I don't know.'

It's then that she stops and stares at me, as though she's only noticing me for the first time.

'Your face,' she breathes. 'What happened to it?'

I'm tempted to tell her the truth, because I'm so upset right now I have a desperate need to be comforted. But common-sense cautions me it's not fair to unburden myself on Elizabeth and by doing so drag her into this. She's in her eighties and vulnerable with health issues. Taking a deep breath, I steady my tone so the lie is more convincing.

'I did it last night at work, covering a music awards ceremony at Alexandra Palace. I'm not used to wearing heels and I lost my balance and caught my cheek on the back of a chair.'

My neighbour looks slowly from the mess of my face to the mess of flowers on the floor and I suspect she's weighing up whether I'm telling the truth or whether the two are somehow connected.

'I shouldn't have thrown them on the floor like that. I've made a right mess,' I say ruefully, following her gaze. 'I'll clean them up before anyone else sees it.'

'You were upset, and rightly so. It's despicable, sending a mother a wreath of flowers like that for her child,' she says indignantly. 'I've a good mind to ring the florist and give them a piece of my mind.'

It's reassuring to have someone in my corner, but if anyone's going to ring the florist to find out who sent the arrangement it's going to be me.

'I'm going to call them now,' I say. 'But thank you.'

Elizabeth pats my forearm. Her touch is so frail I barely feel it. 'Make sure you do. Don't let whoever did this get away with it.'

'I won't,' I reassure her.

She bids me farewell with an invite to pop round to hers

for a cup of tea whenever I feel like a natter. I thank her again then go inside my apartment to fetch the dustpan and brush and a bin liner. I drop to my knees in the corridor and start sweeping the flowers up, but first I remove the card. Anger surges through me again as the words of the message drill into my brain. It's one thing to come after me, but quite another to include Daniel.

If I were in any doubt the flowers were related to me chasing Isaac Naylor's whereabouts, the reference to 'story time' on the card confirms it. It seems it's not enough for Aden Rowlock to send someone to physically harm me as a warning, now he's instigated a psychological assault using my son as bait. I sit back on my haunches for a moment and contemplate whether the story is worth the risk and the answer is of course no. Yet a voice in my head quietly chides me all the same. *Don't forget it's because of Daniel you need this story. You need money to fight Spencer. If you give up now, you're giving up on your son. And the fact Rowlock wants you to give up so much means it's a story so huge there will be shockwaves when you reveal it.*

I exhale noisily. I can't let myself be intimidated into stopping now and I know Daniel is protected where he is, in school and at home. Spencer is the type of hovering, neurotic parent who views every stranger as someone with the potential to do our son harm. He wouldn't let anyone he didn't know get within two metres of him. Also, it's telling that the card didn't mention Daniel by name and that's because I never feature him on my public social media accounts apart from the odd glimpse of the back of his head. I'm assuming that's how whoever sent the flowers discovered I had a son, but I'm scrupulous about never naming Daniel to protect his privacy so while I'm upset he's been dragged into this I'm also certain there is no online trail that could lead anyone to where he and Spencer live; everything in my life that requires an address is registered to

Maida Vale now. Nor do I share the same surname with Daniel, having reverted to my maiden name of Glass.

I stuff the card into the pocket of my joggers and continue sweeping.

I deposit the flowers in the communal bins on my way out half an hour later. There's nowhere I have to be, I just can't stay indoors. I need fresh air and space to collect my thoughts and calm my racing heart. I turn out of my street onto Elgin Avenue and head in the direction of Regent's Park, my feet in trainers and the rest of me clad in a tea dress with a faded print that identifies it as second-hand. I've plastered on foundation to cover my bruised eye and I'm also wearing sunglasses but my cheek is still visible and I notice a few wary glances as I pass people on the pavement. It must look worse than it feels, because the pain has lessened to a dull ache since last night.

Just as I reach the Outer Circle road on the fringes of Regent's Park, Spencer calls me back. I debate whether to answer but know that putting it off will only inflame his ire.

'What was that phone call about?' he asks testily. 'I had a client meeting straight after and I could barely concentrate wondering what the hell was going on with you.'

I can't tell him about the flowers, he'd flip, and rightly so. Instead I invent an explanation I hope sounds plausible.

'I had a bad dream, a nightmare, about Daniel, and it freaked me out because it felt so real. I'm sorry, I shouldn't have panicked you like that.'

'No, you shouldn't. What if he had been with me when you called?'

The thought of my son hearing me shrieking like a demented banshee about him being alive fills me with shame. But Spencer's not finished.

'He was very distressed as it was after your last contact. I've

97

talked to him about it and given it some thought and I feel it's in his best interests that he doesn't stay overnight at yours again until he feels comfortable doing so.'

I grind to a halt on the pavement. 'What?'

'I've spoken to my solicitor and he agrees that because of the incident last week with the neighbour shouting at Daniel and the effect it had on him, there should be no overnight visitation at the moment. We've applied to the court for a temporary adjustment to the custody agreement. Just until I can be sure he feels mentally secure with you.'

I react furiously. 'Mentally secure? It was just a neighbour being arsey with him playing outside – don't blow it out of proportion. I've spoken to him since and he's been fine.'

'Only because you brought him home. He's not comfortable staying overnight if people can scream and shout at him. He told me that himself.'

I try never to cry in my dealings with Spencer because it always has the effect of hardening his stance towards me, because he thinks I'm putting it on. But I can't help myself today. I'm worn out, rattled by last night's attack and this morning's flower delivery, and another trip to court is the last bloody thing I need.

'Please don't do this,' I tearfully beg.

'I'm not stopping you seeing him,' says Spencer huffily. 'I'm just saying he can't stay overnight because of what my solicitor agrees is a volatile environment.'

'It was a neighbour moaning about a flowerbed,' I exclaim. 'You won't win. I'll fight it.'

'You'll have to get a move on. The hearing's scheduled for half an hour's time. Didn't your solicitor tell you? Mine forwarded a copy of the application last Thursday, the morning after we submitted it.'

Oh god. I've been ignoring calls from my solicitor because I thought they were chasing me about the final portion of their bill I owe. Instead they must've been ringing to tell me about this. I imagine they've emailed too but I've been diverting messages from their address so I'm not constantly confronted by money-chasing queries until I'm in a position to pay.

I check my watch. Our case is assigned to the family court in Wandsworth, south of the river. There's no way I can be there in thirty minutes to represent myself. Defeated, I tell Spencer I won't object to the custody change, as long as it is only temporary. It's also just occurred to me, although I can never tell Spencer this, that it might actually be for the best right now – would it be safe for Daniel to stay with me in Maida Vale in the light of that wreath being sent? I'm not sure it would.

'Can I still see him on Wednesday?' I ask. 'I could pick him up from school and take him out for tea.'

'As long as he's back well before bedtime,' says Spencer grudgingly.

I hang up and give in to more tears. I must look a right state, sobbing on the side of the road, because a cyclist slows to a halt at the roadside and asks me if I'm OK. I brush him off and dart into the park, embarrassed to be caught crying.

I don't put my phone away though. Wiping my cheeks dry, I ring the florist and demand to know who sent me flowers in sympathy for my child because he is most definitely not dead. The woman who answers is mortified and apologises profusely for what she insists must be an innocent mix-up, but unfortunately data protection rules prohibit her from telling me who ordered the arrangement and I end the call even more frustrated. The confirmation that they originated from Rowlock would've proved a point.

I keep walking on, through Queen Mary's Rose Garden and out the other side until I hit the Outer Circle road again. It's a gorgeously sunny day and the park is full of office workers making the most of the lunch break by flopping down on the grass with shirtsleeves rolled up and shoes kicked off. On cue, my stomach rumbles to remind me I haven't fed it since last night's awards dinner so I head across Park Square towards Great Portland Street to find somewhere I can buy a sandwich from.

It's at that moment, standing at the traffic lights waiting to cross Marylebone Road, that I experience a feeling of being watched. I cautiously glance to the right, but the only person near to me is a woman about my age fussing over the hood of the buggy she's pushing, trying to pull it down further to block the sun from her sleeping toddler's face. Yet still the hairs on the back of my neck spike. There's no one on my left, so I twist round to check behind me and there is a couple heading my way, but they're engrossed in conversation with one another. I scan behind them to see who else is in the vicinity, but then I hear the beep signalling it's safe to cross so I turn round and hurry forward.

There's a Pret across the road and I dart gratefully into its air-conditioned interior. Sandwich and coffee paid for, I hoist myself onto a tall stool by the window so I can keep a watchful eye out. A couple of passersby cast glances my way – perhaps because I'm wearing my sunglasses inside, or more likely the heat has melted my make-up and my bruise is more visible – but the feeling I'm being watched begins to dissipate and I chide myself for being so nervy, even though it's hardly surprising I'm paranoid given what happened last night.

However, a few minutes later, as I wipe the crumbs from my dress and ball up the cardboard carton my sandwich came in, I notice someone is staring at me from across the road – and with a start I realise I recognise him.

It's the cyclist who stopped earlier to ask if I was OK. He's standing on the pavement across the road, his bike leaning against railings. The benefit of wearing my sunglasses indoors is that I can turn my head to appear as though I'm looking away from him but still glance sideways to fully take in his appearance. He isn't wearing a cycle helmet, just a red peaked cap pulled down low over his face, and he's dressed casually in shorts, a T-shirt and trainers. The bike, I can see now, is one of those scarlet for-hire ones.

He's definitely staring at me though.

My pulse quickens. I want to reach for my phone but fear keeps my hands clamped in my lap. What if he's been sent by Rowlock to finish off what the thug last night started? This man is shorter and out of shape, but that doesn't mean he couldn't still do some serious damage.

I'm frantically debating what to do – should I call the police, shout for help – when a woman clambering onto the empty stool next to mine jostles my elbow. I scoot across to make room for her and by the time I look out of the window again the cyclist is nowhere to be seen.

The only sign he was ever there is the bike, propped up and discarded against the railings.

Chapter Twenty

Extract from *Making Waves: The Highs and Lows of Isaac Naylor*, the unauthorised biography by Tamsin Taylor (Promulgate Publishing, £5.99)

It's A Crying Shame

Playing Knebworth was a pivotal moment for the band. No longer could their harshest critics claim they weren't one of the greats. Isaac said afterwards that having a nightly audience of 125,000 fans sing the words to 'Early Morning Cry' back at him was life defining and a photograph of him falling to his knees and sobbing helplessly on the final night while the crowd sang to him has become an iconic image in music, like Freddie Mercury with his arm and microphone aloft on the Live Aid stage or The Beatles crossing Abbey Road.

People thought the display of emotion was Isaac getting caught up in the moment – certainly that's how Ospreys manager Derrick Cordingly and the band's illustrious publicist Sherry Caputo were at pains to paint it afterwards – but the rest of the band and its crew knew otherwise.

Isaac had hit rock bottom. Years of sustained drinking

and drug-taking were wreaking havoc with his health and he'd started having the kind of blackouts his loved ones feared he wouldn't wake up from. His memory was impaired and his motor functions permanently set at sluggish. He couldn't begin the day without a shot of vodka and a line of cocaine to wake him up and while he was still managing to pull it together enough to rehearse and perform, in his downtime he had become a shell of the magnetic teenager who Derrick Cordingly knew could be one of the biggest stars on the planet the moment he clapped eyes on him.

In fact, Derrick was perhaps the only person who watched Isaac on that stage at Knebworth and recognised the moment for what it really was: a cry for help. It was he, after all, and not Isaac's band-mates, who had to play nursemaid to Isaac throughout his addiction highs and lows, making sure he fulfilled his contractual commitments. Putting Isaac on the stage at Knebworth was something he wrestled with for weeks in the run-up, and the decision to go ahead went up to the wire. Derrick knew what it would mean to cancel the gigs, given it would be charities and backstage crew and not the band that were going to benefit financially from them, but he was really worried for Isaac.

'It was only on the morning of the first gig that I thought he could do it,' Derrick told a friend of his afterwards. 'We sent him to a spa retreat in Switzerland the week before to chill out and relax and it seemed to do the trick. He was really amped up about performing and doing a good job for the fans and apart from the odd slip-up he did well.'

Isaac telling the crowd that Derrick wanted to force him into rehab stung the manager though. 'No one likes to hear themselves being booed by a crowd that size,' Derrick confided in his friend. 'I was really hurt. I did everything I could to keep Isaac healthy and happy and to hear him slag me off like that at the biggest gig the band would ever perform was like a punch to the gut.'

To those who knew them both, it felt like a very public fracture in a relationship that, until that point, had been almost paternal in nature, with Derrick filling the gaping chasm in Isaac's life left by his father's death. From the moment he'd seen The Ospreys play on a *Manchester Evening Echo*-sponsored tour for emerging bands in 2000, Derrick had recognised Isaac's fragility and knew he needed to be protected. In a joint interview the pair of them did with *GQ* in 2009, when Derrick won the magazine's Business-man of the Year category at its annual Man of the Year awards, Isaac had paid tribute to his mentor's ability to nurture him no matter what.

'I know I make it hard for him, and myself, with my behaviour,' said Isaac, acknowledging how his drug habit was by then making him as infamous as he was famous, 'but without Derrick I'd be lost. Or dead. I owe him everything.'

Derrick, not known for being humble in his ruthless pursuit of success, was visibly moved by Isaac's comments according to the *GQ* interviewer. Once he'd composed himself, Derrick responded by describing why he felt so protective of the singer.

'I have twin sons and they mean the world to me,' says Derrick, who divorced his wife, Jenny, in 1995 after five years of marriage, when the twins were two. 'When it comes to Isaac, and the rest of the band come to that, I always think "what I would want someone in my position to do if it was my boys?" The answer is simple: do what-ever it takes to keep them safe and well. I might struggle with the latter, but I'll always keep Isaac safe.'

Friends described Derrick as a 'broken man' after Isaac committed suicide and many wondered whether he would be able to continue working afterwards. Unlike other big-name managers, Derrick didn't handle any other bands, although he did talent-spot and would encourage wannabe artists to send demos to his offices in Soho Square, where colleagues would take on the best. It was actually his sons, Alex and Gavin, who encouraged him to think about continuing with The Ospreys, saying he owed it to Isaac not to give up. 'I think Isaac would've been gutted if he'd known how destroyed Dad was by his death,' said Alex, who now works for Derrick's company. 'Clearly he wasn't thinking when he took his own life, otherwise he'd have realised before it was too late that Dad would always have been there for him and would've got him through the police investigation into Emily Jenkins' death and whatever came after that. But I think he'd have wanted Dad to go on, and for The Ospreys to carry on. Just because he was sadly no longer on the scene didn't mean they had to disappear too.'

Chapter Twenty-One

THURSDAY, 13TH

I stay indoors for the next four days, even cancelling seeing Daniel after school yesterday because I don't feel safe venturing out, much less taking him out in public where he could be at risk too. I provide Spencer with the excuse that I'm not feeling well and it's almost the truth, except it's my mind that's under the weather. I have no proof the cyclist at Regent's Park was following me, but on the heels of being sent the flowers for Daniel and being attacked at Alexandra Palace, my fear of what might happen next is elevated beyond what's normal. Every time I hear a noise reverberate somewhere in the building I think it's someone coming for me. I've stopped answering the doorbell and if my mobile rings I'll only pick it up if I recognise the caller. The landline, which my godmother insists on maintaining despite me never using it, is now disconnected at the socket.

I couldn't even be enticed out for an impromptu Tuesday night drink with my school mum friends, which they found quite baffling because they've never known me to turn down an evening of booze and chat even though I live across London from them now. Our WhatsApp group blew up with questions and the more I protested that I was fine, the less they believed me. One of them, Jo, even asked outright if it was because of Spencer, because they know how much grief he's given me in the past year. I said no, but still refrained from saying what's been going on: as desperate as I am to confide in them, I don't entirely trust that it won't get back to him. I know their partners and husbands still get on well with him.

Yet despite being concerned by what harm might befall me should I dare step outside or answer the phone, I have carried on with the Isaac story during my self-imposed lockdown. It turns out I can no more resist the tug of the story than I can stop myself breathing. With nothing else to focus on, I am consumed with wanting to know where he is, who helped him fake his suicide and where he's been hiding all these years. The questions endlessly scroll through my mind like ticker tape newsreel at the bottom of a TV screen, demanding my attention and demanding to be answered.

In the early hours of this morning, after I was spooked awake by a car backfiring outside and decided to work instead of pointlessly tossing and turning and failing to get back to sleep, I had a breakthrough. I believe I've found the identity of the person who organised the backstage pass for Emily Jenkins. If correct, her name was Pippa and she was one of The Ospreys' most ardent fans.

I found mention of her while trawling through reams of historical posts in a chat room dedicated to the band. One particular discussion was centred on Emily's inquest and the fact the friend who gave her the pass had never been traced and how weird that was, a sentiment I agree with. This friend may have had some valuable insight into events leading up to Emily's death and yet she went undiscovered. Then up popped this comment:

I BET YOU ANYTHING IT WAS ONE OF THE LITTLE BIRDIES.
THEY ALWAYS GOT BACKSTAGE PASSES TO GIVE OUT TO
OTHER GIRLS. I THINK THE MAIN ONE WAS CALLED PIPPA.

It was the first time I'd seen any reference to 'Little Birdies' in any cuttings about The Ospreys. Two hours of digging later and I find only a couple more throwaway mentions online – certainly no explanation as to who or what the Little Birdies are, although presumably the name derives from the band's album *A Little Birdie Told Me*. It takes the £2.99 ebook purchase of an unauthorised biography, hastily written and released by a Fleet Street hack only two months after Isaac's death, for me to learn it was the nickname bestowed upon a group of female fans who followed the band on tour during that period. The author stops short of calling them groupies but does infer lines were crossed. I started speed-reading the book at six-thirty this morning; it's almost eleven now and I've just finished. Disappointingly there are no further references to the Little Birdies anywhere else in the book and they remain a misogynistic footnote in The Ospreys' history.

I find it even more baffling this Pippa character managed to elude being tracked down after Emily was found dead though. How could I find her name yet the police couldn't? If she was friendly with the band and the conduit for handing out VIP passes to other girls, why didn't anyone connected to The Ospreys come forward with that information? If she hung around with the band on tour, there's every chance she was even at the hotel herself that evening and privy to what happened. She might have orchestrated Emily going to Isaac's room, having already snared her the backstage pass. To me, her account of what happened seems really important and I don't understand how she was disregarded in the course of the investigation. Then again, I suppose once Isaac was presumed drowned, the police had no reason to pursue her. As far as they were concerned, it was case closed, but I am yet again reminded of Neil's comment in The Groucho: if Isaac didn't give Emily Jenkins the heroin, someone else must have.

To trace Pippa now will be next to impossible without anything else to go on though. I need to know more about her so I decide to leave a comment on the fan forum thread. The comment about her was posted four years ago but maybe someone with knowledge of her might still reply. I register with the username FriendlyEar and type in the following:

PIPPA WAS A FRIEND OF MINE BUT WE LOST TOUCH. DOES ANYONE KNOW WHERE SHE'S LIVING THESE DAYS?

As I watch the comment load, it dawns on me that I do have another avenue I could explore in my bid to track Pippa down and I reach across the coffee table for the business card Derrick Cordingly gave me at the awards. I've held off phoning him because meeting up would involve me leaving the apartment and I've been too unsettled to do that, but if I'm to find out more about Pippa I should talk to someone either in the band or close to them – and who is closer than their manager?

Derrick answers on the second ring with an abrupt 'Yes.'

'Mr Cordingly, this is Natalie Glass. I write for the nationals, we met at the awards on Sunday—'

'Natalie! Good to hear from you. I was wondering when you were going to call.'

His warm greeting disarms me. 'Um, sorry, I had work deadlines, lots to do,' I reply, flustered. 'But I'm clear now and I was wondering if we could arrange the interview we discussed?'

In the background I hear the tapping of fingertips on a keyboard.

'I've got an hour spare tomorrow morning,' he announces. 'Can you get to our offices for nine?'

My stomach clenches at the thought of leaving the security of the apartment and its many deadbolts, but I know I need to do this. 'Sure, no problem.'

'We're just off Golden Square, 116 Upper John Street.'

I make a note of it. 'Thank you,' I say. 'I'll see you at nine.'

'Excellent. Tell you what, I'll order some breakfast in for us. There's a great cafe round the corner that does a nice line in pastries.'

I can almost hear him smiling down the phone and I'm a bit bemused by how avuncular he's being, since this is only the second time we've spoken and he has a reputation for loathing journalists. I once heard he called up an editor to demand a writer's sacking because he didn't like a review they'd written. Then I catch myself for being negative: I saw how upset he was when I brought up Isaac, he's just trying to make what might be a tough interview a bit more bearable.

'That sounds lovely,' I say. 'See you tomorrow.'

Talk of pastries propels me into the kitchen after we hang up. It's nearly lunchtime and I'm hungry. But a cursory glance inside the fridge reveals slim pickings when it comes to meal options, because I haven't ventured to the supermarket since the weekend. Deciding I can't face pasta with pesto stirred in for the fourth day running, I pull on my trainers and sling my handbag over my shoulder. Then, adopting the manoeuvre I always use when walking home late from the Tube station, I thread my door keys through my fingers, ready to forcibly jab anyone who might be lying in wait to accost me as I nip down the road to the nearby Sainsbury's Local.

But there's no one waiting for me outside or lurking anywhere on my route to the supermarket. I know, because my eyes are on stalks the entire way and I almost trip up looking over my shoulder to check who's behind me. I return home and dive inside the mansion block, a full-to-bursting bag of groceries in hand, and shove the heavy wooden door shut behind me. I lean my back against it, close my eyes for a moment, and let the tension shudder from my body.

I am safe, for now.

Chapter Twenty-Two

FRIDAY, 14TH

My meeting with Derrick necessitates an early start, my usual slapdash make-up routine requiring more time and skill to hide my bruised cheek. The purpling has, thankfully, faded but it still takes a thickly applied layer of foundation to camouflage the worst of it. I cannot entirely disguise that my face has been battered but the make-up should make it less of a talking point.

I had planned to catch the bus to Marble Arch and walk from there but there's been a fatal accident at the junction with St John's Wood Road and the traffic in the area is gridlocked, so I'm forced to take the Tube. Friday morning on the Bakerloo Line is a fraction less busy than on other weekdays due to people working from home or starting long weekends, but not much. The southbound platform is already teeming with commuters as I make my way along it but I manage to find a space to position myself close to the yellow line.

In my hand I have a printout of the questions I plan to put to Derrick and I go over them as I wait for the next train to arrive. Most of them are crafted with the aim of getting him to discuss

Isaac's contribution to The Ospreys' success and how the band members managed to pull themselves together so they could continue without him after his suicide. Even though it wasn't actually my intention to write a feature on them when all this started, I do think it will make good background material to the piece I eventually write about Isaac's return. And inserted within my printout is the question I am most keen for him to answer – does he remember a girl called Pippa being one of the Little Birdies and, if he does, why was her name never given to the police as the person likely to have sourced the backstage pass for Emily Jenkins?

A low rumble from deep within the tunnel opening nearest to me signals the next train's approach. I slide the questions into my handbag and square my shoulders, ready to elbow my way onto the train to grab a seat. But as I turn my head to watch the train as it trundles into the station, I see him, standing further along the platform. His clothes are different but he's wearing the same red cap as yesterday. My heart lurches. It's the cyclist who stopped when I was crying and who followed me to Pret.

I raise a shaky finger towards him. 'You!' But my voice comes out as a croak and is lost in the noise of the train pulling to a stop and the doors opening. I step into the carriage but when I turn around the cyclist is heading along the platform towards the exit, a blur of red as he dashes by.

Derrick's running late so I use my wait in the plush reception of his management company to talk some sense into myself. Now I've calmed down I'm not so sure it was the same cyclist I saw by Regent's Park – more likely it was just someone wearing a similar cap. I'm spooked by what's been going on and I'm seeing danger where it doesn't exist. That's all this is—

My phone rings. It's Lucy, but there's no time to answer her because Derrick Cordingly chooses this moment to stride into reception. I kill the call then get to my feet to shake his hand. Almost immediately my phone pings to indicate I have a voicemail message.

'Do you want to check that?' asks Derrick.

'It can wait.'

'Let's go to my office then. It's this way.'

Derrick leads me through glass double doors and along a corridor that has an unpolished concrete floor that's all the rage now in hip office settings. To me it just looks unfinished.

His office has the same flooring, but at least there's a sofa that's comfortable to sit on, to the side of his glass-topped desk. The floor-to-ceiling windows offer a panoramic view of Soho's rooftops and covering the walls is a vast array of gold and platinum discs and framed magazine covers. It's the latter that catch my eye, and in particular two *Rolling Stone* covers hung side by side.

The first one is a full-length image of The Ospreys with Isaac Naylor very much centre stage and the others crowded either side of him. There is a swagger to their pose, a sense of 'yes, we are the biggest band in the world right now, your point is?' and their attire is defiantly jet-black from head to foot, giving the impression their bodies are merging into one. Yet melded though they may be, it is Isaac who draws your gaze, his glacial blue eyes demanding the fullest attention. The other cover, by contrast, shows the three original Ospreys seated on the edge of a stage, legs dangling but backs ramrod straight, half a metre of space between each of them. Jem Spencer, Isaac's replacement, is crouched almost deferentially behind them. None of their clothes match in style or hue.

Derrick follows my gaze and sees what I'm looking at, but wrongly assumes what I'm thinking.

'They were much more settled second time round with *Rolling Stone*,' he says. 'That cover was taken about a year after Jem joined and they were really gelling.'

To me, it appears the opposite. The second cover feels awkward and affected, whereas on the first the band appear languid in their familiarity with each other, limbs loose, faces at ease. I understand why Derrick would push the second one as the truest version though: as their manager he needs the public to believe Isaac's loss was not the momentous setback it was and that the band are as united without him. Yet side by side these covers prove a picture really can speak a thousand words.

Derrick tugs at his shirt cuffs beneath his jacket sleeves as he settles himself on the sofa next to me. Like Bronwyn, he appears to favour formal tailoring in the work place, although he has dispensed with a tie. I know he's in his fifties but close up he appears much younger, wrinkles negligible, and I suspect some chemical intervention at play. His hair is also dubiously free of grey but the darkening to mid-brown is subtle. He's nice looking, if a bit too slick for my tastes.

'Are you fine for me to tape the interview?' I ask, holding up my digital voice recorder. I'm aware it makes me something of a relic to use such a device when you can download all manner of voice recording apps to your phone these days, but my old-school sensibilities won't allow me to rely solely on them. So I do use an app, but only as backup to my trusty handheld device. Its solid presence and the little red light that indicates it's recording allows me to relax; I've always been of the view interviews should be more like a conversation you'd have with a friend than an interrogation.

Derrick smiles benignly. 'Sure. But let's eat while we talk. These are the pastries I was telling you about.'

He gestures to a platter of baked goods that's been laid out on the low table next to the sofa. I'm not hungry but I don't want to appear rude, so I help myself to a Danish whirl but leave it untouched on my plate. Mindful that my allotted hour is ticking by, I ask if we can start by him sharing his favourite memory of Isaac. Derrick nods.

'There are so many to choose from, but at a push, if I had to pick one, it was when the band signed their first deal. We were getting stuck into the champagne when Isaac suddenly excuses himself from the room. Twenty minutes go by and he's not back, so I go to look for him and he's up on the roof terrace, just standing looking out over London with tears pouring down his face. I was shocked, I thought something was wrong, but then he turned to me and said it was the best day of what had been a pretty shitty life up until that point and I'll admit I got choked too. So it ends up with the two of us, grown men, standing on the top of the record label building blubbing like babies.' Derrick flashes me a sad smile. 'He wanted success so badly. It meant everything to him.'

I'm about to follow up, but Derrick insists I try my pastry.

'I'd rather crack on,' I say. 'I've got a lot of questions to get through.'

'Don't worry about the time,' he says, apparently sensing my concern about the hour running out. 'I can be late for my next meeting. Go on, try it.'

I nod and take a bite of the pastry and it tastes every bit as good as he promised.

'If you have to be somewhere after, I can arrange a car for you.'

'There's no need,' I mumble through a mouthful. He doesn't appear to hear me though.

'Tell you what,' he says, rising to his feet, 'let me get my assistant Alice to book the car now.'

I shake my head, spraying crumbs everywhere in the process. 'You don't need to,' I say, coughing as a flake of pastry catches in my throat.

'Nonsense. Let me just do this and then we can get back to your questions.' He goes to his desk and is about a press a button when the door to his office swings open. 'Ah, Alice, I was just about to buzz you. Can you—' He stops mid-sentence. 'What's the matter?'

His assistant, an attractive young woman with long dark hair so shiny I can almost see my reflection in it, looks ashen and her bottom lip trembles as she tells Derrick she has some bad news to share. His face blanches.

'What kind of bad news? Is it the boys?'

I wonder if he's referring to his sons or The Ospreys.

'No, it's not them. It's someone else you know.' She casts a wary glance in my direction.

'It's OK, you can say it in front of Natalie,' he reassures her.

'I just saw it on the *Evening Standard* online,' says Alice. 'There was a mugging outside The Soundbank last night. Someone who works there was stabbed.'

I freeze, the pastry halfway to my mouth.

'Jesus,' breathes Derrick. 'Who?'

'The paper says it was Bronwyn, the studio manager.'

I let out a cry of shock and let go of the pastry. It misses the plate and falls to the floor, crumbs exploding across the unpolished concrete. 'Did you say Bronwyn?' I croak.

'Do you know her?' Derrick asks me, his face paling.

I nod and try to get to my feet but my legs won't support me. Bronwyn's been stabbed? That can't be right, it just can't. Then I remember the missed call from Lucy and my heart lurches. Was she ringing to tell me?

'She's my best friend,' I manage. 'Is she OK?'

'I'm so sorry,' says Alice, a sob escaping. 'They're saying she's dead.'

Chapter Twenty-Three

Evening Standard, Friday 14 June

Breaking news> London

Victim of Camberwell studio stabbing dies in hospital

Tilly Sinclair / 1 hour ago / 0 comments

A 41-year-old woman stabbed during an apparent mugging out-side a south London recording studio has died from her injuries, police have confirmed.

The woman, named on social media as the studio manager Bronwyn Castle, was leaving The Soundbank on Tyrrell Street at 10.30 p.m. yesterday evening when a man on a pushbike approached her and threatened her with a knife if she didn't hand over her bag. According to an eyewitness at the scene, she tried to resist but was stabbed three times in the abdomen. Her attacker escaped empty-handed.

Ms Castle was taken to Guy's and St Thomas' Hospital where she underwent emergency surgery, but police issued an update this morning revealing she had died from her injuries in the early hours. Next of kin has been informed.

Detective Chief Inspector Dan Clarke of the Major Crime Unit based in Southwark has issued a plea for more witnesses to come forward.

'This was a despicable, cowardly crime attacking a defenceless woman as she made her way home after a long day at work,' he said. 'Sadly, the victim was unable to recover from her injuries and this is now being treated as a murder inquiry. We urge anyone who has information to come forward.'

A description of the assailant has been issued: he was white, average height, in dark clothing and a cap and he was riding a bike with a chrome frame. He rode off down Tyrrell Street in the direction of Peckham Road.

The Soundbank is one of the capital's most in-demand studios, with Freddie Xerox and Loco Motive both recording their latest albums there. According to her LinkedIn profile, Ms Castle began working there as studio manager in 2016, after moving from The Premises Studios in Hackney.

The Soundbank declined to comment when approached by the *Standard*. However, some artists who've recorded there have already posted tributes to her on Twitter and Instagram, including newcomer Jo-Jo Jones, who said she met Ms Castle while recording at the studio for the first time earlier this week. Jones tweeted to her 18,000 followers: 'Devastated to hear the tragic news about @BronwynCastleSound. Met her for 1st time this week laying down tracks @TheSoundbank and she was so lovely and welcoming. I hope they catch whoever did it. #RIP.'

* Anyone with information about Ms Castle's murder should call CrimeStoppers on 0800 555 111.

Chapter Twenty-Four

I don't recall which of us is the first to say we should postpone the interview, but I couldn't continue now even if I wanted to. Bronwyn is dead. Murdered. It feels so unreal and yet I know it's not, because I've pulled up the *Standard*'s story on my phone and read it for myself, the journalist in me wanting facts to make sense of the horror.

'It says she tried to stop the mugger taking her bag and that's when he stabbed her,' I relay in a hoarse voice to Derrick. Alice has already respectfully withdrawn from the room; there's nothing more she can say now she's imparted the news.

'Fucking hell. Sorry, excuse my language. But it's just so . . . so,' he gropes for the right word, 'senseless.'

I can't answer him. My head is pounding and I'm trembling. Derrick takes off his suit jacket and gently places it on my shoulders but still my body shakes as though I am freezing cold.

'I can't believe it,' he keeps saying.

'Her wife tried to call me. That was the message notification you heard, in reception. It was from Lucy.'

Derrick looks shocked. 'Do you want to listen to it?'

I shake my head and fresh tears spill over, rolling down my cheeks unbidden. I don't think I can bear to hear Lucy confirm the awful news. 'They have two kids, little ones. I don't know how they'll cope without her.'

Sadness fills his face. 'We'll do something for them, as an industry. Make sure they don't go without.'

I wipe my cheeks dry with my fingertips. 'I should go to see her wife.'

He nods. 'Let me get you that car.'

I wait outside on the pavement for my ride to arrive, despite Derrick's protestations I should stay inside until it's here. I can't bear him and his staff watching me and I want to call Lucy back without them eavesdropping. My stomach knots as I wait for her to pick up, but the call goes unanswered. I leave a message but can barely get out the words and break down halfway through. 'It's me. I can't believe it. I'm so sorry. Call me when you can.' I still don't listen to her voicemail though – I can't bear to hear her utter the words that Bronwyn's dead.

The driver is professional enough to acknowledge my upset, passing me a box of tissues from his glove compartment, but not to quiz me on it and for that I'm grateful. He does ask me to confirm my destination though, which gives me pause. While I desperately want to see Lucy and the children, I'm hesitant to turn up on her doorstep until I've spoken to her first, so I ask to be taken home. Yet by the time we reach Oxford Street the traffic is so slow moving that we only get as far as Selfridges before I have to ask him to let me out. I'm feeling panicky and anxious and I need fresh air. The driver is concerned about stopping, but acquiesces when I tell him I think I'm going to be sick on his pristine leather back seat.

I weave unsteadily through clusters of shoppers and tourists until I reach Marble Arch and the entrance to Hyde Park. Crossing the grass past Speaker's Corner, heading towards the glittering expanse of the Serpentine, I can finally catch my breath and gulp down a lungful of air. But I'm still in shock. My best friend is dead. Gone. I'll never see her again, never be able to talk to her again.

Just shy of the Serpentine I spy a tree set far back from the path and throw myself onto the ground beside its trunk. Then I draw my knees up to my chest, bury my face in them and cry with abandon. I don't think I've ever felt grief like it. It's as though my chest has been hollowed out.

I don't know how long I cry for, but two people stop to ask me if I am OK and I manage to convince them I am and that I just want to be alone. Eventually – finally, my tears begin to abate and I take my phone from my bag.

First I google Bronwyn's name to see if there are any further updates but the other news outlets appear to have lifted their copy straight from the *Standard* and there are no new details. Then I try Lucy again, but as before the call goes to voicemail. I feel a physical stab of pain when I think about how she and the children must be feeling. The kids! Oh God, I have to tell Daniel, I realise. He's going to be so upset, he adored Bronwyn. I wonder if Spencer knows yet, so I call him.

'I've just seen the news. I was going to call you,' he says before I can say anything. 'Nat, I'm so sorry. I know how close you were.'

The tenderness in his voice floors me. This is the Spencer I loved, before all the ugliness. I'm not sure I can cope with him being kind on top of everything else and I have to grip my phone tightly to steady myself.

'We need to tell Daniel,' he adds and the way he says 'we' brings fresh tears to my eyes.

'I don't know how,' I say, my voice breaking.

'I can do it, when he's home from school, but he's going to want to see you once he knows, so maybe you should be here too? We could eat together afterwards.'

I am shocked by how nice he's being. 'That would be lovely,' I stutter.

'Can you get here for five?'

'Yes, I can.' I pause. 'Spencer?'

'Yes?'

'Thank you, for this.'

'Nat, Bronwyn was your best friend and she's been there for you through everything. I know how much you must be hurting and I'm really sorry for that,' he says, his voice thick with emotion.

My vision blurs with more tears. I can't bear this, so I tell him I'll see him later and end the call. I sit quietly for a while, blinking hard to stop myself breaking down again, and that's when a particular thought breaks free from the many thundering back and forth through my mind: what if there's more to Bronwyn's death than has been reported? Derrick used the word senseless to describe it . . . but what if it wasn't?

I can't believe I didn't make the connection immediately, but the shock of being told she was dead was so overwhelming I couldn't think of anything else. But now, my mind a bit clearer, the timing chills me to the core. It's only eight days since Bronwyn passed me Aden Rowlock's address at the studio. Four days since she lambasted me at the awards for putting her job on the line after he sent that legal letter. Four days since I was attacked at the awards. Three days since someone sent me a funeral wreath telling me my son is dead. As my mind scrolls through the timeline of our interactions and what's followed, I am forced to think the unthinkable: what if it wasn't a mugging, but was engineered to look like one? What if the aim was to silence Bronwyn because of what she knew? She recognised what a good story the mystery songwriter was because I told her that in order to persuade her to source Rowlock's address. Then it hits me: this was all my doing. I made her make that call.

124

The accusation rattles around my head with such ferocity that I start to cry again. If I'm right and this wasn't an opportunist mugging gone wrong, it's my fault Bronwyn's children woke up with only one parent this morning.

Chapter Twenty-Five

TUESDAY, 18TH

The next few days pass in a blur of tears while a terrible, aching sadness consumes me. Until she died, I hadn't appreciated just how much I'd come to rely on Bronwyn to be my ballast. I took our friendship for granted and I wish desperately I could tell her how much I loved her and how thankful I am for her supporting me during the darkest days of my divorce and beyond. Instead, I am haunted day and night by the knowledge that our last words to each other, at the awards, were spoken in anger and upset. Every time I think about the look on her face as she walked off inside Alexandra Palace I break down again.

Spencer was true to his word and together we gently broke the news to Daniel that Bronwyn was dead. I'm not sure Daniel grasped the finality of what we were saying and the few tears he did shed I think were most likely prompted by him seeing me upset, because he perked up immediately on hearing we were having tea together. It was a lovely meal all things considered, with Spencer serving us an old favourite of chicken and pea risotto, and for a moment it felt like we were a family again, sitting there together listening to Daniel telling us about his day. But the minute we finished eating Spencer began clearing the plates and told me it was time to go, and the fairytale dissolved.

Lucy and I have spoken as well now. I never played her message back, but she told me during our first conversation, that evening after I got back from Clapham after telling Daniel, both of us sobbing so much it was a wrench to speak, that it was simply her asking me to call her. She didn't want to break the news in a voicemail. I went to see her the next morning and now we are talking constantly on a practical level about the funeral arrangements, because being officious is the only way I can dull the excruciating anguish I feel at losing my best friend.

The funeral is to be held at St Mary's in Battersea next week, the same church where Bronwyn and Lucy had their marriage blessing eight years ago. On that occasion I was their attendant, this time I'll be doing a reading. Lucy wants to deliver the eulogy herself, insisting she's strong enough, but I am concerned she's putting too much pressure on herself and that there are plenty of other people in Bronwyn's life who could step up. Meanwhile their sons, Wolfie and Harrison, are too little to comprehend what's happened: one moment they are bewildered by Bronwyn's absence and the steady trickle of mourners arriving at the house to pay their respects, the next they are oblivious.

I hadn't expected the funeral to be so soon, but the coroner released the body after the post-mortem, saying the cause of death was conclusive and the necessary evidence has been recorded to assist police in any future criminal proceedings. Yet already it feels as though they've decided they're unlikely to catch the person responsible. They think it was a mugging gone wrong and the few witnesses who saw it happen have given varying accounts that have muddied the waters, according to the family liaison officer assigned to Lucy and the boys. The police also revealed the place where Bronwyn was killed was a CCTV blind spot – a development that does not feel oppor-tunist or coincidental to me. Someone who intended to do her serious harm would've made sure they couldn't be caught on camera, in the same way I was attacked away from prying eyes at Alexandra Palace.

Which is why I am outside 17 Rushton Avenue again, about to confront Aden Rowlock about the campaign of fear and aggression I am convinced he's been conducting to stop me revealing Isaac as the mystery songwriter. He might not have meant for Bronwyn to die, but she did, and anyone who gets others to do his dirty work is ultimately a coward, and cowards buckle when they're forced to face up to what they've done – at least that's what I'm banking on. I feel I owe it to Lucy and the boys to try, and for my sake it needs to stop, now.

I don't mind admitting I'm trembling with misgiving though. It's mid-morning and the streets are emptied of commuters and school-run parents and carers and as I glance up and down the road either side of me I can see there are no passersby in the vicinity to help me if things turn sour. I haven't mentioned Rowlock's name to the police either. I did think about it and even went as far as to ask the family liaison officer when I was at Lucy's whether they were looking into any of Bronwyn's associates who might have a motive for wanting her dead, but he looked at me as though I'd sprouted two heads and Lucy reacted with equal astonishment, quizzing me about why on earth I thought anyone they know would want to hurt Bron-wyn. I dropped it then, anxious not to stoke her distress any more than I already had.

Steeling myself, I press the buzzer for Rowlock's flat but instead of saying his name I ask for Bibek, the man I spoke to the last time I was here. I don't want Rowlock to know it's me yet; I want to get inside his office first and confront him there and my plan is to force my way in once Bibek opens the door.

Yet it's not him who answers and says he'll be right down, and when I see who opens the front door my jaw drops.

It's the cyclist in the red baseball cap.

I reel backwards in fright, almost losing my footing, but I manage to grab the railing by the side of the steps to right my balance and as I do, fury kicks in.

'Why have you been following me?' I hurl at him. 'I know you have been, so don't even try to deny it.'

He looks stunned then reaches out as though trying to make a grab for me. I step back beyond his reach.

'Tell me the truth or I call the police right now,' I say, taking my phone out of my bag and holding it aloft.

'You've got it all wrong. I'm not following you, not like you think.' His speech is rushed and anxious, which confuses me.

'I don't believe you,' I say, but with less certainty. 'Are you Aden Rowlock?'

His face mottles. 'You think I'm him? No, no, you've got it all wrong. I had an appointment with him but he's not here.'

'Don't lie. You just came downstairs from his office.'

'I did, but only after one of the other residents let me in. I went up to his office but he's not there,' the man adds. 'I'm not Aden Rowlock. You're barking up the wrong tree.'

I experience another rush of anger. 'If you're not Rowlock, who the hell are you and why have you been following me?' I shout at him. 'I know it was you by Regent's Park the other day and then at the Tube station. You're wearing the same cap.'

He lifts it off to reveal longish, mousy brown hair that's flecked with grey and slathered against his scalp by sweat. Better able to see his face, I would put him in his late thirties. There's something familiar about him and a few seconds later I find out what.

'I didn't mean to scare you, I swear,' he says. 'But I was told you're a journalist and that you're writing a story about

Isaac Naylor and I wanted to see who you were. That's why I followed you.'

'Who told you I'm working on a story?' I demand to know. 'Who are you?'

'I'm Isaac's brother. I'm Toby Naylor.'

Chapter Twenty-Six

I have no idea of the number of shocks the average person can safely absorb in the space of a week but I'm pretty sure I've reached my limit. I grab the railing for support again, my legs rendered jelly-like by the revelation I didn't see coming.

'You're Isaac's brother?' I echo.

He nods. 'I'm sorry I haven't introduced myself before now. I'm sorry if I scared you.'

I need a moment to digest what he's saying and so lower myself onto one of the steps. Balling the baseball cap tightly between his hands, Toby sits down on the same one, but on the far side, so there's a sizeable gap between us. I stare across at him. The family resemblance is obvious now I know where to look. Pudgier in the face, Toby has the same beaky nose and the same eye shape as his brother, but his eyes are brown compared to Isaac's blue. Then I look down at his right hand and confirm his index finger is missing its tip – just as I expected.

I know exactly how Toby lost the tip because there is a chapter devoted to the accident that caused it in the trashy biography I downloaded. Toby was only three when older brother Isaac cajoled him into sticking his finger through the bars of an electric heater to 'see what would happen'. Unfortunately, what happened was the skin melted away from Toby's toddler finger like ice cream left out in the sun and no amount of medical intervention could save it, although the nail did remain intact and grew in a curve over the missing tip. According to the biography, Isaac never got over the guilt of causing the injury because it meant Toby could never master playing guitar like he did. It was, the author claimed, a defining childhood moment for them both.

Toby clears his throat. 'The reason I've been following you is that I've been plucking up the courage to talk to you.'

'Why?' I say it forcibly, to make it clear I am still very angry, despite him being who he is. Three times he's scared me now and I don't forgive easily.

'I was told you were writing a piece on my brother and I was curious, because I've read your stuff and I like how you write, so I wanted to find out more.'

'How do you know about that?' I ask, although I've already guessed. 'Did Derrick Cordingly tell you?'

'Yes . . . him. He emailed. He thought you might approach me for a comment and wanted to warn me.'

His wording unsettles me. 'What do you mean, warn you? Why would he have to do that?'

'He knows I hated dealing with the press,' Toby replies flatly. 'They hounded Isaac in life and then hounded me after his death. It was relentless. Everyone wanting an interview, no one caring that I was grieving.' He takes a moment then exhales. 'That was then though. I have a different perspective now. I'm ready to talk, and seeing as you're interested in my brother I think you'd be a good person to talk to.'

My mouth drops open in surprise. Toby casts me an uneasy look. 'If you want to interview me that is.'

I nod, excitement supplanting my earlier annoyance. Toby Naylor wants to grant *me* his first ever interview about his brother. This is big.

'I'd love to,' I say. Then, trying to play it cool, I add, 'You could pick any journalist you wanted though.'

'I've read your work. I like how you write. I want people to remember the good stuff about Isaac and I think you're the writer who can help me do that.'

My jubilation at being handed an exclusive on a plate suddenly deflates. If I do the interview, how can I continue working to prove Isaac is alive? How would Toby react if he knew what my real agenda was?

'I'm not sure I am,' I say reluctantly.

'Oh. OK. Is it because you don't think what I have to say will be interesting enough?'

He gives me a look that falls just on the right side of bashful. The biography described him as the shyer of the two brothers and an introvert even in company, happy to follow in Isaac's formidable wake as his personal assistant on the road and at home. It also revealed that after his brother's suicide, Toby became a recluse, returning to their hometown of Jarrow in the north of England to live alone in a house Isaac had bought on its outskirts a few years previously.

'It's not that at all,' I say hastily. 'I think it would make a great interview. I just don't know if I'm the right journalist for it.'

Toby looks down at the cap still balled between his hands. He's gripping it so fiercely his knuckles have whitened. 'If you say no I won't do it with anyone else.'

I realise I have a decision to make, and fast. If I turn Toby down he might disappear into obscurity again and so too would any further chance of interviewing him. Or he could have a change of heart and approach another journalist and then I'd kick myself for not saying yes.

'I'd really like you to do it,' he repeats. 'I thought you'd want to.'

I hesitate again, unsure which way to turn, until a voice in my head pipes up that, actually, I *could* do both. Regardless of whether Isaac is alive or not, an interview with his brother who has never spoken publicly before would make a fascinating read. Then, once I am able to confirm Isaac is the mystery songwriter, I'll have an established contact with Toby that would ensure I had a ringside seat for his reaction to the news and could report on it before anyone else. I wouldn't be exploiting him, I reason to myself, just hedging my bets for now.

'I'll do it,' I say firmly, and he breaks into a smile. 'I only hesitated because I was surprised to be asked—'

We both jump as the front door suddenly opens behind us. Bibek crosses the threshold towards us and he does not look happy.

'Why are you still here? I tell you Mr Rowlock isn't here,' he says abruptly to Toby, as we spring to our feet. Then he realises who I am and scowls. 'Why are you talking to a journalist?' he asks him.

'I don't think that's any of your business,' Toby replies congenially.

Business. That reminds me. 'Why *are* you here to see Rowlock?' I ask him.

Bibek glares down at us from the top step as Toby explains. 'He's an old friend of the family from back home. He did a lot of legal work for our dad when we were kids, after our mum died.'

Joan Naylor's premature death is another slice of family history I learned from the biography. She died only three weeks after being diagnosed with breast cancer when Isaac and Toby were twelve and nine respectively. Her sudden demise all but broke their dad, John, and after falling into depression he never worked again and much of what motivated Isaac to become famous and rich was the desire to give Toby some security after the remainder of their childhood was spent living on the breadline. Sadly, John Naylor died not long after The Ospreys' first album went to number one. His death was from natural causes, but Isaac stated in more than one interview that he believed his dad had died from a broken heart.

'I don't visit London often, every couple of years if that, but I make a point of coming to see Aden when I do,' Toby continues.

'Didn't you tell him you were coming today?' I ask. 'Why isn't he here?'

'He must've forgotten.' Toby shrugs. 'It wouldn't be the first time.'

Bibek takes a step forward and waves his arm like he's wafting away a bad smell. 'Go now, both of you. Mr Rowlock won't be back today.'

Toby gives him a long, appraising look then turns to me. 'Fancy a drink? There's a pub at the end of the road.'

It's only noon but the thought of an ice-cold beer makes me salivate.

'Sounds good,' I nod. 'Lead the way.'

Toby does, but not before he addresses Bibek for a final time. 'Please tell Aden to give me a call.'

From Bibek's disgruntled expression I'm not sure Toby should trust him to pass on the message.

'What about you?' Toby asks me. 'Do you want Aden to call you too?'

I realise I'm being gifted another opportunity. Rowlock won't leave me alone while he thinks I'm still chasing the mystery songwriter story and not being able to confront him today still leaves me vulnerable and my loved ones potentially at risk. Yet Toby turning up like this and offering himself as an interviewee gives me an out, or rather a diversionary tactic to stop Rowlock sending any more of his thugs after me.

'I don't need to speak to him. The story I was working on

doesn't matter any more. The interview with you is all I'm interested in now.'

'Are you sure?' Toby presses me.

'Absolutely.' I fix my gaze on Bibek, hoping he understands my emphasis and will feed it back to the man he has made it his business to protect. 'Any dealings I had with Aden Rowlock are over.'

Chapter Twenty-Seven

Toby and I make polite, stilted chitchat on our short walk to the pub, covering the weather – still baking hot – and how well we each know the area – not that well. It's as though the spectre of his brother is looming over us and I can't relax until we've talked about him. Toby, I imagine, is just as nervous because he's in the company of a journalist. It's a relief to get inside the pub and order a drink and I note with satisfaction that he gulps down a third of his pint with the same speed I do mine. God bless alcohol, the great liberator.

The pub is one of those long-standing London locals that has been spruced up to attract a more metropolitan clientele but still falls short. The decor is nice enough – stripped back to brick walls, reupholstered seats that actually match – but the only cask ale it sells is Greene King IPA, a television on the wall in the corner is playing *Sky News* on mute and there's not a wasabi peanut to be seen among the hanging display of Scampi Fries and Mr Porky packets.

We seat ourselves at a table close to the door, which is propped open to allow air to circulate inside. By now my beer is only a third full and I'm already thinking about the next one. But first, I have a question for Toby.

'Does Aden really run his solicitor's firm from that address?'

'Yes. Why do you ask?'

'It's not exactly premium office space.'

He chuckles. 'No, you're right. It's actually a bedsit that doubles as his office. But he manages.'

'The firm's not listed anywhere online either,' I casually drop in. 'I wanted to check the address before I went but when I googled it there was no record.'

Toby shrugs. 'Beats me why not.'

'Why did he move to London?'

I know I'm pushing it with these questions but I'm understandably curious about the man who appears to keep putting me in harm's way.

'Bad divorce, I think. Or maybe someone told him the streets of London were paved with gold.'

If only they were, I think sourly.

'Did he ever represent Isaac or the band?'

'Um, not his bag – Aden does family law.' He takes another sip of beer. 'Why were you there to see him?'

My defences silently rise and click into place. Their friendship means I need to be careful what I say now.

'I don't recall me saying I was,' I respond noncommittally.

'Natalie, you were outside his address and you thought I was him, so I'm going to respectfully suggest it's not a leap of imagination to say you were.'

It's the first time he's used my name and I like how he says it. I also like how his tone is gently mocking. It suggests he has a sense of humour about things.

'OK, you got me.' I pause for a second, conscious of not wanting to let slip anything about the mystery songwriter to Toby. 'I came across his name in a cutting and I thought he'd be a good person to talk to for the piece I was planning to write about Isaac.' A lie, but a necessary one I feel.

Toby frowns. 'There was an article about Aden?'

'No. His name was just mentioned in a piece.'

'What were you going to ask him?'

Toby's questions are making me nervous. I try to answer him as breezily as I can manage. 'It's irrelevant now, because I can't seem to get past his bodyguard.'

'Bodyguard?'

'Bibek, the one who just bawled us out on the doorstep.'

'Oh, right.' I wait for another question about Rowlock, but Toby surprises me by asking what happened to my face. Self-consciously I touch my cheek, blushing beneath the bruising and the make-up.

'It looks like you really hurt yourself,' he adds.

I shrug as though it's no big deal. 'I lost my footing wearing stupidly high heels I'm not used to walking in and went smack into the back of a chair. It hurt like hell at first but it's not too bad now.'

He seems taken in by my explanation. 'Another one?' he asks, gesturing at my now empty pint glass.

'I'll get them, it's my round.'

Waiting at the bar to be served, I keep an eye on Toby in the mirror behind the row of optics. He appears pensive, clutching his cap in his hands like a child's comforter, and I wonder how he'd react to the blind item if he knew about it. Then a startling thought occurs: what if he knows Isaac's not dead? The two of them were incredibly close; it's more than feasible Toby knew the suicide was faked . . . and was even in on it? He could easily be the person Isaac trusted enough to help him flee the country. My stomach churning with apprehension, I order the drinks and pay for them. I need to tread very carefully now, because for all I know Toby and Rowlock could be working together and this offer of an interview could be a set-up. I think about what happened to Bronwyn and my hands start to shake as I return to our table and put the pints down.

'I was thinking, after we've drunk these, shall we get something to eat and start the interview?' asks Toby.

His comment stops me cold. 'You want to do it today?'

'Now I've made my mind up to do it, there's no point waiting. Eight years is long enough to sit on the truth,' he says grimly.

'The truth?'

He fixes me with a stare and my blood chills a fraction more.

'Do you like surprises, Natalie?'

'Um, I guess that depends on the surprise? What is it?'

He smiles pensively. 'You'll have to wait and see.'

Chapter Twenty-Eight

Sunday Times Culture Magazine, December 2011

ROCK/INTERVIEW

EXCLUSIVE INTERVIEW: ISAAC NAYLOR OF THE OSPREYS COMES CLEAN ABOUT THE BAND'S NEW ALBUM AND WORLD TOUR AFTER REHAB PULLS HIM BACK FROM THE BRINK

INTERVIEW/MAX JENNINGS

The first picture to emerge of a sober, drug-free Isaac Naylor ended up being a tabloid sensation – but not, unfortunately, to celebrate his road back to rude health. Taken in February in the grounds of a private rehab facility in California by another in-patient in possession of a contraband phone, it showed the formerly louche, hollow-cheeked and skinny-jean-loving lead singer of The Ospreys wearing grotty grey jogging bottoms and a Deep Purple T-shirt that strained to cover a visible paunch.

The red-top tabloid which ran the image risked a nailed-on privacy claim to do so, under the auspices that it was revealing Naylor's new look, as though it was something he had deliberately cultivated for the band's new album cover rather than being the consequence of eating properly for the first time in years after coming off a meal-substitute regime of inhaled heroin.

Yet Naylor shows no rancour towards the person who betrayed him while in recovery, nor towards the newspaper that printed the image. In fact, he tells me, over a coffee and a doorstep BLT sandwich at a cafe near to his north London home, during a break from band rehearsals for their forthcoming world tour, he's grateful to them both.

'The world needed to see me no longer ascribing to the image it had of me as the poster boy for "heroin chic",' he says. 'So I had a bit of a belly on me, so what? I was fucking *alive*. Before I went to rehab, I was a dead man walking. If I'd carried on the way I was going, I doubt I'd have made it to my next birthday.'

I don't disbelieve him. Naylor's descent into drug abuse is well documented to the point it feels unnecessary to give chapter and verse again here. 'I never injected though,' he's at pains to tell me. 'People might shrug and say "So fucking what, you still took heroin, you muppet", but it's an important distinction that I only smoked' – he qualifies *only* using air quotes – 'because, to me, not injecting meant I never quite hit rock bottom. I was like Tom Cruise in that scene from *Mission: Impossible* – hovering fucking inches from the ground but luckily never completely crash landing.'

His drug addiction reached its zenith around the release of the band's opus, *A Little Birdie Told Me*, three years ago. Naylor is mired in regret that it overshadowed what should have been a time for celebration for him and his band-mates, Danny Albright, Archie Samuels and Renner Jones, given the rapturous critical and commercial response to the album. 'I'd have kicked me to the kerb years ago, but lucky for me they are nice, forgiving people,' he says, his Jarrow accent as discernible now as it was when he left home at sixteen to pursue his music career. 'I put the boys, our manager Derrick and my brother Toby through so much shit and it says more about them than it does about me that they're all talking to me still.'

But talking they are, and in the case of Albright, Samuels and Jones they've forgiven him enough to continue performing with him. The British leg of The Ospreys' sell-out *Right Back at You* Stadium Tour begins on Saturday in Scotland, when they take to the stage at Glasgow's 51,866-capacity Hampden Park. Then they'll head to America and Australia but will be back to headline Glastonbury for a second time before completing the tour in Europe. Naylor certainly looks as though he has the stamina for such an arduous schedule, but it does beg the question whether he's mentally prepared for the rigours of so many dates and of being away from home for almost a year.

'I wouldn't be doing it if I wasn't ready,' he says, shaking his head emphatically. 'I wouldn't do that to myself or to the band, because if I fuck this up we're done. But my therapist and doctors have given me the green light and I'll have the support of my NA [Narcotics Anonymous] sponsor.' He pauses then breaks into a grin. 'Jesus, I sound a right knob. Therapist and sponsor I'll have you. Next I'll be fucking practising yoga.' Is that likely? 'Nah, I'm not flexible enough. I did try it once in rehab but I pulled a muscle. Never again.'

CONTINUES ON PAGE 23

143

Chapter Twenty-Nine

The pub's menu is too unappetising for Toby's tastes, so he suggests we venture out to find somewhere alternative to eat. I'm not keen, wishing he'd tell me what the surprise is first, but he's insistent and so we stumble outside into the searing heat of the midday sun which, combined with two pints of lager, immediately makes me feel listless. We trudge up the road to where there are more cafes, but Toby is unenthusiastic about them all.

'What do you want to eat?' I ask.

He smiles sheepishly. 'It sounds mad in this weather, but I'm really craving macaroni cheese. It was my favourite when I was a kid. Our mam used to make it all the time.'

I realise this could be an opportune moment to test whether Toby knows Isaac's alive and where he is.

'I've been reading a biography of Isaac and it mentions your mum a lot. It must've been so hard losing her so young.'

Toby's expression tightens. 'It was.'

'You were lucky you had a big brother to look out for you. It sounds like you two were really close.'

'We were. After our mam died our dad went downhill and couldn't look after us, so Isaac had to take over. He pretty much raised me.'

'You must miss your brother so much.'

'Like you wouldn't believe,' he nods, eyes glazing with tears. 'I know it sounds soft, but I've been so lost without him. Even now I go to pick up the phone to call him and then I remember, and it kills me that he's dead. I wish I could turn back the clock—' His voice trails off and he self-consciously wipes his eyes dry with the backs of his hands and I am convinced his grief is genuine, which both pleases and horrifies me. He can't be in league with Rowlock if he thinks Isaac is dead, but if the blind item is right and the suicide was faked, how could his brother deceive him for all these years?

'Have you ever lost anyone close to you?' he suddenly asks.

'Me? I—' I think of Bronwyn, lying cold and still in a funeral home, waiting for her formal goodbye. I force myself to shake my head though. I don't want to tell Toby about her. I don't know why, it just doesn't feel right, and I don't want my grief to distract him. 'My grandparents,' I say, which isn't a lie.

'Right.' Neither of us knows what to say now, so I'm relieved when Toby breaks the mood by pointing to the next cafe along. 'If this one doesn't have macaroni cheese on the menu either, we'll have to give up.'

I have an idea. 'Why don't we go back to my place in Maida Vale and I'll make you some? I have a little patio so we can sit outside to eat and do the interview after.'

Toby's eyes light up. 'You can make macaroni cheese?'

'I have a nine-year-old. It's a staple of his diet.'

'I didn't know you had a kid.'

'Why would you?' Then I pull a face. 'Although you have been following me, so—'

We both grin at that and I feel the last remnants of tension ease from my shoulders. This is going to be fine. I'll get this interview in the bag and then keep working on the other story and hopefully in the meantime Bibek will pass the message to Rowlock to leave me alone.

'I am sorry about that,' Toby repeats, 'but it's worked out well now.' He looks up and down the road. 'Which way's the Tube station again? I can never remember. Unless we get a cab back to yours?'

I baulk at the suggestion, knowing I should offer to pay, as he's the interviewee, but knowing I can ill afford it. 'The Tube will be quicker,' I say.

'It'll be really hot and stuffy though in this heat. Look, let me pay for the taxi. If you're going to make me lunch it's only fair.'

Before I can protest he flags down a taxi that's coming towards us and opens the door to let me in first.

'Thanks,' I say, and flop gratefully into its air-conditioned interior. I give the driver my address as Toby settles in the seat beside me.

'Talking of the Tube, why did you run off that day?' I ask him as the taxi pulls away from the kerb. 'Why didn't you tell me who you were then?'

Toby laughs. 'Are you kidding? You pointed at me like I was the devil or something, I thought I was going to get lynched. Plus, if I had said who I was, other people might've reacted and, well, I don't like the attention. Isaac loved people knowing who he was, but not me.'

When the cab drops us off Toby peels a £20 note from a roll of them and it reminds me what a wealthy man he is. He inherited the bulk of Isaac's estate, bar an undisclosed sum that was paid out to Emily Jenkins' family and is assumed to have run into seven figures.

'Do you want to sit outside while I get lunch ready?' I ask, after letting us into the apartment.

'Sure. Have you got anything to drink?'

I'm not sure more booze is a good idea but I suspect he wants it for Dutch courage rather than a desire to get drunk; we've not started the interview yet but already he's twitching with nerves.

I fetch him a glass of wine from the kitchen then show him outside to the patio. 'I won't be long,' I say.

I quickly whip up the macaroni cheese and after shoving it under the grill so the grated cheese on top bubbles and browns, I decide to make a salad to go with it. Five minutes later I carry both outside on a tray, where I've already laid the patio table with plates and cutlery.

'I hope this is OK,' I say as I set the tray down. Toby looks delighted and thanks me profusely for making his favourite dish as he helps himself to a plateful. I do the same, then we chat about what it's like living in Maida Vale while we eat. After a second helping Toby takes an enormous slug of wine then clears his throat.

'So. Where do you want to start?'

Normally I spend a couple of days at least preparing for an interview like this. I find researching my subjects as enjoyable as writing about them, if not more so, and I pride myself on digging up under-reported facts about them that I craft into interesting questions. Usually, for an hour's time slot, I'll have a list of at least twenty-five questions ready, plus more on my back-up list if I think I can squeeze extra time out of the publicist who's set the interview up. But for this, what might prove to be one of the most significant interviews of my career, I have nothing prepared, only my scrappy notes. But I do know what I want to ask.

'Do you mind?' I ask, gesturing to the voice recorder I've already placed beside my plate.

Toby flinches. 'You want to tape it?'

'Well, my shorthand isn't up to much, so if you want to be quoted verbatim this is the best way.'

He still looks worried.

'If you want, you can record it on your phone as well,' I suggest. 'I don't mind. Then you'll have your own version of exactly what you said.'

'It's not that—' He glugs down another mouthful of wine, emptying his glass. I refill it from the bottle sitting in the wine cooler I put on the table earlier.

'What is it? Are you having second thoughts?'

'No. It's just, well, I don't want anyone else listening to the tape afterwards. It would feel intrusive.'

It's not a concern my interviewees usually have, but it's easily remedied.

'The only way anyone else would hear the tape was if you contested how I quoted you, such as if you thought I'd put words into your mouth that you never said. Then the lawyers for whichever paper runs the interview would have to listen to the tape to see if your claim was legit.' I pause. 'Why don't you record it yourself and I'll also give you a read-through.'

'What's that?'

'It's when I read the interview back to you over the phone to check for accuracy before it goes to press. It's not copy approval – you don't get to change the way in which I write the piece – but if there are any details I've included that aren't correct you'll be able to say.'

'Will the newspaper agree to that?'

I smile. 'If they want your exclusive interview they will.'

My assurances seem to relax him and after setting up his

phone to record on the table next to his plate and both of us having another fortifying slug of wine, I'm ready with my first question.

'Toby, do you believe your brother killed Emily Jenkins?'

Chapter Thirty

Toby breaks into nervous laughter. 'Whoa, go straight for the jugular why don't you.' I laugh too.

'OK, it might seem like that, but there's a reason I've started with that question.'

'Go on,' he answers cautiously.

'I've been reading up on what happened and two things are clear.' I tick them off on my fingers. 'First, Isaac had been sober for nine months before that night, and second, he never inject-ed drugs. In the light of that, and as one of the people closest to him, if not the closest, I want to know if you think Isaac was responsible for Emily's death.' I pause. 'I am going to ask what he was like growing up, The Ospreys getting signed, how he coped with fame, etc., but I want to know your take on the evening his world imploded, because it informs everything else. So, do you think your brother killed her?'

Opening with a killer question is not the interview technique I normally apply. Usually I go in soft and ask a slew of back-ground questions first to ease the subject in. But this is different, because we've already spent time in each other's company and therefore I do not feel I need to warm Toby up. And if he trusts me enough to grant me the interview, he should trust how I conduct it.

Toby slowly nods. 'I understand. I just haven't really talked to anyone about it since the coroner's hearing into Isaac's suicide.'

'I've read the reports from the hearing. You were with him at the venue and remembered Emily being brought backstage,' I prompt.

'That's right, she was among the fans who watched the gig from the side of the stage and were invited to meet the band. My job as Isaac's assistant was to have a quick word with them first and lay down some basic ground rules about photos. He could get a bit arsey if fans were over-familiar and I had to make sure they understood what was allowed and what wasn't.'

'Did Emily stand out among the fans?'

'No, she didn't. I don't mean that in a horrible way though,' Toby adds hastily. 'You can see from her pictures how attractive she was. What I mean is there were always lots of pretty girls coming backstage to meet the band and I wouldn't say she stood out more than any other.'

I see the opening and dive right through it. 'The Little Birdies were special though, weren't they? Special enough to be given a nickname by the band.'

Toby's mouth slackens in surprise. 'Christ, I'd forgotten about them!' He winces. 'Shit, we wouldn't get away with calling them that now.'

'Do you remember if any of the Little Birdies were there the night Emily came backstage? In particular one called Pippa.'

I watch him keenly for signs of recognition of the name, but his expression remains frustratingly impassive.

'They probably were there; a group of them showed up for every gig. But I don't recall a Pippa, sorry.'

'I haven't been able to confirm it yet, but there's a possibility that a Little Birdie called Pippa was the one who supplied Emily with the backstage pass. If that's the case, she may have also encouraged her to go back to the hotel with Isaac. I'm trying to track her down.'

Toby shakes his head emphatically. 'Emily met Isaac along with the other fans who had passes for the meet and greet. She wouldn't have been given access any other way. It wouldn't have happened through a third party.'

I study Toby for a moment, trying to weigh up if he's being honest with me. The Ospreys are by no means the first band to have a dedicated groupie following they encouraged and exploited, but in the #MeToo era no one is going to want to admit to it. It wouldn't look good for The Ospreys now if I write about the Little Birdies, but I wonder how much loyalty Toby still has to the band to try to deflect me from doing so. We shall see.

'What else do you remember about Emily and Isaac meeting for the first time? Did she take much persuading to go back to the hotel with him?'

Toby stares out beyond the low hedge into the communal garden. He lifts his hand to rub his chin and I see the flesh on his disfigured finger is pink and wrinkled, like it's been submerged in hot water for too long. 'So much from that night has been misreported,' he says softly.

'How?'

He turns away from the garden and his eyes meet mine. He looks so sorrowful I chide myself for not appreciating how difficult this must be for him. I need to temper the way I'm asking my questions, I'm being too abrupt.

'Emily didn't go back to the hotel on her own with Isaac. There were others in the car. It wasn't like he spirited her away on his own. Christ, she was barely legal. He wasn't stupid.'

'Who else was in the car?'

'Me, Danny and Derrick and another girl.'

'But not Pippa.'

'No. I don't remember the girl's name but I know it wasn't that.'

'It must've been a big car,' I remark.

That makes him smile. 'It was one of those big bastard SUVs. There was plenty of room.'

I wait a beat, wanting to frame my next question in a way that doesn't sound like I'm blaming him.

'It was widely reported only Emily and Isaac were in the car. If you and the others were in the vehicle too, I'm wondering why the mistake wasn't corrected at the time?'

'I – I guess I wasn't paying attention. Isaac was missing and I was frantic with worry. It was only after we knew for sure he was gone—' Toby swallows hard, 'that I read all the press coverage.'

'Derrick Cordingly should've said something then. As Isaac's manager you'd think he'd want to set the record straight.'

'You'd think, but all he cared about was protecting his remaining assets,' says Toby with evident bitterness. 'If the press found out he and Danny had been in the car with Emily too, they'd have been tainted by association, for being part of the entourage that took her back to the hotel where she died. As it was, no one ever found out.'

'You must have been very upset about that.'

'I was. I still am. It wasn't fair. Isaac had already borne the brunt of so much shit for that band.'

'In what way?'

'There was so much expectation on him as lead singer. The others were almost bystanders. The label and Derrick wouldn't let Renner, Danny and Archie do anything without Isaac being there too, which meant his schedule was relentless and he never got a break. The worst occasion was our dad's funeral.'

'What happened?'

'Me and Isaac arranged to have the wake at our old local in Jarrow and loads of people from the area who we hadn't seen for years were coming along after the service. It should've been a brilliant evening, seeing all those old faces, catching up, having a few drinks.'

'Should have?'

Toby straightens up in his seat, patently riled by the memory he's about to share.

'Derrick booked the band to be on breakfast news the morning after the funeral to plug the album. Isaac's call time was five-thirty in the morning, so we couldn't stay in Jarrow – we had to come back to London that same evening. There was a car idling outside the wake for the whole half an hour we were able to stay before we had to leave. The others said they could do the programme without Isaac but Derrick refused, saying it was too important. He and the label didn't care we'd just put our dad in the ground; it was all about shifting records for them.'

'That must have been really hard for you. He was your dad as well.'

'This isn't about me. I want you to know what it was like for Isaac. It wasn't easy for him being in The Ospreys and he suffered, more than you can imagine.' He pauses. 'I want you to think good of him.'

'It's hard to, when faced with what we know,' I say as gently as possible. 'Even if he didn't inject her himself, Isaac still ended up in bed with a young, impressionable fan who died while taking drugs in his presence.'

Toby releases a tremulous sigh. 'That's the biggest mistruth of all. Isaac didn't go to bed with Emily Jenkins.'

'What do you mean?' I ask, confused.

'Isaac wasn't in the room when Emily got into his bed – and I know that because he was already asleep in mine.'

Chapter Thirty-One

To say I am stunned is an understatement. It takes a few moments for his words to sink in, then I lean over to check the red light on my voice recorder is definitely on, because I know I don't want to miss a word of this.

'You're saying Isaac went to sleep in your hotel room?'

'I am.'

'But he woke up in his own bed with Emily's body beside him.'

'He did.'

'So he got up in the night and went back to his.'

Toby shakes his head. 'No, that's not how it happened. He went to sleep in my bed and the next thing he knew he'd woken up in his suite.'

'How did he get there?' I ask sceptically.

'The only explanation I can think of is that someone drugged him and moved him. Isaac was sober when he went to bed, but he woke up off his face in his bed with Emily dead next to him. He didn't take the drugs himself.'

I let out an incredulous laugh, unable to help myself. 'You do know how crazy that sounds?' I say.

'I know, but I'm telling you that's what happened.'

Toby's face is set with such grim conviction that suddenly I don't know what to believe. It all sounds so preposterous and yet . . .

'If what you're saying's true, Isaac was set up. He was framed,' I say slowly.

'It's the truth,' Toby says firmly.

'But who would've done such a thing? More to the point, why?'

His expression pinches. 'I can't be sure.'

'You must have some idea,' I scoff. 'Why have you said nothing all this time and let them get away with it?'

My question comes out far blunter than I intended and Toby reacts accordingly, crossing his arms defensively across his torso.

'I told the police at the time. They didn't believe me.'

Probably because it sounds so ridiculous, I think. 'They would have had a duty to investigate if you told them Isaac was in your room—'

He cuts me off. 'I couldn't prove he was. I still can't.'

'How can I be sure it's the truth then?'

Toby looks to his empty glass of wine, then to me. 'Got another bottle? I think we're going to need it.'

The hotel where The Ospreys stayed on the night of 10 December did indeed have a VIP lift that allowed its famous guests to bypass reception and go straight from the basement garage up to the top floor where the biggest suites were situated. The group that included Toby, Isaac and Emily had disembarked from the SUV right beside its sliding doors. Toby remembers the lift being a bit of a squash and slow moving enough to make him break out in a claustrophobic sweat and they were all relieved when the doors opened on the top floor to spew them out.

Toby's room was actually one floor below, though. 'I didn't warrant a fancy suite,' he smiles ruefully. 'The reason I went to that floor was because I was going to Isaac's suite to borrow his

157

laptop, as my own had given up the ghost on the flight from London to Glasgow and I hadn't had time to get it repaired or replaced.'

'Where did the others go?'

'I didn't pay attention; I just followed Isaac. It was definitely only the two of us in his suite though. Anyhow, Isaac said he wasn't feeling well and was going to crash out straightaway, so I took the laptop and as I left he was getting into bed.'

'Hang on, you said he went to sleep in your room.'

'He did. About half an hour later I got a call from Ben, one of the road crew. He and some others were in a pub around the corner from the hotel that held lock-ins after last orders and they asked me to join them,' he explains, adding that while he would never have admitted it to Isaac, he had a much better time hanging out with the roadies than he did with the band, because the atmosphere was more laidback and friendlier. He felt he fitted in with them more.

'I said I'd meet them, but first I decided to run the laptop back upstairs to Isaac in case he changed his mind about wanting it. I had the spare key card to his room so I was just going to slip in and leave it. But when I got to his floor I could hear loud music coming from one of the other suites and Isaac was awake and really pissed off because he was feeling ropey and he couldn't sleep because of the noise. So that's when I suggested he get his head down in my room instead.'

'Ropey in what way?'

'He said he felt dizzy and sick.'

I stare at him. 'Dizzy and sick like he'd been drugged?'

Toby meets my gaze. 'Yes. I didn't think that at the time though – I just thought he was done in after the gig. Normally he'd have got so high afterwards he wouldn't have noticed how knackered he was, but this was the first concert he'd done sober in years and he wasn't used to it.'

'Then what happened?'

'I needed to get my jacket from my room to go out, so Isaac got the lift down with me and when I left he was crashed out on my bed and already asleep. I was a bit worried about leaving him when he felt unwell, so I asked his security detail to check on him and to call me if there was a problem and I'd come back.'

'What time did you return?'

Toby grimaces. 'This is the issue I have with proving what happened. I didn't go back to the hotel until the following morning, when I got the call to say Emily had been found and the police were on their way. Me and Ben ended up chatting to some girls who lived locally and we went back to their flat to carry on the party and I crashed out there.'

'You don't know for sure Isaac fell asleep in your bed then,' I point out. 'He could've stirred after you'd gone, headed back upstairs and at that point bumped into Emily.'

'That's true, but I know he didn't.'

'How do you know?'

'Because I believed my brother when he told me he didn't remember how he got back to his room and he had nothing to do with Emily dying.'

The air between us suddenly feels heavy and thick and I shift awkwardly in my chair. Of course Toby wants to believe Isaac wasn't capable of hurting her. Which sibling wouldn't, in his shoes? But I can't ignore what came next, the twist in the tale that turns his theory on its head.

'If Isaac had nothing to do with it, why take his own life?' I ask. 'Someone as convinced of their innocence as you say Isaac was would surely have wanted to clear his name.'

Toby flares up. 'He did it because he thought he'd lost everything! Do you have any idea what it was like for him, waking up with that poor girl in his bed and knowing it had nothing to do with him but everyone thinking the worst, everyone assuming he'd got high again and forced her to take drugs with him? He was terrified he was going to prison.' Toby's outburst rattles me and he notices and apologises. 'I'm sorry. I didn't mean to shout at you. It's just so upsetting to talk about it still. Isaac did what he did because he thought there was no way back for him, not because he knew he was guilty.'

'I don't understand why the police didn't listen to you when you said he'd gone to sleep in your room.'

'I suppose they thought the same as you – that he could've got up at any point and gone back upstairs to his suite. But I know he didn't.'

Toby pours us both another large glass of wine. I take a small sip from mine, aware of how much I've had to drink already and that I should be keeping a clear head. He shows no such restraint and knocks back half of his in one gulp.

'I should've kicked up more of a stink at the time but after Isaac absconded I was too focused on finding him to worry about it. I thought once we found him we could sort it out, make everyone see he hadn't done anything wrong. But then his stuff was found on the beach and, well,' he blinks back tears, 'I was too devastated to think straight. I was a wreck. By the time I came through the other side of my grief, months had passed and it was impossible to re-write history.'

'And now?'

'I want people to know Isaac didn't kill that girl.' Toby drunkenly jabs his injured finger at me. 'And I want *you* to help me find out who did.'

Chapter Thirty-Two

NME.COM

'Isaac lied about his recovery'

The Ospreys have shed new light on Isaac Naylor's state of mind before the infamous night during which a fan was found dead in his hotel room

By Steve Marshall

First uploaded 3 March 2017

To mark the release of The Ospreys' greatest hits next week, drummer Robert 'Renner' Jones, manager Derrick Cordingly and the band's long-time stylist Cicely Harris were guests on Lola Maurice's award-winning Downbeat podcast. Part 1 saw them discussing how the band rebounded after Isaac Naylor's suicide, Part 2 drills down into the events that led to it – and how Renner's deepest regret is that he didn't see Naylor's relapse coming. Below is a partial transcript. Click here to listen to the audio extract.

Lola: *I know it's hard raking over what happened the night Emily Jenkins died, but has hindsight given any of you a different perspective on it?*

Renner: *Fuck yeah. I wish I'd paid more attention to how Isaac was feeling about the tour. I think he was coping with the performances, because on the surface it was business as usual. He was in great shape, had been clean for nine months, he was on fucking fire. But I never asked him if he was happy – happy to be back in the band, happy to be on the road again. We all took it for granted that he was, but he can't have been to fall off the wagon like he did.*

Cicely: *I feel the same. I mean, he went from nought to sixty in a blink of an eye and we should've realised the crash was coming.*

Lola: *By zero to sixty you mean him going from being clean to injecting heroin?*

Cicely: *Yes. It was no secret Isaac smoked heroin and he also drank like a fish, but he was proud of the fact he never injected. It was like a badge of honour for him. He'd look at someone like Pete Doherty and he'd say, 'At least I'm not as bad as him.'*

Renner: *Plus he couldn't stand needles. He must've been so out of it to stick one in his own arm that night, let alone Emily's.*

Derrick: *Or he was simply desperate. I have a different view to these two. I spoke to Isaac a lot about his mental state in the run-up to the tour because naturally I had a responsibility to him and everyone else to make sure he was strong enough to go ahead with it. I also had regular conversations with his sponsor and the* doctors who treated him in rehab. What we could all agree upon was that Isaac was very adept at disguising how badly he was coping. He was a proficient liar. So I honestly don't think anyone could've anticipated how fragile his recovery was. Certainly the professionals meant to be looking out for him didn't.

Lola: *But there was always going to be a risk that he'd relapse, surely? I remember reading an interview with him where he admitted he'd been taking drugs since his teens. That's nine months sober compared to years of abusing his body chasing a high.*

Renner: *This is what saddens me the most. Isaac was so grateful to be clean at last. He'd tried before a few times, but his heart hadn't been in it. This time it honestly felt different. The only thing that jarred is the lads and me offered to clear out all the booze from backstage and from the tour buses and planes but Isaac wasn't having any of it. He was adamant he wouldn't be tempted to drink or do drugs because he finally could see the benefits of being sober.*

Cicely: *Renner's right, Isaac was in a good place, or so it seemed.*

Derrick: *None of us will ever know what persuaded him to inject smack that night, much less administer it to a seventeen-year-old girl—*

Lola: *Sorry to butt in, but technically no one knows for sure that he did inject Emily himself. The police didn't find his fingerprints on the syringe or on the drugs.*

Derrick: *The physical evidence was inconclusive, that's true. But there was proof.*

Lola: *Really? What was that?*

Derrick: *The fact he ran away. If he hadn't done anything wrong, why didn't he stay?*

Chapter Thirty-Three

I need a few minutes to process everything Toby's told me so far, so I suggest we take a break while I make us coffee. He gets up from the table at the same time and that's when I realise he's weaving drunk now, because he staggers into the hedge on his way inside. Morally I know I can't continue the interview this afternoon: if he's too inebriated to walk in a straight line he's not going to be in control of what he's saying either, and while I am obviously keen to get the best interview I possibly can out of him, I don't want him to later claim it was conducted under duress. I'll get some coffee down him then call for a cab to take him back to wherever he's staying.

As I fill Gayle's coffee grinder with fresh beans my mind begins to spin. Could it be true? Could Isaac really have gone to sleep in Toby's room and someone else was responsible for moving him back to his suite and for the state Emily Jenkins ended up in? But I keep coming back to the same glaring truth: Isaac skipped police bail and did a runner rather than face the consequences. Then – of this I am certain now – he faked his suicide as an act of contrition. Why go to such lengths if he had nothing to be sorry for?

A few minutes later I carry the prepared coffee on a tray from the kitchen into the reception room – only to find Toby lying prone on the sofa, fast asleep. I set the coffee down on the table and debate whether to wake him, but then I spot the baseball cap in his hands, fingers digging into the fabric, and I decide to leave him be. The man's a walking ball of tension and clearly needs some rest. I fetch a glass of water from the kitchen and put it by the sofa, then leave him where he is and take my coffee over to the breakfast bar where my laptop is. I check my emails and my heart leaps when I see I've been sent a notification from MusicJabber – someone's answered the query I posted about Pippa.

I DON'T KNOW WHERE SHE IS NOW, BUT PIPPA'S PARENTS LIVED IN RICHMOND. HER SURNAME IS MIRREN.

The poster's name is WhatACarrion123. When I search the rest of the forum for any of their previous posts I'm surprised to find none; either they've changed their name to reply to me or this is the first time they've posted on the site. But whoever they are doesn't really matter: what matters is the information they've provided, because a few minutes later, via an online electoral register site, I've confirmed an address for a Stephen and Belinda Mirren in Richmond, which is in south-west London. I decide to head down first thing in the morning: as it's the weekend I may have a better chance of catching them at home if they both work. Besides, I can't go anywhere right now when I've had too much to drink myself and there's a man I barely know passed out on my sofa.

I use the time while Toby's sleeping to write up my notes from the interview so far. I find it baffling no one would listen to him about what room his brother fell asleep in that night and I wonder what Derrick Cordingly would say if I put it to him.

*

166

By the time I finish working, the apartment has grown dark, long shadows drawn out of their daytime hiding places by the advent of dusk. Toby has shifted position once or twice but he's still out for the count and for now I'm happy to leave him where he is.

I'm fixing myself another coffee in the kitchen when suddenly I hear the crash of breaking glass. I tear into the lounge, thinking it might be Toby knocking the water glass over, but he's still fast asleep and the glass intact. Then I hear voices in the corridor outside and the sound of someone hammering on a door. Grabbing my keys, I rush outside to find a couple of other neighbours trying to get into Elizabeth's apartment two doors down. One, a man who lives on the floor above but whose name I don't know, rounds on me.

'Did you hear the smash? Someone threw a brick through Elizabeth's French doors.'

'Oh my god, is she OK?'

'She isn't answering the door.'

'How do you know it was someone throwing a brick?' I ask.

'I was on my balcony when I saw this man pelt across the garden. I didn't realise what he was doing at first, then I saw the brick in his hand and he threw it.'

He resumes hammering while the other neighbour, Suki, who I know because she lives next door to me with her husband and two children, calls Elizabeth's name again. When there's no response from the other side of the door we exchange fearful looks.

'Does anyone have a spare key?' I ask her.

'I think Julia at number seven might. They play bridge together,' she says, hitting the door with her fist again. 'Elizabeth, can you hear me?'

I leave them to their hammering and shouting and race along the corridor to apartment seven. Thankfully Julia's in but she becomes distressed when I tell her what's happened and it takes me a few moments to calm her down enough so I can make her understand we need the spare key to get into Elizabeth's apartment. She hands it over then asks me to return when I have news; she has poor mobility and can't walk far to check for herself.

The man from upstairs goes into Elizabeth's apartment first. He reaches the mouth of the hallway that leads into the lounge and lets out a cry. 'We need to call an ambulance.'

I push past him. Elizabeth is unconscious on the carpet next to broken glass from the missing pane in her French door. I rush over and kneel down beside her.

'Is she dead?' asks an ashen-faced Suki, who's joined me on the carpet.

I check Elizabeth's pulse and feel a faint beat, then put my hand to her chest and feel it rise and fall ever so slightly. 'She's still breathing.'

'The ambulance is on its way,' says the male neighbour, who is hovering on the threshold to the hallway, too nervous to step inside. I take hold of Elizabeth's hand and reassure her that help is on the way.

'Did the brick hit her?' asks Suki. 'I can't see any blood.'

We check around Elizabeth's head and body, careful not to touch or move her, in case she's hurt and we make it worse. 'There's no wound,' I say.

That's when I see it. Half hidden beneath the sofa where it must have skidded to a halt is the offending brick. I bend down for a closer look and to my surprise I see there's a note attached to it with the aid of a rubber band. I let go of Elizabeth's hand and crawl towards it.

'Don't touch it, I've called the police as well,' cautions the neighbour from upstairs.

But I don't need to touch it to see what the note says. It's perfectly visible, written in thick black marker and bold capitals.

STOP DIGGING.

I reel back, horrified. I think the brick was meant for me.

Chapter Thirty-Four

Stifling a sob, I get to my feet and stagger my way out of Elizabeth's apartment, ignoring Suki's cries of 'Where are you going?' and shoving past our other neighbour standing by the door. Outside in the corridor I run slap bang into a bleary-eyed Toby, roused from his nap by all the commotion.

'Hey, what's wrong?' he asks as we disentangle ourselves.

My chest heaves with distress as I explain that someone's thrown a brick through Elizabeth's patio door and the shock has made her collapse.

'That's awful,' he exclaims, more alert now. 'Why would anyone do that?'

I grab his hand and drag him back into my apartment and shut the door firmly behind us. Then I press an ear against it and look through the peephole to make sure no one is directly outside. Toby stares at me with a bemused look on his face while I do this.

'What's going on?' he asks.

'The brick was meant for me,' I whisper.

'What do you mean?'

'Whoever threw it was either a really bad aim and missed my window, or they were told the wrong address.'

'Why would anyone chuck a brick at your flat?'

'Someone's being trying to shut me up and I think they killed my best friend as well.'

'Killed?' exclaims Toby, now wide-eyed with shock. 'How?'

'She was stabbed. The police said it was a mugging but I don't think it was. They want me to stop working on the story,' I say, my voice coming in juddering gasps. 'They warned me and I didn't listen and now Elizabeth's out cold and barely breathing. It's my fault.'

Toby grabs me by the shoulders. 'Natalie, you need to calm down. You're not making sense.'

I try to catch my breath but I can't. 'It was the blind item about Isaac, that's what started it.'

'Isaac?' he echoes. 'What about him?'

If I weren't so upset right now and more able to process my thoughts rationally, I would absolutely caution myself not to say a word about the mystery songwriter to Toby of all people, but I'm not, so I don't, and I blurt out everything I know in a long, rapid torrent.

'About ten days ago I started working on a story to prove your brother is still alive and since then I've been threatened, assaulted, had funeral flowers delivered to me to commemorate my son, who thank goodness is alive and safe with his dad, and my best friend was killed and now there's been a brick lobbed through my neighbour's window with a note on it saying "stop digging" and I know it was really meant for me, because they want me to stop looking into the story.'

Reaching the end, I breathe out, relieved at having unburdened myself – until I see Toby is staring at me as though I have two heads.

'You're trying to prove my brother's alive?' There's no mistaking the anger in his voice.

'If you let me explain—' I begin.

He holds up his hand to stop me. 'No, I don't want to hear

it. Christ, Natalie, I thought you were a serious journalist, but you're just another bloody tabloid hack trying to dig up dirt.'

'I'm not, I swear. I didn't go looking for the story. Please, come and sit down, let me explain.'

He doesn't budge, but he doesn't walk out either, which I take as an encouraging sign.

'Look, I found something online, a website post about your brother faking his suicide.'

His mouth drops open. I don't think he could look more surprised if I'd just slapped him across the face.

'Are you for real?' he croaks.

'That's what the post said.'

Toby paces back and forth in the hall, then turns on me.

'I can't believe you'd be so stupid to swallow some crap that's been written on the internet,' he seethes through gritted teeth. 'My brother is dead. He went into the sea and drowned himself.'

I feel terrible I'm upsetting him. He's practically vibrating with anger and is close to tears. I need to back off so I do, literally, taking a step away from him.

'I'm so sorry, I shouldn't have said anything.'

He shoots me a dark look. 'Well, you've started now so you may as well carry on. I'm all ears.'

I am standing with my back against my front door and I don't like it. I feel trapped.

'Can we sit down?' I start edging past him towards the lounge and I'm pleased to say he follows me without argument. The sofa is still warm from where he was asleep on it only minutes ago. I sit but he stays standing in front of me, furiously balling the cap in his hands again, his fingers rhythmically clenching and unclenching.

'How exactly is my brother supposed to have faked his own death?' he asks, his voice swollen with emotion.

'The blind item wasn't about how Isaac had faked his death as such: it was about a mystery songwriter who has been anonymously providing lyrics to producers in London via his lawyer. It said the songwriter had been successful in the past but had disappeared from public view a few years ago.' I swallow hard, acutely aware of how flimsy the blind item was on detail now I'm retelling it – and of how Toby is staring down at me with ill-disguised disgust. 'It was suggested the songwriter could be Isaac, so I started to look into it and that's when I found out via someone who works at a studio that the lawyer submitting the songs on the songwriter's behalf was your old family friend Aden Rowlock.'

His hands stop clenching. 'Aden?'

'That's what I was told – that Rowlock's the lawyer acting for the mystery songwriter, so any producer who wants to record the songs has to go through him. I went to door-knock Rowlock at his address in Kentish Town, but he wasn't there, but within hours of me doing that he'd fired off a legal notice to the studio about his client's privacy being invaded because a journalist – me – had been asking questions.'

I can tell from Toby's expression that his anger is now being tempered by intrigue. I relax a little.

'A couple of days later I was at an awards show when I was threatened and punched in the face.'

'Is that why your face is bruised? You didn't get it falling over into a chair? You lied,' he challenges me.

'I said that because I didn't want people asking awkward questions, but yes, a man attacked me and told me to leave the story alone.' I tell him then about the funeral wreath and repeat my suspicions about Bronwyn being stabbed.

'The police think it was a mugging gone wrong but I'm not convinced,' I say. 'She was the person at the studio who got Rowlock's address for me and now she's dead.'

Toby eyes me sceptically. 'You think Aden's behind all this?'

'I do, and that's why I think the online story is correct and Isaac is very much alive. Why go to so much trouble to shut me up if it wasn't true?'

'Show me the story on the website.'

'I can't. It's been taken down.'

'Right.' He looks angry again. 'For all I know you could be making this up just to get a quote out of me.'

Then I remember. 'I screen-grabbed it. Here, let me show you.' I get my laptop and find the item. Toby reads the story and the comments below, which I also captured, but I have no idea what he's thinking because his expression is inscrutable.

'See, I'm not making it up,' I say.

'What you're saying is crazy though.'

'Is it? Rowlock is probably desperate to stop the story breaking too soon. The police would very likely re-arrest Isaac over Emily Jenkins' death and if Rowlock's been protecting him all this time, he could face charges himself for perverting the course of justice or helping a suspect abscond. He will have wanted to manage the story coming out, but I've messed up his and Isaac's plans.'

Toby erupts, his face turning puce. 'You're wrong about Isaac!'

'They never found his body,' I retort.

'That's because it was swept out to sea!' he shouts at me, which makes me quail, but I stand my ground.

'If it's not true, how do you explain what Rowlock's been doing?'

'What you *think* he's been doing. You have no proof,' he says scathingly. 'The mystery songwriter could be anyone. You're assuming it must be Isaac because a few internet trolls have put the idea into your head. You're adding two and two and coming up with ninety-nine.' He shakes his head. 'Christ

174

almighty, Natalie, I thought you were a serious journalist.'

The way he says it sends a shudder of doubt hurtling through me. What if I have got it completely wrong? 'But how do you explain all the stuff that's been happening to me?' I ask, far less sure of myself than I was a few moments ago.

'It could be someone else with a grudge against you – maybe someone else you've written about and they didn't like it. Someone else you've hurt,' he adds pointedly.

An image of Spencer flashes before my eyes but I force it aside. My ex might be doing his damndest to diminish my involvement in our son's life but he wouldn't hurt me. He's not calculating enough and he wouldn't be so cruel as to send me a funeral wreath for Daniel. Besides, there's Bronwyn's murder to consider. No way could Spencer be behind that.

'You might have a point,' I respond, 'but the threats have referred specifically to a story of mine and the only one I've been working on up until I met you was the one about Isaac not being dead.'

'You think my brother pretended to kill himself leaving me on my own to deal with everything?' Toby asks. 'Exactly *why* do you think he'd have done that?'

'The obvious answer is to evade justice. The police had arrested him and were building a case against him. Charges were likely. So, rather than stand trial, he fled.'

'Where to . . . and how? It's one thing to fake a suicide but another to spirit himself out of the country. What's your explanation for that?'

'He had the means to pay for help. It's amazing what money can buy. A fake passport, for one.'

Toby stares at me. 'Natalie, do you realise how preposterous this all sounds? No one will ever believe it.'

'I know, which is why I had no intention of telling you about the blind item until I knew for sure whether it was true or not. But I've found some other stuff online and I think Isaac could've ended up in Nepal—'

Toby draws himself up to full height and squares his shoulders. 'Stop. Enough. I've heard some crap about my brother in my time but this is something else.' He makes for the door and I scuttle after him.

'Please don't leave—'

'You think I'm going to stay and carry on with the interview now? You're even crazier than this story you've concocted, which, by the way,' he adds snippily, 'you couldn't print a word of. Not without proof.'

'Not yet,' I admit. 'But I'm working on it.'

His face twists in anger. 'You were the one journalist I thought I could trust. Now I find out you're just like all the rest, peddling stupid rumours to get your name in the papers. I'm an idiot to think you were different.'

'Toby, please—'

But I'm too late. He's gone, slamming the door behind him.

Chapter Thirty-Five

Evening Standard, Friday 21 June

News> London

Music's biggest stars donate to family of Camberwell mugging victim

Tilly Sinclair / 1 hour ago / 0 comments

Some of the biggest names in music have contributed to a trust fund set up for the children of murdered recording studio executive Bronwyn Castle.

The fund was put in place days after Ms Castle was attacked outside The Soundbank studio in Camberwell last Thursday evening. The 41-year-old was leaving the premises, where she worked as studio manager, at around 10.30 p.m. when a man on a cycle tried to steal her handbag and stabbed her three times in the stomach when she resisted. She was taken to Guy's and St Thomas' Hospital where she underwent emergency surgery, but later died of her injuries.

Ms Castle, who lived in Battersea with her wife Lucy and their children, Wolfie, four, and Harrison, eighteen months, had worked at The Soundbank since 2016 and was popular with the artists who recorded there. Since news of her murder broke last week the industry has come together to set up a fund for her children, with stars including Ed Sheeran, Harry Styles and Ellie Goulding said to be among the generous benefactors.

Derrick Cordingly, manager of The Ospreys and one of the fund's trustees, said Ms Castle was well regarded for her unflappable manner and for how she went 'above and beyond' to make sure everyone's needs were met.

'Bronwyn made recording at The Soundbank the easiest experience imaginable. She was a lovely woman and I know I speak for many in the industry when I say we all feel desperately sad for her family and want to help in any way we can,' he told the *Standard*.

A memorial service for Ms Castle is being held next Thursday at St Mary's Church in Battersea and many of the names that worked with her are expected to attend. A private burial for family only will take place afterwards.

The police are meanwhile stepping up inquiries into her murder. Detective Chief Inspector Dan Clarke of the Major Crime Unit based in Southwark told the *Standard* that the bike used by the mugger was found abandoned on wasteland in Murphy Road, close to the studio.

'We now believe the assailant continued his escape on foot and we ask anyone who might have seen him running or walking from the direction of Murphy Road any time after 10.30 p.m. to come forward.'

Ms Castle's killer is described as white, of average height, wearing dark clothing and a cap and he was riding a bike with a chrome frame. He rode off down Tyrrell Street in the direction of Peckham Road.

* Anyone with information should call CrimeStoppers on 0800 555 111.

Chapter Thirty-Six

THURSDAY, 27TH

The poem Lucy has chosen for me to read ends with a line about love 'going on' after a person has died. I've been rehearsing it endlessly since she emailed it to me, anxious to be word perfect so I don't let her down, but now, facing the packed congregation in the church local to her and Bronwyn's home in Battersea and within spitting distance of the bank of the River Thames, I cannot get the words out.

'Or you . . .' I start to falter, my tears obscuring the words on the printout I'm holding. 'Or you . . .' I look up, stricken, knowing I can't continue. To my left lies Bronwyn in her closed coffin and if I reached out with my hand now I could touch the polished wood. But I can't bear to look at it, knowing my best friend's inside it and knowing this is the last time I'll ever be this near to her.

The celebrant comes over and touches my elbow.

'Let me finish,' she whispers, and she does, reading the last few lines again while I weep beside her. Then I feel a hand gently take mine and I look up and it is Spencer, come to lead me back to our pew, and I have never been so grateful to see him.

'I'm sorry,' I whisper to Lucy as we pass her in the aisle. I feel ashamed I didn't finish when she was so strong herself delivering the eulogy, even managing to make us laugh as she described the future plans she and Bronwyn had that will never come to fruition now, of the memories they will never make with their children. 'It's OK,' she whispers back, tears streaking her cheeks.

But it's not OK. This will never be OK.

I follow Spencer back to the pew and slide in beside him. His hand stays wrapped in mine and it feels both comforting and alien at the same time, so long is it since we've touched. I didn't ask him to come today, he asked to. Theoretically he knew Bronwyn for as long as I did and before our split they did get on. Daniel isn't here though: he's at school and will be going to a friend's house afterwards, from where Spencer will pick him up later. I'm hoping he'll suggest I go back with him and we have tea together again, as there's no wake happening today. Lucy has requested family only at the burial and afterwards they will return privately to her house. Instead, she's planning a separate wake next month. 'I want to celebrate Bronwyn's life in a fancy bar drinking champagne and wearing colourful clothes, not right after the funeral when everyone's feeling morose,' is how she explained it.

After a final hymn the celebrant draws the service to a close and a combination of undertakers and family members steps forward to raise Bronwyn's coffin onto their shoulders to bear it out of the church. As the coffin draws level with our pew my breath catches in my throat and I turn to press my face into Spencer's shoulder. I cannot bear to watch it pass, knowing Lucy and the boys are following behind. Spencer wraps his arm around me and leaves it there until it is our turn to leave. When his touch falls away, I miss its solidness and warmth.

Outside, people gather quietly in small groups and I am once more grateful Spencer is with me, until, that is, I see him reading a text on his phone and his face takes on a curious expression. It's as though he wants to smile but is trying hard not to.

'Everything OK?' I ask.

'Yeah. I need to dash though. Something's come up. Work.' Spencer slips his phone into his suit jacket pocket. 'Will you be all right if I go?'

I want to say no, I won't be, and to beg him to stay, or to let me go with him, but pride stops me and I nod. 'Thank you for being here.'

To my surprise he leans over and kisses me softly on the cheek. 'She was a great person, Nat. See you.' I watch him leave the churchyard and I don't know if I have ever felt so alone. Then I spy someone I know, Emma, a friend of Bronwyn's from university who I've been on a number of nights out with, and I go over to say hello. I can see how worn out with grief she is – it's what I see when I look in a mirror. The delicate skin beneath Emma's eyes is red raw from crying, while her blonde hair hangs limply and un-styled around her pallid face.

She hugs me and for a few seconds we cling to one another, united in our distress.

'It's so awful, isn't it,' Emma says as we let go.

'I can't believe she's gone. I keep expecting her to bowl up asking what all the fuss is about.'

Emma smiles sadly. 'She hated people fussing.' She bites down hard on her lip and I can see she's trying hard not to cry and I grab her hand to comfort her. 'I was on the phone to her when it happened,' she says.

My stomach falls to my feet with a whoosh. 'What?'

'We'd been trying to arrange getting together but kept missing each other so she called me as she was leaving work. I'd only just answered when the . . .' She stumbles over the word, ' . . . mugger came up to her.'

'Oh God, Emma, that's awful,' I say, horrified.

Tears spill from her eyes. 'I heard her say to him, "I told you to leave me alone", and then she screamed—' She's sobbing now and I pull her into another hug, but I'm dry-eyed as I comfort her and my heart is racing. Emma heard Bronwyn say to her attacker, 'I told you to leave me alone'? That sounds to me as though Bronwyn had met him before or knew him, that there had been a previous interaction between them. I want to press Emma on it but I wait until she's composed herself. Then, carefully, I say what's on my mind.

Emma's response is to look bewildered. 'It couldn't have been anyone she knew. Bron didn't have any enemies. He'd probably bothered her before for money but this time he didn't give up.'

I so desperately want her to be right. Yet, after all that's happened in the past couple of weeks – my neighbour, Elizabeth, was discharged from hospital after three days and is now recuperating at her daughter's home in Epsom, the hospital confirming it was shock from the brick being thrown through her window that triggered her collapse – I'm struggling to accept Bronwyn's death was a tragic coincidence.

'Sorry, I have to go, my lift is ready,' says Emma, gesturing to where another of Bronwyn's friends is waiting. Then she pauses. 'Look, I know we'll see each other at the wake, but let's meet for a drink as well. I think Bronwyn would want us to stay in touch, don't you?'

I nod, my throat thick with tears. 'I'd like that.'

Emma says goodbye with a promise to ring me, but as she walks away I realise she's presented me with a dilemma of epic proportion by telling me Bronwyn's final words. The right thing to do now would be to go to the police and tell them everything that's happened to date: I shouldn't let Rowlock get away with any of it. Yet I have no proof, only a hunch and a series of incidents that, even when you string them together, could easily be dismissed as unrelated. As a lawyer Rowlock would probably have a field day blowing holes in my account.

'Natalie?'

I turn round to see Derrick Cordingly coming towards me, with his assistant Alice in tow.

'Alice said it was you,' Derrick greets me with kisses on both cheeks. 'You did so well with that reading. It must've been tough.'

'It was,' I say.

'Bronwyn would've been proud, I'm sure,' he adds and I am struck again by how intrinsically paternal he is, bucking the stereotype that music managers are exploitative or must be a Svengali to succeed.

We fall silent then, which makes me feel awkward, so to fill the void I mention I've been meaning to call him to re-arrange our cut-short interview. 'I'd still like to talk to you for my piece,' I add.

'He's very busy at the moment,' Alice butts in.

I look to Derrick.

'She's right. I don't have time next week, but maybe the one after that? Give Alice a call to sort it out.'

I try not to look disappointed, but it's hard not to because I'm starting to worry the story is slipping away from me, what with Toby storming out and Derrick now stalling. Then inspiration strikes. Since the row with Toby I've been trying to track down where he's staying in London but to no avail, because I don't have any contact details for him. I never thought to ask after bumping into him as I did. Derrick does though.

'Sure, we can meet whenever you're free next,' I say. 'In the meantime, can I please get Toby Naylor's email address from you?'

Derrick stills, head cocked to one side. Alice flashes him a look.

'Toby?' he repeats.

'Yes. I'm hoping he'll talk to me too,' I say, neglecting to mention we've already been in touch.

'Why would you assume I have his email address?' Derrick's response throws me, as does the bluntness of his tone. 'I haven't been in touch with Toby for years. He changed his phone number and I've never had an email address for him.'

'But—' I'm about to blurt out it was Toby himself who told me Derrick had emailed to warn him I was writing an article about Isaac, but manage to stop myself. Instead, I shrug to cover my growing unease. 'I just thought you might have it. It doesn't matter.'

Derrick's demeanour shifts. He smiles. 'Sorry I can't be of more help.'

I nod, then make a show of looking at my watch. 'It's getting on and I have to go. It was nice to see you both.'

I can sense them watching me as I walk along the path towards the street but I daren't turn round in case my expression betrays my alarm. Toby told me he'd received an email from Derrick, but Derrick claims to have not been in touch with Toby for more than a decade.

Which of them is lying?

Chapter Thirty-Seven

Thrown by the encounter, and wrung out from crying, I decide to go home. However, as I continue out of the churchyard and turn right, in the direction of the main road where I can catch a bus, I see a group of people chatting by the kerbside and among them is Neil Caffrey, my PR friend. I should've known he'd be here: he knows everyone in the industry and Bronwyn was no exception. When he sees me coming towards them he breaks away from the group and beckons me over.

'We're going to the pub to toast dear Bronwyn and I insist you join us. You did so well up there reading that poem, my sweet.'

'Thanks, but I'm not feeling very sociable.'

'I understand, it's been a difficult day, which is why a drink will do you good.' Neil drops his voice to a low murmur. 'See the tall chap behind me?'

It's not hard to spot the person he's referring to because the man towers above everyone else in the group. He must be at least 6ft 4, but he'd be even taller if age hadn't curved his shoulders into a hunch in the same way it's whitened his hair and lined his face.

'Who is he?' I whisper back.

'His name is Gregory Robertson. He's the friend I was telling you about who was with Isaac Naylor that day. He's a sound engineer.'

My eyes widen. 'Seriously, that's him?'

'Yes. I've told Gregory you'd like to talk to him but he's a bit nervous about it. He doesn't trust journalists. I think if you came to the pub with us now you could win him round though. A few Scotches should loosen his tongue, if you get my meaning.'

Neil's comment about not trusting journalists makes me think of Toby and how I upset him. This might be my chance to get the story back on track.

'OK, I'll come. I have to make a phone call first, so I'll catch you up. Which pub are you going to?'

'It's called The Merry Widow, would you believe. No wonder they didn't want to hold the wake there.'

Don't ask me how he did it, but when I arrive at the pub ten minutes later, having called my mum as I promised I would after the service because she was worried about me doing the reading, Neil has manoeuvred the seating arrangements so the only spare place is next to Gregory. There is a vast array of drinks already on the table, so when I ask if anyone wants anything at the bar everyone demurs and Neil bats away my offer with an order to sit down. Then, casual as can be, he pours me a large glass of white wine and introduces me to Gregory. The sound engineer's forehead creases as the question of who I am sinks in, but he does not appear unduly ruffled. There is an almost finished glass of neat Scotch on the table in front of him, so perhaps Neil was right about it taking the edge off.

For the next hour or so we chat as a group. There are eight of us altogether, a mismatch of two journalists including myself – the other one works for *Mixmag* – Neil and another PR called John, a session drummer called Pete, two backing singers called

Ingrid and Tally, and Gregory. Our commonality is, of course, Bronwyn and I sit quietly as the others share bittersweet memories of working with her. Her innate professionalism no matter who she was dealing with is shared by the *Mixmag* writer and Neil and his publicist colleague, while Gregory, Pete, Ingrid and Tally talk about how she would think nothing of staying at the studio all through the night if a recording session was going badly, to make sure everyone from the producer down had what they needed to sustain them.

'She always made us session singers feel as important as the talent,' Tally tells the group, choking up. 'I still can't believe she's gone.'

As the conversation turns to Lucy and the children and how they'll cope without her, I sip my drink in the hope it will quell the churning in my stomach. I feel sick every time I think of her darling boys and the future they face without her and how it might be my fault because I asked her for a favour and she was too nice to say no.

'So you're Bronywn's best friend?' Gregory asks me so quietly I almost don't catch what he's saying. His voice is soft but gravelly, as though his throat is parched. 'That's why you did the reading?'

'Yes. I'm also godmother to her youngest son.'

'Why aren't you at the burial?'

'Immediate family only. It's what Lucy wanted.'

'Right.' Gregory takes a sip of his Scotch then stares at me contemplatively. 'Neil says I can trust you.'

I manage a smile. 'I didn't pay him to say that, in case you're wondering. But I'm a music writer, not a news hack, if that helps.'

The corners of his lips tug upwards but he remains silent.

'Can I get you another drink?' I ask.

'It depends.'

'On what?'

'What you want to ask me about Isaac.'

I sneak a look at the others but no one is paying us any attention, they're all listening to Neil as he regales them with one of his stories. I take a deep breath and plunge right in.

'I want to ask why you think someone might've wanted to set him up to take the blame for Emily Jenkins' death. I've spoken to someone close to him who swears blind he couldn't have given her the drugs.'

Gregory stares at me and for a horrible moment I think I've gone too far. Then he smiles.

'You want to print the truth, in other words.'

'Yes, I do.'

'Well it's about time someone did.'

Chapter Thirty-Eight

'We can't talk here,' I say in a low, urgent voice. 'I don't want anyone overhearing.'

'There's a pub called The Alex on Westbridge Road. Make your excuses and leave now and I'll meet you there in fifteen minutes.'

My face must betray my doubt that Gregory will keep to his word and I won't end up sitting there alone like an idiot, because he tells me he means it. 'I need to do this,' he adds.

The remark puzzles me but I file it away for later. 'OK. I'll see you there.' I pick up my bag to go when Gregory leans towards me again.

'Get the drinks in when you get there. Mine's a Scotch on the rocks. Double.'

Neil makes a song and dance about me leaving, but when I go to peck his cheek to say goodbye he whispers in my ear, 'I said you could win him round.'

'Thanks,' I whisper back. 'I owe you.'

He chuckles. 'Add it to the list.'

The Alex is less than a two-minute walk away. I pay for our drinks then find a table in the beer garden out the back. It's three in the afternoon and with most people still at work it's empty and quiet, save for a ruddy-faced pensioner nursing a half as he reads his newspaper. It's nice and shady out here though and I'm grateful not to be sitting in the glare of the sun.

On cue, exactly fifteen minutes later, Gregory bowls through the open doorway into the garden, stooping low to pass under the frame.

'When I couldn't see you inside I thought you'd changed your mind,' he says, accepting the Scotch I slide across the table to him. The ice has melted now but he does not remark upon it.

'No chance of that,' I say. 'I'm dying to hear your take on what happened to Isaac.'

'Before we start I have one condition. I don't want to be named in any article.'

This is a blow, but not unexpected. Gregory has a professional reputation to preserve, an excellent one from what Neil said, so he's not going to risk his livelihood for the sake of my story. Producers and studios might baulk at hiring him if they see he talks to the press.

'That's fine, you have my word I won't name you, but I still want to record the interview.'

'I'm going to need more than your word. I'll need it in writing.'

I reach for my phone and open the email app and ask for his address. Once he relays it, I tap out an email confirming I will quote him only as an unnamed source and nor shall I refer directly to his profession, so there is no chance of jigsaw identification.

'What's that?' he asks, reading the email on my phone once I've finished composing it.

'Jigsaw identification means putting details into the piece that when added together means people would be able to work out it's you. I'll need to say you saw Isaac the same day this all happened, but I'll be careful not to say where or in what context.'

Technically my email isn't legally binding, but Gregory's lawyers would have a strong case against me if I break my written promise. But I won't do that, because I know how important it is to protect good sources.

Gregory re-reads the drafted email and nods. 'Send it to me,' he instructs.

Email dispatched, I switch my voice recorder on. I also have my notebook ready in which to jot down points I may want to follow up.

Gregory knocks back a mouthful of Scotch then winces. 'Fire away.'

'What did you mean when you said you need to do this?'

He regards me for a moment. 'Isn't it obvious? For years the narrative has been that Isaac killed that girl by filling her full of drugs then took his own life. I don't believe he did either.'

I'm startled. There is so much to unpack in those few sentences that I almost don't know where to begin. 'You don't think he's dead?' I ask.

Gregory shakes his head. 'Even when he was fucked up on drugs Isaac was never suicidal.'

'You last saw him *before* Emily Jenkins died though. Finding her body, being arrested – those two things alone could've tipped him back over the edge.'

'Ah, but as you said earlier, if he didn't have anything to do with her overdosing, why would he need to top himself?'

I pause. It's a good point, but I do have a counter-argument.

'OK, putting that aside for a moment, Isaac would've been acutely aware of what the reaction would be to a seventeen-year-old girl overdosing in his bed. Even if the police ruled out his involvement eventually, the scandal would've haunted him for the rest of his life. Any time anyone wrote about him or The

Ospreys, her death would be mentioned. Maybe he couldn't live with that being his legacy? Everything he'd worked for, all that success, boiled down to one tragic event.'

Gregory takes a pack of cigarettes from his suit pocket and offers me one. I decline and watch impatiently as he lights up. He takes a deep drag then sends a thin rasp of grey smoke spiralling into the air above our table. Finally he's ready to talk again.

'That's not why he ran. Isaac wanted to escape and the girl's death gifted him the opportunity. No offence to her or her family,' Gregory adds with a shrug, 'but when you look at it pragmatically, it was the chance of a lifetime for Isaac to escape the tyranny of being in the band.'

Suddenly I wonder if I've made a mistake in interviewing Gregory. I can't write my story based on supposition, which is what he seems to be offering me. What I need is facts, so I attempt to steer him back towards more solid ground.

'Before we get into what might have happened afterwards, can you tell me about your meeting with Isaac that day?'

Gregory sends a flume of smoke in my direction. 'Sure. I'd worked with the band before, on their first and second albums. I got on well with them all, but Isaac was the easiest to deal with and me and him really clicked. We liked the same music, had the same sensibilities.' He washes down another drag of his cigarette with a mouthful of Scotch. 'I think it was in mid-September of that year or thereabouts – a couple of months before they were going on tour again anyway – that Isaac rings me himself out of the blue and says he's been working on his own stuff and would I listen to it because he would value my input.'

'He was planning to go solo?' I interject.

'He didn't spell it out, but yes, that's the impression I got from talking to him. But it wasn't like what often happens when bands get huge and the lead singer starts to think they're the star of the show and they should go it alone,' says Gregory. 'Isaac didn't want to record the songs himself, he was done with being on stage.'

'I don't understand.'

'He wasn't writing for himself, he was writing with others in mind. He wanted to see if I thought the material was decent enough to approach a few big-name artists.'

My excitement rises. What Gregory's telling me fits with the blind item about Isaac staging a comeback as a lyricist for other singers and bands – his ambition was to quit performing and go behind the scenes.

'All that stuff in the papers afterwards about the others planning to chuck him out of the band was bollocks,' says Gregory gruffly. 'He'd have happily left if they'd asked. He was done.'

'He actually said that to you?'

'Yes, he did, that morning, when we were in the studio together. He'd sent me the songs a few weeks before, I'd given him feedback and then he paid for me to fly up to Glasgow to go through them in person. He couldn't wait to get them finished and get them sent out. It was his way out of the band. He was done being in the limelight and he wanted to protect his recovery. He'd worked really hard to get sober and he knew he was risking it staying in The Ospreys.'

I remember something Neil said when we met at The Groucho and he first mentioned Gregory to me.

'Neil told me you went to the police with all this but they didn't follow it up.'

'They said the same as you, that addicts lapse and all the drug paraphernalia in Isaac's room pointed to him using again. They weren't going to be swayed by anything I said so I let it drop.'

'If what you're saying is true, why did he want to leave the band so much?'

'Getting clean gave him clarity and he was writing stuff that wasn't right for The Ospreys but would have been amazing sung by other artists.' Gregory grinds the butt of his cigarette into the ashtray in the middle of the table. 'I wish you could've met Isaac then. Free of drugs, he was a genius songwriter. But you know that, don't you, because of the blind item.'

My jaw drops. 'You saw it?'

'I was in the studio with Bronwyn when you sent it to her.'

Chapter Thirty-Nine

Procurator Fiscal Evidence Log

The last Facebook entry of Emily Jenkins, submitted as evidence to the Procurator Fiscal at the Crown Office, Glasgow, on 22 February 2012

Emily Jenkins
3 December 2011 at 11:06
I am SO excited I think I might actually burst!
15 comments 104 Likes

Chloe Morris Whassup??
Like • Reply • 1 minute

Rich Pauley Spill!
Like • Reply • 1 minute

KTKitt Is this what I think it is???
Like • Reply • 1 minute

Emily Jenkins HELL YEAH!
Like • Reply • 1 minute

KTKitt I'm sooooooo jealous!
Like • Reply • 1 minute

Matty Rose Don't keep us hanging, share with the class!
Like • Reply • 2 minutes

Emily Jenkins I'VE GOT A BACKSTAGE PASS FOR
THE OSPREYS TONIGHT! I'M GONNA BE MEETING
ISAAC NAYLOR!!!!
Like • Reply • 3 minutes

Matty Rose No fucking way! HOW????
Like • Reply • 3 minutes

KTKitt SCREAM!
Like • Reply • 3 minutes

Emily Jenkins Met someone in fan forum chat room who
knows the band well and she's sorted me out.
Like • Reply • 4 minutes

Chloe Morris Errrrr . . . that sounds well dodgy! How can
you be sure she's who she says she is? Have you paid her
yet???? Don't give her any money until you know!
Like • Reply • 4 minutes

Rich Pauley Chlo's right, could be any old perv.
Like • Reply • 5 minutes

Emily Jenkins She's not, I've spoken to her on the phone.
She's really nice and she knows the band because she follows
them on every tour. She's matey with them too and goes
backstage all the time. The pass is real – she emailed me a scan

of it and my dad said it's legit. I CANNOT WAIT! This is going to be the best night of my life. I sent her my picture and she said Isaac would love to meet me. Get me!
Like • Reply • 5 minutes

Chloe Morris IN is cute but he's also a total druggy. Don't do anything stupid!
Like • Reply • 7 minutes

Emily Jenkins Can't promise that! I lurrrve him. LOL.
Like • Reply • 7 minutes

Sean Jeffrey Really can't see what there is to get excited about. The Ospreys are a glorified pub band and a steaming pile of shite.
Like • Reply • 8 minutes

Rich Pauley LOL.
Like • Reply • 9 minutes

Chapter Forty

Gregory was the person talking in the background at The Soundbank during my call with Bronwyn after I emailed her the screenshot, he tells me. 'It was just the two of us in the studio, no one else was there,' he adds. 'Bronwyn swore when she read it and then showed me, thinking I'd find it funny. When I said I thought it was true and you should be careful not to repeat it, that's when she called you.'

I sit back in my seat, stunned. 'You think Isaac is the mystery songwriter too?'

'I've suspected it for a while. I got wind of a songwriter working anonymously who'd scored a couple of hits so I did some digging, asked about.' His eyes bore into mine. 'I found out which songs of his had done the rounds and a couple of the ones that have been recorded are identical to the tracks Isaac played me, give or take the odd word. The production is different, but the lyrics are the same. They're Isaac's.'

I am astounded, and thrilled. The identical songs are all but confirmation Isaac is still alive and is attempting a comeback. 'Why have you kept quiet about this until now?'

He takes another long drag on his cigarette. 'If Isaac wants to stay under the radar, who am I to fuck that up for him? It's what he wanted all along.'

'Meaning?'

'Isaac was craving a break from being Isaac Naylor. We talked about it a lot and he told me that he didn't feel like himself any more, it was like he'd been reduced to playing a role. There was so much expectation on him to be the swaggering drug-addled rock star that he reckoned everyone around him had lost sight of who he really was. That's why he was stoked at the idea of writing for other people and having a break from fame. The girl's death gifted him the chance to run away and start again.'

I pull a face. '"Gifted"? I'm not sure her parents would see it like that.'

'No, I don't suppose they would, and knowing Isaac as I did he would've struggled with that. I've often thought that's why there was a two-week lag between him disappearing and his stuff ending up on that beach – because he was wrestling with his conscience. In the end, though, nothing would bring the girl back so why not save himself?'

'He must've had help to flee the country.'

'Of course he did. Isaac had the cash for it and the connections.'

'Who do you think helped him?'

Gregory almost answers but catches himself at the last moment, the unspoken words extinguished on his lips as he places another cigarette between them. Undeterred at his stalling, I ask him again what he means by Isaac having connections.

'He knew lots of people.'

'Anyone in particular?' I persist. 'I know it wasn't his brother, he thinks Isaac's dead. But it had to be someone he trusted just as much.'

Gregory chooses his words carefully. 'I can't give you a name, but what I will say is that Isaac knew a lot of people who had nothing to do with the music industry. Start with them.'

What the hell does that mean? Frustration wells up inside me but I force myself to ignore it, telling myself that Gregory

199

isn't being cryptic on purpose to annoy me, he's just trying to protect himself. Considering everything I've been subjected to since I took up the story, I could probably learn a thing or two from him.

'Where do you think Isaac has been in the interim?' I ask.

Gregory shrugs. 'Could be anywhere. I just hope he found some peace and quiet while he was there.'

'Somewhere like Nepal?'

He shoots me a look. 'That's specific. It sounds like you know more than you're letting on.'

It's on the tip of my tongue to tell him about the research I've done that's pointed me towards Nepal, but I hold back.

'If he went to all that trouble to disappear, I don't see why he's now attempting a comeback as the mystery songwriter though,' I say. 'If he's found out he could be re-arrested.'

'Well, that's what I don't understand either. Man, if I were Isaac and managed to escape, no way would I come back. That's why I told Bronwyn to get you to leave it alone, to leave *him* alone. Then Neil called to say you wanted to speak to me and I knew you hadn't.'

For a horrible moment I am seized with fear that Gregory isn't someone I should trust. He is clearly annoyed I didn't listen to his warning to ignore the blind item: could he and not Aden Rowlock be behind the other warnings, out of loyalty to Isaac and a desire to protect him? Then, to my relief, he slowly grins.

'But it's a great story, I get it. I don't blame you for following it up; I'd have done the same in your shoes. Bronwyn thought it was a good story as well, because she forwarded it to someone else, despite me telling her not to.'

'To who?' I ask, surprised.

'She didn't say, but whoever he was he wasn't happy, because he called back a few minutes later and I could hear him ranting and Bronwyn had to leave the studio to speak to him privately.'

'You're absolutely sure she didn't say who it was?'

'No, and I didn't ask. Didn't feel like my business to.' Gregory swills the remaining Scotch in his glass and knocks it back. 'I should go now.'

I'm disappointed, but I don't push it. I can tell he's had enough of being interviewed. 'Can I ask you one more thing before you leave?'

'Sure.'

'How can you be so certain Isaac didn't give Emily the lethal dose?'

Gregory sits back in his chair and looks at me contemplatively.

'I just know he wouldn't have. There were a few times Isaac smoked smack while the band was recording and I was there and not once did he try to force me to partake. Instead he talked endlessly about wanting to give up and how I was lucky booze and fags were my only vices. I just can't see him forcing a young, vulnerable girl to do something he wouldn't do himself.'

'You mean inject?'

'Yeah. The thought of it repulsed him,' says Gregory. 'Whoever put that shit in her veins it wasn't Isaac.'

'Who did then?'

'Your guess is as good as mine. It could've been anyone in the hotel that night. Do you know how many people make up a tour crew? Dozens, hundreds even. That's without taking into account the hotel staff.'

'But why set Isaac up to take the blame? If it was someone else to do with The Ospreys, I mean. He was the lead singer, the cash cow. The record label and their manager wouldn't let the others do any press without him,' I add, remembering what Toby told me about their dad's funeral. 'Everything had to revolve around Isaac. It makes no sense that anyone involved with The Ospreys would want him out of the picture.'

'Ah, but it turns out the band could manage very well without him.'

'No one knew that at the time though. The other three thought they were finished after Isaac was declared dead.'

'True,' Gregory concedes as he rises from his seat. 'Whoever set Isaac up didn't care about the impact on the band – or they believed there wouldn't be any.'

Chapter Forty-One

Our interview has come to a natural close, but before he leaves I persuade Gregory to give me his phone number in case anything else crops up that I need to ask him about.

'If I don't answer straight away it's because I'm in the studio,' he adds, after reciting it to me. 'But I will call you back.'

After he's gone I stay seated outside and sip my drink, lost in thought. I mull over everything Gregory's told me, including Bronwyn forwarding the message, and I'll admit I'm a bit annoyed she did that after telling me that I mustn't. I wonder who the recipient was though, and why they were cross enough to call her back and rant down the phone? Why didn't she tell me? What other secrets did she keep from me?

Dwelling on Bronwyn makes me weary and sad again, so I down my drink and decide to head home. I'm itching to get out of these clothes, a skirt and blouse I bought specially for today when I realised I didn't possess anything remotely funereal. I retrieve my phone from my bag to check bus times and that's when I see the missed calls from Spencer. I'd muted my phone before the service and hadn't thought to turn the volume back up. There's also a voicemail message and some angry texts asking where I am. I call back, bracing myself for whatever this new tirade is about, but I can barely hear Spencer's voice over the sound of Daniel sobbing in the background. Hearing it makes my stomach cartwheel with panic.

'What's wrong?' I ask.

Spencer can't keep the upset from his voice. 'How quickly can you get here? Daniel's in trouble.'

The house I once called home is in the middle of a terrace on a tree-lined street one block back from the north side of Clapham Common. While the properties here are far less grand than the imposing houses that line the common itself, it still used to baffle me that a thirty-second walk from our street to the next could make the difference in price of almost a million.

But I don't dwell on it now as I hurry along the street as familiar to me as the veins on the back of my hands. I am desperate to reach Daniel so I can see for myself he's OK. Spencer offered only the scantest of details on the phone, saying there had been an incident and the police had been called, but it quickly turned into a denouncement of why the hell hadn't I answered my phone sooner. Spencer was so het up I couldn't get a word in edgeways.

I no longer have a key to let myself into the house, even though it's still half mine in name and I have every legal right to enter whenever I want. I relinquished my means of access against my solicitor's advice but at Spencer's insistence because he felt it would be inappropriate to let myself in without knocking first and I agreed for the sake of keeping the peace.

My heart skips a beat as I near the house and see a police car parked in the bay directly outside. Racing up the path I'm almost at the door when it suddenly swings open and Spencer appears.

'Where's Daniel?' I pant.

Spencer pulls the door to behind him so it's ajar by only a slither.

'He's inside. Why didn't you answer your phone?' He leans forward and sniffs. 'Oh, so you were in the pub getting pissed and couldn't be bothered.'

The snipe enrages me. 'For crying out loud it was Bronwyn's funeral. I went for one drink afterwards and I'm here now. What's happened?'

'Daniel was caught throwing stones at passing cars. Someone called the police.'

I reel back in surprise. 'He did what? Where?'

'On the edge of the common.'

'Who involved the police?'

'I don't know,' replies Spencer tetchily. 'One of the drivers or a passer-by presumably.'

I stare at him, shocked. I can't believe our sweet-natured little boy is in trouble with the police. 'He must've realised what he was doing was wrong,' I say. 'What was he thinking?'

'I don't know. But don't go in all guns blazing, Nat. He's upset enough as it is.'

I nod. 'What was he doing on the common anyway? I thought he was going to a friend's house after school?'

'He and his friend were walking home from school.'

'On their own? Who said he could do that? He's only nine!'

'He's Year 5 now, it's allowed. I gave permission.'

'I bloody well didn't,' I snap. 'Let me see him. We'll talk after.'

With obvious reluctance Spencer steps aside and I push past him into the hallway, the worn wooden floorboards greeting me with their usual loud creak. I can hear the rumble of voices in the front room, so it's there I head, Spencer close behind me.

Daniel leaps up from the sofa and runs to me as I step into the room and I'm reminded of how fast my little boy is growing up as his solid frame slams against mine. We hug each other tightly and I sink my face into the top of his head until I'm almost dizzy from the smell of him. Then I look up and see there are two uniformed police officers in the room with us. One, male, is sitting in the armchair next to the fireplace drinking tea from a cup balanced delicately on a saucer. The other, female, is standing on the opposite side of the fireplace, one hand resting on the mantle, back-dropped by a bookcase stuffed with paper-backs, her cap tucked under her arm. Together they look like a Banksy version of a Norman Rockwell painting.

'What's going on?' I ask them.

'Daniel was caught throwing stones at cars travelling along the common. Luckily we were called before it caused an accident,' says the female officer, though not harshly. It's obvious that Daniel is beside himself with remorse and her softened tone appears to reflect that.

'I'm sorry Mummy, we didn't mean to hurt anyone, we were just aiming at their tyres,' Daniel sobs.

'We?'

'Hi Natalie,' says a familiar voice from behind me.

Perturbed, I look round to where the sofa is pushed up against the wall and sitting there is Jo, one of my school mum friends, and her daughter, Maya, who's been in the same class as Daniel from Reception. I'm surprised to see them here, as Daniel and Maya have never been particularly close and Jo and I keep our fraternising to grown-ups-only evenings in the pub.

'Hello. What are you doing here?' I ask her.

'Jo offered to have Daniel after school,' says Spencer.

The male officer interrupts. 'Mrs Cummings, Daniel and Maya were both involved.'

'It's Ms Glass,' I correct him.

'The children need to appreciate how serious this is,' he continues.

'I think Daniel's got the message,' I say, nodding down at my son who is still sobbing and repeating the word 'sorry' over and over. I glance over at Maya, his apparent partner in crime, but she just looks bored.

The female officer shoots a look at her colleague. 'I think he has too. Daniel, before we go, do you promise not to do anything like it again?'

'I do, I promise,' he cries. 'But Maya needs to promise too, it was her idea. She said if I didn't throw stones as well she'd stamp on my iPad and break it.'

'I did not!' shrieks Maya, finally roused from her bored stupor.

'Daniel's exaggerating,' replies Jo coolly, getting to her feet. 'But clearly we made a mistake in thinking they were responsible enough to walk home alone. We'll make sure they're supervised from now on.'

'I think that's our cue to go,' says the male officer, and to my surprise, he hands his cup and saucer – both items I bought – to Jo. 'We'll leave you to decide an appropriate punishment for the children.'

Spencer sees them out while Jo and I wait in the front room together.

'I'm really sorry about your friend, Nat,' she says. 'It's so sad.'

'Thanks. And thank you for looking after Daniel.' I pause. 'You don't live this side of the common though, so why were they walking back here?'

'Spencer thought Daniel might be a bit upset because of your friend and would want to come home, so we agreed I'd wait for them here instead of at mine.' Spencer comes back into the room looking pensive and Jo throws him a look I can't quite interpret – until Daniel spells it out for me.

'Jo is Daddy's girlfriend,' he announces. 'She and Maya have sleepovers here.'

The room stills as Spencer and Jo wait for my reaction. I want to be cool about it, because of course either one of us could have met someone else, yet questions swarm my mind.

How come Jo didn't tell me her own marriage had ended? How long has it been going on with Spencer? Is it serious? How much time do she and Maya spend here? Does Daniel like Jo more than me?

Spencer splinters the silence and has the grace to look embarrassed. 'I should've told you.'

'Yes, you should've,' I parry back. 'I deserve to be informed about who is looking after Daniel. We'll talk about this later, in private.'

'Why don't we get a snack you two,' Jo says to Daniel and Maya and they follow her into my kitchen.

I hear the sound of the fridge opening and Jo laughing and I'm unsettled that someone I thought was a friend has supplanted me in my former home. But Jo can't be one, I decide, because a friend would've checked whether I minded them dating my ex-husband, especially knowing what a bastard he's been since our separation. Then in the back of my mind there's a stirring, like the swirling of mist, and a memory pops up of Jo and Spencer at a BBQ two summers ago hosted by another family from school, when they spent the entire evening laughing together in the corner, oblivious to anyone else, Spencer irritated when I sent Daniel over to interrupt them.

Then another memory pops up, like the next lottery ball forced from the barrel by a squall of air. A mums' night out six or seven months after the BBQ, lots of wine sunk, Jo drunkenly telling me how I was lucky to have a husband as nice as Spencer and how handsome he was. I don't remember my reply but the bad patch we were in at the time most likely meant it was negative. Did she seize upon that and exploit it for her own ends? Or were the wheels already in motion, with Spencer a willing participant or even the instigator? Anger burns in me when I consider he could have manipulated what I said about not being in love with him to end our marriage, when all along he had his next relationship lined up – if not already under way.

'I'm sorry you had to find out about Jo and me like this. Especially today of all days,' he says.

'How long's it been going on?'

'A while.'

I let that sit for a moment. A while could be anything from a few months to the eighteen we've been apart, or more. The thought it could be the latter makes me even angrier.

'Is this why you've been making it difficult for me to see Daniel? Are you hoping I'll get so fed up being dragged to court that I'll walk away and leave you and Jo to play happy families without me getting in the way?'

'Don't be ridiculous. I don't want that,' he says edgily.

'Really? Because you've been at it since day one, making out that Daniel didn't need to see me more than every other weekend. Is it because you think Jo's a better mother than me?'

'Of course not.'

'So why keep Daniel from me?'

'We've been through this. I didn't want him rattling between two homes all the time. He's better off staying in one place for the majority.'

'Does Jo share equal custody of Maya with her ex-husband?'

Spencer blanches. 'I, um—'

'Well?'

'They split it fifty-fifty.'

'So it's OK for her but not for me. You really are a piece of work,' I sneer.

He makes no attempt to contradict me and an enormous pause settles over the pair of us until I speak again, low enough that I can't be overheard from the kitchen.

'When I said I wasn't in love with you that day, I never meant I no longer loved you at all. You know I did. You were my husband, the man I thought I'd be spending the rest of my life with. The only reason I said it was because we were in a really shit place and arguing all the time. I never wanted us to end. I wanted us to work through it.' My tears are falling faster than I can wipe them. 'I have driven myself crazy wishing I could take back what I said, but you wouldn't let me. You just pulled the plug as though all those years we spent together, us having Daniel, didn't count for a thing. Until today I couldn't understand why you were in such a rush to do that, but now I think I do.'

Spencer's cheeks begin to colour as I nod towards the kitchen where my replacement is tending to my son.

'You made me think it was all my fault, when all along, behind my back, you were inflicting more damage on our marriage than I could ever conceive of doing.'

He quickly shakes his head. 'It's not what you think. Nothing physical happened until after you left.'

A dry, hollow laugh scrapes its way out from the back of my throat. 'You expect me to believe that? What do you take me for?' I stare at him for a moment, wondering exactly when it was he became a stranger to me. 'You're not airbrushing me out of Daniel's life, Spencer. I'm his mum and either you stop fighting me for shared custody or I will tell everyone you were having an affair all along and that's what really killed our marriage.'

He looks aghast, and a sense of triumph washes over me. I know Spencer and I know he cares more about what other people think than is healthy. Everything he does is through a prism of whether others will approve. My moving out meant he could conveniently paint me as the villain of our divorce – he would hate for those roles to be suddenly reversed.

'You wouldn't,' he says, voice croaking.

'Just watch me.'

My piece said, I call to Daniel and he comes scurrying out of the kitchen with an anxious-looking Jo in his wake. Ignoring her, I drop to a crouch again and smile. Being at face level with my son, where the world is reduced to just him and me, is my happy place.

'I have to go now, but I'll be back first thing on Saturday to take you out for the whole day,' I tell him.

His face lights up. 'All day?'

I glance up at Spencer, daring him to say no, but instead he meekly nods. He knows that me discovering his affair changes everything. 'All day is fine,' he says.

'Too right it is,' I reply scathingly.

'What about Melissa's party in the afternoon?' Jo interjects. 'He and Maya are both invited and I was going to take them.'

'Nat can take him herself,' he says. Jo opens her mouth to protest, but he sternly cuts across her. 'Nat's his mum and she can take him.'

I rise to my feet and smile grimly at them both. 'Good. I'm glad we're on the same page at last.'

Chapter Forty-Two

MONDAY, 1st

My Saturday spent with Daniel makes me so happy that I carry my good mood all through Sunday and into this morning. Jo cried off taking Maya to Melissa's party in the end, citing illness for them both, and a couple of friends I caught up with there admitted they knew about the relationship, but Jo had made them promise not to say anything, saying she and Spencer would 'deal with me'. They also said she was cagey about when it began, but neither revelation made me as angry as I think my friends expected they would. I'm more relieved the fighting will be at an end, because now I know Spencer's true motive for ending our marriage so hastily I can use it to my advantage. Not in a getting even kind of way, I'm done with the arguments, but to make sure I receive equal time with our son and also my half of the proceeds from the house sale.

The latter isn't going to materialise overnight, though, and with the morning post bringing a new batch of bills for me to fret over, I need to knuckle down with the Isaac story on the back of Gregory's revelations, which is why I'm presently on an Overground train cutting a swathe through London on my way to Richmond. I'm planning to doorstep Stephen and

Belinda Mirren, who I hope are the parents of Pippa, the girl who organised the backstage pass for Emily Jenkins. Pippa's Little Birdie status could have afforded her valuable insight into how Emily ended up in Isaac's hotel suite and I'm hoping that if they are related they'll put me in touch with her.

The Mirrens' house is only a short walk from the station and I am thankful for it because it's another potboiler of a day, with the thermometer nudging twenty-nine degrees. On the news this morning a meteorologist proclaimed it to be an extraordinary heatwave for this early in the summer, because it has lasted twelve days now without interruption. As I trudge along the hot pavement, the soles of my feet slick with sweat in my sandals, I don't think I'll be alone in wishing for a sudden deluge to cool things down.

Arriving at the house I glimpse a woman moving about inside through the downstairs front window. I don't think she sees me though, because it takes quite a few minutes for her to come to the front door after I ring the bell. Then my eye is drawn to the walking stick she's gripping, at odds with the sleek exercise leggings and matching tank top she's wearing, and I wonder why she has it. I'd put her age at mid-fifties, which seems no age at all to require a cane for support.

'Yes?' she asks me expectantly.

'Hi. I'm Natalie Glass and I'm trying to track down Pippa Mirren. I believe this is where her parents live?'

An odd look crosses her face. 'Pippa? I – well, yes. I'm her mother. Sorry, who are you?'

I launch into the spiel I've been honing in my head all the way here.

'My name is Natalie Glass and I'm a music writer. I'm putting together a piece about The Ospreys and why they were so popular and I was told Pippa used to be a huge fan of them and that's why I'd like to talk to her. I'm sorry to turn up

213

unannounced, but I didn't know how else to get hold of her and this is the last known address for her.' I don't mention how I got hold of it and hopefully Belinda won't think to ask.

'Pippa can't help you.'

'I just want a quick chat. Can I leave you my number to give to her?' I ask, holding out the business card I've been clutching in my sweaty fingers since exiting the station.

Belinda Mirren recoils from my hand. 'What do you think you're playing at?' she snaps.

Her reaction makes me flounder. 'I – well, I just hoped Pippa might talk to me.'

She stares at me with such intensity I feel the heat rise in my cheeks.

'What do you know about my daughter?' she asks.

'Only that she was a fan of The Ospreys. Look, I'm sorry I disturbed you. If I can just leave my card—'

'There's no point. I can't pass it on to her.'

'Oh. OK,' I say, unable to hide my disappointment.

She peers at me again. 'You really don't know, do you?'

'Know what?'

'My daughter's dead and has been for three years.'

It was a car accident. Pippa and her parents were driving through Scotland on their way home from visiting relatives for Christmas when their car hit a patch of black ice and skidded out of control. Pippa was killed instantly, while her parents suffered life-changing injuries. Belinda's leg never recovered from being pinned in six places and her husband Stephen now lives in a specialised facility, the brain injury he received requiring round-the-clock care she simply cannot manage within their home. It's a devastating story to listen to, but Belinda tells it dispassionately, as though time has blunted her emotional response to the terrible event that shattered her family. Then she administers the final punch – Pippa was six months' pregnant at the time and the baby, a boy, died when she did.

'I'm so sorry,' I rasp, clutching the mug of tea Belinda made me after she saw how shocked I was to learn that Pippa was dead, and invited me into her home. 'I can't imagine what you've suffered.'

She nods. 'I miss my daughter and my husband very much. Sorry, that must sound strange, because Stephen's very much alive, but he's little of the man I married.' She gestures to a framed family portrait on the sideboard, of the three of them posing against a beach backdrop. Pippa is primary school aged and as I study her freckled, smiling face, framed by a pillow of unruly light brown curls not dissimilar to mine, it's hard to equate the little girl she was then with what was inferred about the Little Birdies in the biography I downloaded.

'It was terrible for Pippa's husband Mark as well,' Belinda continues soberly. 'He hadn't made the trip with us because of work. He's doing better now though. He's met someone else, so that's good.'

I fear anything I say in reply to that will sound trite, so I keep quiet and sip my tea. Belinda emits a smile, her first since my arrival.

'I'm sorry you had a wasted journey. Pippa loved The Ospreys and would have been thrilled that a journalist wanted to interview her about them. I didn't care for their music myself, too frenetic.'

Did Belinda know how involved her daughter was with the group, I wonder? I won't sully Pippa's memory by asking, that's for sure. I do question, though, if Pippa ever mentioned knowing Emily Jenkins. Belinda's face clouds as I say Emily's name.

'I asked Pippa after it happened and she said she didn't, but it really shook her up and she stopped following the band soon

215

afterwards.' Belinda grimaces. 'I'm not naive, I knew she got up to stuff with The Ospreys but she was twenty-two and knew how to look after herself. Unlike that poor girl.'

With no Pippa here to ask directly, I realise I've gone as far as I can with this line of research. 'Thank you for your time, and the tea.'

'I have a box of Pippa's upstairs that contains mementoes from when she followed the band. You're welcome to look through it before you head off,' says Belinda. 'There might be something you could use for your article.'

My pulse leaps in anticipation of what I might find. 'I would love to take a look, thank you.'

Even though there is a stair-lift fitted against the wall, Belinda insists on walking up to the next floor. 'It was put in for Stephen when we thought he might be able to do home visits and if I start using it I may as well give up and join him where he is,' she says grimly. 'I do find it useful though. I put my glasses and books and things on it and send them upstairs first so I don't have to carry them. Otherwise it's just an ugly appendage blighting my lovely hallway.'

I am filled with admiration for this woman who has lost so much and yet remains wilfully stoic. I'm pretty sure I would've crumbled long ago if I were in her place.

'Go straight ahead,' she orders once we reach the landing. 'I need to catch my breath.'

I do as she instructs and enter the doorway in front of me. It leads into a small and sparsely decorated bedroom with a single, unmade bed pushed against one wall and a tall bookcase next to it.

'The box is next to the bookcase,' Belinda calls out. 'You can't miss it.'

She's right; it would be impossible to. The clear plastic box, about six times the size of the average shoebox, is covered in pictures of The Ospreys. Isaac Naylor stares insolently up at me as I prise the lid off.

Inside is a veritable treasure trove of pictures, ticket stubs and backstage passes on lanyards. I pick carefully through the mementoes, mindful I'm lucky Belinda has trusted me to go through them and also so I don't miss anything. I'm almost near the bottom of the box when I pull out a photograph of a group of people that makes me double take. Belinda has joined me in the room now and peers over my shoulder for a better look.

'Is that Pippa?' I ask, pointing at a young woman in the centre of the image who resembles the pre-teen in the portrait downstairs but her straightened, raven-black hair and heavily applied make-up make it hard to be sure.

'Yes, and those were her best friends back then,' she says.

'Even this one?' I ask. The photograph is a group shot of four women and one man.

'Oh yes. He even visited here a few times when the band were recording in London. A lovely young man, very polite and well-mannered.'

'Were they ever a couple?'

'I don't think so, but they were close.'

They certainly look it. Standing next to Pippa in the line-up, one arm wrapped tightly around her waist and smiling shyly for the camera from beneath a baseball cap, is Toby Naylor. The same Toby Naylor who claimed not to recognise Pippa's name when I asked him.

First the email he never received from Derrick, now this. Why has Toby lied to me again?

Chapter Forty-Three

Back on the Overground I furiously check online for any mention of Toby and his current whereabouts. Why did he deny knowing Pippa when clearly they were good friends back in the day? Has he known all along she was involved in procuring the pass for Emily? After we went back downstairs I discussed with Belinda what happened between Emily and Isaac but she knew no more about it than I do, other than to say Pippa was devastated by his suicide and when the band took a break to mourn his loss, her interest in them and their music waned and eventually she made new friends and met her future husband. Belinda said she lost touch with Toby and the others in the picture pretty quickly after Isaac killed himself.

Frustratingly, I draw a blank on Toby's whereabouts, hindered by him being that rare breed of person who doesn't document every cough and spit of their life on social media. The only thing I discover of note, that I'm kicking myself for not finding earlier, is that two years ago he sold the house in Jarrow he inherited from Isaac. The seven-bedroom detached property set in five acres of land went for £2.2 million – an eye-watering amount for that part of the country. The local paper ran a story about the house being sold, but there was no reference to where Toby moved to afterwards. Without a current address or any clue about where he might be staying in London, I'm stuck—

As inspiration strikes, I slap my palm to my forehead and groan. Why didn't I think of it sooner? I fish Derrick's business card out of my purse and dial his mobile number.

'It's Natalie Glass,' I announce when he answers.

'I know, I've saved your number,' he says. 'Are you ringing to reschedule the interview? I'm in the middle of something now so you really should call Alice. I don't have my diary to hand.'

'Oh, yes,' I say, realising I've completely forgotten about arranging a new time to meet and I am annoyed with myself that I have. I mustn't neglect the Isaac leads I've already established and the last thing I want is Derrick to think I'm no longer interested in what he has to say. 'I'll email Alice right away. But before we meet, I have a question you might be able to help with—'

'Make it quick.'

'Did Isaac have a favourite hotel in London?'

Derrick sounds surprised. 'That wasn't what I was expecting.'

'It's just for background,' I say.

'You couldn't wait until the interview to ask me?'

He's got me there. 'You're right, it could've waited, I'm sorry. I'll message Alice now—'

'Wait, I didn't say I wouldn't answer. Yes, he did, the York & Albany in Camden. It's a Gordon Ramsay hotel and restaurant now but before that it was the kind of place you could hole up in without being bothered. That's why Isaac loved it, plus it was close to the rehearsal space we used back then.' Derrick pauses. 'Does that help?'

'It does,' I respond effusively. 'Thank you.'

'Good. Email Alice about the interview,' he adds then hangs up.

I take a moment to mull over what he said.

It was the kind of place you could hole up in without being bothered.

The kind of place Isaac's brother might still like to hole up in? There's only one way to find out. I stand up to check the route map above the seats opposite mine. The next stop is Kensal Rise, which is where I'd been planning to get off to catch a bus back to Maida Vale. However, if I stay on the train for another eight stops I can disembark at Camden Town and walk the short distance to the hotel.

I sit back down.

Forty-five minutes later I find myself in the York & Albany's bar nursing an orange juice and a dented ego. No amount of cajoling could elicit even the tiniest hint from the employee manning the hotel front desk that Toby is currently a guest here. I even described him in detail but still her expression didn't crack. It crossed my mind I should offer a financial enticement, but I only had a forlorn-looking £5 note in my purse and I didn't think sliding it across the desk the way they do in films would have held much sway. There's only £1 of it left now, the orange juice costing the rest of it.

I don't notice the waiter sidle over until he's right beside my table because as usual I'm head down scrolling on my phone.

'I don't want anything to eat, thanks,' I smile up at him, assuming that's why he's approached me again. I expect him to nod and leave but instead he bends at the waist to lower his face towards mine.

'You were asking at the front desk about a guest called Toby Naylor?'

'Um, yes, I was,' I say, taken aback.

'I think I know who you mean. In his thirties, stubble, bit chubby, wears a red baseball cap all the time?'

'That's right,' I answer cautiously.

'You said he was a friend and you were worried about him? Sorry, I was passing through reception and overheard you.'

Telling the receptionist I was a friend concerned about Toby's wellbeing and needed to check on him was the first approach I tried on her to no avail.

'Oh, yes, that's right. My friend was meant to call me when he arrived in London and he hasn't and I'm very concerned something is wrong.'

The waiter leans even closer. 'If it was my friend I'd want to know, so between you and me the man you described was staying here but he checked out a few days ago. But he wasn't registered under the name you said.'

Disappointment trickles through me. 'It can't be the same person then. My friend is definitely called Toby. Thank you though.'

The waiter straightens up. 'My mistake, I apologise. From your description it did sound like him.' Good deed thwarted, he smiles ruefully then makes to leave.

'Wait,' I call after him. 'Do you know what name he did use?' It's not unheard of for famous people to use aliases in hotels and while he's not his brother, Toby is still paranoid about people knowing who he is.

The waiter doubles back, clearly not wanting to raise his voice. He smiles conspiratorially and leans forward again to tell me the name. I'm so shocked my voice catches in my throat.

'Are you sure?' I croak.

'Yes, one hundred per cent,' confirms the waiter. 'Your friend checked in as Aden Rowlock.'

Chapter Forty-Four

Extract from *Making Waves: The Highs and Lows of Isaac Naylor*, the unauthorised biography by Tamsin Taylor (Promulgate Publishing, £5.99)

Brothers in Arms

The Ospreys' early success was built on a foundation of friendship and loyalty, forged back in school when Isaac met Danny in Mrs Stanton's music class. Yet the band's most loyal member was arguably its unofficial fifth member, Toby Naylor. People who knew both brothers say Toby was everything Isaac wasn't: quiet, considered, meticulous about detail, a planner, a thinker and someone who would always have your back, no matter what you'd done.

Never was that more apparent than in the summer of 1998. It was the year Isaac sat his GCSEs and the poor results he received – he spent more time and effort in the school music room than any other classroom, earning him a slew of Ds and Es in his other subjects – meant his future options were limited in terms of further academia. Not that it mattered to Isaac, as he was focused solely on pursuing his ambition to make it big. But what the sixteen-year-old never stopped to consider was that even budding rock stars need to make sure they don't fall foul of the law before they've made it famous.

Like many kids in Jarrow, the Naylor brothers skirted around the fringes of petty crime, as much to stave off boredom from living in a town where nothing much happened as to profit from it. But a week after Isaac received his disappointing GCSE results he became embroiled in an illegal activity that almost cost him his future – until Toby stepped in to save him.

Hot-wiring cars to take joyriding was something neither boy had done before and no one will ever know for sure what convinced them to do it that August evening in question. A friend who was with them at the time, who declined to be identified, said they and a group of six or seven other teens who lived alongside the boys in Wenlock Road had spent a couple of hours in the park after teatime drinking cheap lager that an older boy had bought from the corner shop – even Toby, who was only thirteen, had been drinking.

Sometime before 11 p.m. the suggestion was made to steal some cars to take joyriding. Defences lowered by the alcohol they'd consumed, the Naylor brothers were enthusiastic participants and when they found a suitable vehicle, a Vauxhall Nova, Isaac got behind the wheel. What happened next had a grim inevitability about it: Isaac lost control while haring about a supermarket car park and crashed into a wall. He was uninjured, as was Toby in the back seat, but the boy in the passenger seat suffered injuries to his pelvis and legs and an ambulance had to be called, along with the police.

While Isaac panicked that he was going to jail, Toby managed to keep a clear head and when the police turned up, he stepped forward to claim he had been driving. The assembled Jarrow crowd, protective of their own as always, corroborated his false version of events.

Afterwards, Toby told his friend he knew the youth court would be far more lenient on him as a thirteen-year-old than they would on his older brother. 'He was right too,' said the friend. 'The court gave him the equivalent of what's known as a referral order these days and it was wiped from his record after a couple of years. It was a slap on the wrist compared to what Isaac might've got. The passenger had some nasty injuries and chances are he'd have received a sentence for causing them.'

That Toby was willing to risk his own liberty to protect his brother speaks volumes for his character. Even when word of the incident and the brothers' switcheroo was leaked to the press after Isaac became famous, Toby continued to maintain it had been him behind the wheel and it was his fault. As for Isaac, it was yet another secret he took to his watery grave.

Chapter Forty-Five

I send the glass of orange juice flying across the table in my haste to get up. I have to leave, now.

'Are you OK?' says the waiter worriedly. 'Did I say the wrong thing?'

I don't answer as I lurch past him. I run out of the bar and through the reception and only when I'm on the pavement outside the hotel do I allow myself to stop and gulp down huge, juddering breaths to calm the dizzying shock now engulfing me.

Why the hell did Toby stay at the hotel under the name Aden Rowlock? My brain gropes for a plausible explanation and the best one I can come up with is that Rowlock booked the hotel in his name as a favour when Toby said he was coming to London. Yet it doesn't ring true for reasons I can't quite put my finger on, just a creeping fear that it's too easy an answer. The next thought I have sends a chill rippling through me: what if Toby has known all along what Rowlock has been doing, that Rowlock's the one behind all the intimidation, the attacks, sending a wreath in the name of my son? I shudder again. If that's the case, should I take it to mean Toby knows Isaac faked his death and he was only pretending to be furious when he blew up at me for daring to suggest it? What if he and Rowlock are in on this together, to protect Isaac?

Someone nearby emits a loud cough, which makes me jump. I hurry away from the hotel in the direction of Camden High Street, agitated and upset. I cannot believe I misread Toby so wrongly and that I blithely trusted him without fully considering what his motive might be for offering to be interviewed. I fear he never intended to set the record straight with me – he just wanted to know what I suspected about his brother being alive. Christ, he even made a point of telling me how much he hated the press because journalists had harassed him after Isaac's suicide. The biggest red flag of all and I'd stupidly ignored it.

I reach the junction with the high street and stop. The muggy air is vibrating with the clamour of buses, taxis and cars rumbling along the road. Pedestrians also stream past me in droves but still I don't move. My indecision has nothing to do with where I go next, but rather what I should do. This binding of Toby to Aden Rowlock has thrown me into such a spin I don't know how I should proceed. Throw in his friendship with Pippa, the girl he denied knowing, and his lying about Derrick emailing him, and suddenly Toby is the person I fear the most. And he knows where I live.

A teenage girl with a sullen face and a matching attitude shoulder-barges me as she goes by, then swears loudly in my direction as though it was my fault. The jostle does at least force me out of my daze and I make a decision: I'll go back to the apartment and collect my thoughts there before I decide what to do next and if Toby pitches up, I'll call the police. But as I cross the junction to the Tube station, a young man I recognise is coming out of the exit. It's the tenant from Aden Rowlock's address who came into the hallway looking for his post when I was talking to Bibek during my first visit. As I watch him stroll ahead, an idea begins to form. I could follow him and try to strike up a conversation about who lives in the building and whether he's seen Toby visit Rowlock before last week's visit, which Toby claimed was his first in a couple of years. I might even show him a photo of Isaac, just to see how he reacts.

I trail the tenant from a safe distance. I'm expecting him to head towards Kentish Town, but instead he veers off in the direction of Camden Market, one of the biggest tourist attractions in London – and also one of the most rammed. I pick up my speed, anxious not to lose him in the heaving crowd, but it's hard because he manages to fluidly sidestep people whereas I stop and start to get past them. I just about keep my eyes on him until we reach the covered section of the market, beneath the railway bridge, but then he's gone, swallowed into the mass of people browsing the stalls laid out in there. Frustrated, I plough on, eyes darting left and right, hoping to catch a glimpse of him again.

I complete four circuits of the indoor section before I clock him again. By now I'm a sweaty, red-faced mess, outside's sultry temperature raised at least another two degrees in here. The tenant, however, appears cool and composed when I find him inside a stall. He must work there, as he's now busy serving a customer. I watch him from across the way, tucking myself in beside another stall so I'm not getting in anyone's way. I know there's someone else in the stall with him but I can't tell if it's a man or a woman because they're right at the back, beyond my view. All I see is a hand shoot out to take a £10 note from the tenant and pass back some change for him to give to the customer.

'You want to buy something?' a voice suddenly rings in my ear. I jerk round to be confronted by a man emerging from the stall I'm standing beside.

'Oh, I'm just looking,' I say.

He follows my gaze across the walkway to the stall I've been watching.

'We have an even better selection than they,' he says. 'Mine comes from the villages around Ghorahi, Nepal's finest city.'

It's so noisy inside the market that for a moment I think I've misheard him. 'Sorry, you sell products from Nepal – and that stall does too?'

The stallholder gives me a bemused look. 'Did you not look at my stall?' he asks.

I do then, and realise what I'm standing beside is a display of richly woven blankets, patchwork jackets and wraps. I look over at the other stall, where the tenant is now serving another customer, and I realise their stock is almost identical.

'You're from Nepal?' I ask.

'Yes I am,' the stallholder replies.

'Is he?' I point across at the tenant.

'Yes, that is Soumy.'

I decide to take a gamble. 'Do you know Soumy's friend Bibek?'

'He comes here occasionally, but I haven't seen him for a while. Now, what can I interest you in?'

My mind jangles as another piece of the puzzle slots into place. The most credible sighting of Isaac I found was in Nepal. The solicitor who I believe represents him as the mystery song-writer is based in a house alongside what appears to be a clutch of Nepali nationals, including one who is fiercely protective of him and who possibly works for him. Then there is Gregory's assertion that Isaac knew people outside the music industry who could have helped him flee the country – what if he met those people right here, in Camden Market, a stone's throw from the hotel where he frequently stayed? What if, somehow, they spirited him all the way to Nepal, where he's lived ever since, protected by them and their fellow countrymen?

'You don't want to buy anything?' the stallholder asks me again. I must be getting in his way but he's being very polite about it. I'm about to apologise when I suddenly spy a familiar face heading through the market and my lungs seize in panic. There is no mistaking him from his stature, the way his eyes are narrowed in an angry stare, nor his imposing presence that intimidates people browsing the stalls into moving swiftly out of his way.

It's the man who attacked me at the awards – and he's heading right for me.

Chapter Forty-Six

I want to run, but I fear I won't be quick enough. 'Please help me,' I beg the stallholder. 'See that man? He wants to hurt me. He's done it before.'

The stallholder takes one look at my attacker bearing down on us and needs no more persuading.

'Come this way.'

I follow him into the rear of his stall. Its walls are fashioned from tarpaulin and I think he's going to tell me to duck under the one at the back but instead he motions to the right. He lifts the sheet and says something in what I presume is Nepali and suddenly a hand appears beneath the tarpaulin to beckon me under. It's a tight squeeze to push myself beneath it – the tarpaulin is tethered to the ground at each end of the stall so there's not much give – but once I'm through, another man helps me to my feet.

'Quickly,' he urges, then in English tells the next stallholder along that I need help, that someone is after me, and means to hurt me. I repeat the same manoeuvre, squeezing under the tarpaulin with the help of the next person. This continues for three more stalls and by the time I reach the last one I am sobbing with gratitude, because I can hear shouts in the market itself and I know it's my attacker from the awards looking for me, but these stallholders are keeping me hidden from him and easing my escape.

My final rescuer, a young black woman, lifts not the side, but the tarpaulin at the rear of her stall. 'This will take you outside, through the way where we bring our stock in. Go on, hurry.'

'Thank you,' I cry. 'Thank you all.'

Behind the stall there is an area full of boxes and piles of stock and beyond that is a wide-open door to the outside. My legs kick into gear and I run as fast as I can and I don't stop running until I'm on the street and see a black cab with its orange light on and I fall into the back of it, panting heavily from both the fright and the exertion. But when the driver asks me where I want to go, I'm stumped. The thug might follow me back to Maida Vale if I go there and the friends I know I could count on to put me up are back in Clapham but there's no way I can afford to get south of the river from here.

'I'm sorry,' I tell the driver, reaching for the handle. 'I've changed my mind.'

He's disgruntled at losing his fare, rolling his eyes as he unlocks the door to let me out. 'Have a nice day,' he bids me sarcastically.

Back on the pavement, I quiver with fear, expecting my attacker to suddenly appear in front of me. There are so many people swilling around, passing back and forth, that he could easily creep up on me without me seeing him first. I feel like an easy target standing here and I need to be somewhere with more space, less people—

Suddenly I know exactly where: Regent's Park. Camden is on the other side of it from Maida Vale and it's only a fifteen-minute walk from here. I can find a quiet spot where I'm not surrounded and catch my breath. Head down, I break into a stride. The sooner I'm far from here the better.

★

The spot I've chosen is against the hedge that borders London Zoo on the north side of the park. There's something comforting about the sounds of the animals I can hear, although it does make me think of Daniel and how much he loves going to the zoo and that sets me off crying again because I am scared, tired and worried that this is never going to stop unless I quit chasing this story.

It goes against every journalistic instinct I have to walk away from a sitting duck of an exclusive. Feasibly I could write the story without even finding Isaac and just based on me finding the blind item about the songwriter and what's happened since: me being attacked and my son threatened, finding Toby Naylor, his relationship with the mysterious Aden Rowlock and the confirmed link to Nepal where Isaac has been sighted. I'm pretty sure any of the newspapers I usually write for would be interested in running that. But would it signal the end of the intimidation and threats? My deepest fear is that it wouldn't, then one day, when I'm least expecting it, a 'mugger' might confront me with a knife or I might be sent flying on a Tube platform but there would be no one to pull me back and the headlines will be I tragically fell or, worse, I jumped. How could I let that happen, knowing what it would do to Daniel?

No, the only way to walk away from this unharmed now is to kill the story. I'm done, I realise, tears spilling down my cheeks. It's over.

I cover my face with my hands and sob at having made the decision. It's like tipping water out of a paddling pool – the relief floods out of me until I feel emptied out. Walking away is the right thing to do, because no amount of money is worth this aggro. Plus, with Spencer and I reaching an understanding now, I'll soon have my share of the house sale and financially I'll be secure again. I sit up and wipe my face dry and for the first time in days my mind is calm.

The feeling doesn't last long though. Moments later I hear the faint ring of my phone in the bottom of my bag. Taking it out, the caller ID says 'unknown' and my stomach clenches with apprehension. It could be my bank or another creditor, or it could be something to do with Rowlock. I don't answer and the ringing stops . . . but starts again immediately. Then the same happens again. Whoever is calling is determined to get through and with a start I realise it might be something to do with Daniel and school. Usually they call Spencer but maybe they can't get hold of him? I answer with a tentative hello.

'Is that Natalie Glass?' asks a brisk female voice.

'Yes.'

'Oh, great, hi, you're there. This is Jess, Felix Thompson's assistant.' She pauses, as though expecting me to say something, but I don't, I'm too surprised. Felix Thompson is the producer Bronwyn said had been working with the mystery songwriter and Jess is the assistant who gave her Rowlock's details to give to me. Why the hell is she calling me now? I'm sweaty after escaping the market, moisture pooling at my lower back beneath my T-shirt and my armpits are saturated, but hearing her on the line makes me shiver as though it's freezing cold out.

'Is this a good time?' she asks.

I manage to squeeze out 'sure'. Then, habit kicking in, I delve inside my bag for my notebook and a pen, in case what she has to say is worth taking down.

'This is a bit of a weird one to be honest. I was wondering whether Bronwyn Castle ever spoke to you about a lawyer called Aden Rowlock?' She pauses. 'We were all so sad to hear about what happened to her.'

I am stunned. 'Why do you think she spoke to me?'

'She called me a couple of weeks ago asking for his contact

details and someone I just spoke to at The Soundbank said you were with her that lunchtime. Bronwyn mentioned someone else needed to get in touch with him and, well, this might be a long shot, but I don't suppose that was you?'

I am rattled she knows I was with Bronwyn when she called, and decide lying might make things worse. 'Yes, it was,' I reply cautiously.

'Oh great,' she says, audibly relieved. 'The thing is, I can't get hold of him and I really need to urgently, so I wondered if you've had any luck?'

My face contorts with disbelief. This is not what I expected at all. 'I thought you were working with one of his clients,' I say.

'We are, and that's the problem. Felix has got an artist who's recorded one of the songs, but Aden hasn't returned the contract for the rights and the label can't release the track until that's done. The number we were given for him keeps going straight to voicemail and stupidly we don't have a number for his partner.'

'He has a partner? Who?' In my mind's eye I see Toby's face.

I hear a rustling of paper down the line. 'Here we go,' says Jess. 'Bibek Gautam. He's Mr Rowlock's associate who's been overseeing the contracts.'

Bibek's a lawyer too? The shock of hearing his name renders me speechless but Jess doesn't notice.

'So, do you have any other contact details for them?' she asks briskly.

It's on the tip of my tongue to say no, but then I realise she's gifting me an opportunity. How is Rowlock going to know I've dropped the story and to leave me alone unless I tell him? I have an address but no contact number for him – but Jess has both.

'I do have a number,' I bluff. 'Why don't you tell me the one you've got and I'll see if mine's the same?'

She reads the number aloud and I write it down in my notebook.

'That's annoying. It's the same as the one I've got,' I fib.

'Damn,' says Jess forcefully. 'I was really hoping you could help. It's so weird how he's gone quiet on us. One minute everything was fine, the contact was regular, the next he's disappeared off the radar.'

'When was that?' I ask her.

'When was what?'

'When was it he stopped getting in contact?'

'Um, about two weeks ago.'

Two weeks ago is when I met Toby outside Aden Rowlock's address for the first time.

'I guess we'll have to resort to plan B,' she says tightly.

'What's that?'

'Our legal team will ask Mr Rowlock to explain himself, because the ramifications for Felix are huge. But this is all off the record; you can't print a word of this, OK? I only called you as a last resort, not to give you a story.'

'I understand. I'm sorry I can't be of more help. Good luck finding him.'

I hang up and sit there for a moment, cradling my phone, the mobile number staring up at me from the page of my notebook. If Rowlock isn't picking up calls at the moment, should I text? No, I decide. Nuance can be too easily misinterpreted in a text message – better that I call so my meaning can't be misconstrued. I dial the number and the call is sent straight through to voicemail as I expected it would be. I gather myself as I wait for the beep then clear my throat when it sounds.

'This is Natalie Glass. I have a message for Aden Rowlock. I want you to know I am no longer investigating the story about Isaac being alive, so please stop sending people after me and threatening me. It needs to stop.'

Then I hang up and cry again.

Chapter Forty-Seven

I stay in the park for the next couple of hours, partly to soak up the fresh air but also because I'm not feeling confident enough to return home yet. My phone rings a couple of times but neither of the callers is Rowlock. I probably shouldn't expect him to return my message given he's ignoring the likes of Felix Thompson, but confirmation he has listened to it would be nice. Then I can truly relax and put all of this behind me.

Around five o'clock I'm propelled to my feet by a combination of hunger, stiffness and a pressing need for the toilet. I satisfy the first and last in the nearest branch of McDonald's and by the time I've wolfed down the last bite of cheeseburger the second has dissipated too.

I am feeling much calmer as I head back outside the fast food restaurant and I'm ready to return to Maida Vale. I decide to walk the two miles back to tire myself out; I want a good night's sleep, then tomorrow and Wednesday morning I shall devote every working minute to securing new commissions before Daniel comes to stay after school as usual. My mood picks up at the thought of equal time with him at last and, buoyed by the prospect, I call Spencer to confirm Daniel's staying over and that the process to alter our custody arrangement is in hand.

'Yeah, we'll get it sorted,' says Spencer when I ask him, his tone more affable than it's sounded in a long time.

'It would be good if we could sort it out without involving solicitors,' I say. 'Now we've agreed the new arrangement between ourselves we don't need to involve them. We don't need the added expense.'

'I think we might still have to use them to petition the court to amend the current order.'

'You can do that through yours,' I say forcefully, 'seeing as the order was your doing in the first place.'

'Yes, I can do that,' he responds.

I'm not used to him being this reasonable and I'll admit I'm thrown by it. 'Well, thanks,' I say.

'We'll need to time it with you moving back to Clapham, of course.'

'Sorry, what?'

Spencer emits a confused laugh. 'You'll be living here, won't you?'

'Uh, I hadn't thought about it—'

'Nat, a fifty-fifty arrangement isn't going to work if you're still living on the other side of London. It wouldn't be fair on Daniel. Imagine trying to get him to school every morning from Maida Vale – it would be a nightmare, not to mention making sure he still attends all the activities he does. He'd have to spend hours every day on the Tube or bus and, sorry, that's just not on. You must see that?'

There is no rancour in Spencer's voice though, only concern. Worst of all, I know he has a point. If Daniel is with me for a week at a time, it will be awful commuting back and forth to Clapham with him for school. My solicitor did raise the idea of me living close by in the early days of our court battle but then things turned nasty, and the prospect of shared custody started to feel so unattainable, so I stopped dwelling on the minutiae.

I've neglected to consider there might be conditions attached to this new arrangement – and that the biggest one would be me returning to Clapham to make life easier for Daniel. But how the hell can I afford to move back when I'm swimming in debt? I'd need to earn triple what I do now to afford the rent on a two-bed flat.

'We need to get the house on the market then. I'll need the equity to move,' I say firmly.

'Yes, but that'll take time, so unless you can move down here sooner we'll have to carry on with the current arrangement. For Daniel's sake.'

He's got me over a barrel. If I kick up a fuss and say, no, we split custody now while I'm still in Maida Vale, then it's Daniel who'll suffer being pulled from pillar to post. Then a thought occurs.

'Could you not just buy out my share? Then you can stay put and I can get my own place and it'll be a far quicker process.'

'I don't want to stay here. Jo and I want to buy a new place together. Her house needs to be sold too though.'

'That could take months,' I say, dismayed.

'Can't you rent somewhere closer by?'

'I can't afford it. I need the house sold first.'

'Look, it's June now and the housing market is never great in the summer, so why don't we get it on the market for the first of September. There's a few jobs that need doing and a couple of rooms need painting first, so I can do that in the holidays.'

I'm trying to reign in my temper for the sake of cordiality but it's hard. 'You want to wait another three months? What about me seeing Daniel in the meantime?'

'You can see him as much as you want,' Spencer offers, 'but it's not my fault you don't have the money to rent somewhere closer.'

The dam bursts. 'It is your fault, because I've had to spend thousands on solicitors fighting your court petitions, when all the time you were shagging my friend behind my back.'

'Leave Jo out of this, Nat,' Spencer barks back.

I want to scream blue murder at him, but I can see my outburst is attracting the attention of passersby and the last thing I want is someone thinking it would be amusing to record me calling my ex-husband every name under the sun and putting the footage on social media to go viral. Instead, I hang up. Spencer immediately rings back but I kill the call then switch my phone off.

I am distraught. I can't afford to move to Clapham to share equal custody of Daniel until the house is sold and it could be well into next year before that happens if Jo's sale and their purchase of a new property is part of the chain. I know Gayle would let me bring Daniel to Maida Vale to live half the time if I pushed Spencer to agree, but what kind of parent would I be if I did that, forcing a nine-year-old to commute endlessly back and forth across the city? He'd miss out on so much with his friends and activities.

I'm back at square one, I realise. I have little money coming in, no prospect of paying off my growing debt and no hope of getting shared access of Daniel until I can move back to Clapham, but no means to be able to do that until the house sells. If it sells. Who knows what the housing market will be like in a few months? Which brings me back to the one thing that could get me out of my financial hole, but the one thing I don't want to do: prove Isaac is alive and make money off the back of the exclusive – even though, based on what's happened so far, the story might end up being the death of me.

Chapter Forty-Eight

Filled with despair and unable to see any other way out of my predicament, I do what a lot of people would do in my situation: I go home and start drinking, stopping off to buy two bottles of cheap wine on my way back. Two bottles in one sitting is absolutely not what I would normally drink when I'm alone, especially on a Monday night, but that's how much I want to obliterate how upset I am. It's been an onslaught of one bad occurrence after another and I haven't even begun to process my grief at losing Bronwyn yet. All I want is to put everything aside for a short space of time and so I flop down on the sofa and pour myself a large glass.

Three more later, I drunkenly pull the coffee table my laptop is on towards me, my resolve to switch off weakened by alcohol. Beside the laptop sits my notebook and all the other documents I've amassed since I began investigating Isaac Naylor. I start reading back all the notes I've made so far, until I reach the page on which I first made note of Aden Rowlock's name and address, read out to me by Bronwyn in the cafe next to The Soundbank. That feels like a lifetime ago now, I think morosely.

I'd written Aden's name down in big capital letters and had ringed it three times for emphasis. I stare down at my hand-writing and as I do something clicks in the back of my mind.

There's something about seeing the name written down like that which is triggering recognition, but I can't think what of. I rip a fresh page out of the back of the notebook and I write the name out again and again, over and over, my writing sloppier than usual because I'm drunk. Still my brain can't quite make the connection, but I know it's registering something.

For the next five minutes I force myself to try to remember, but still I draw a blank. Exasperated at my inability to piece it together, I drain my glass then get up to refill it. The kitchen is in darkness, but as I open the fridge door to get the wine bottle, the interior light illuminates my Kindle charging on the work-top next to it. Suddenly I remember: I know where I've seen the name Aden Rowlock before – or rather what it reminds me of. I yank the Kindle from its charger and take it back into the front room. If I'm right about this, it changes everything.

Heart pounding, I activate the Kindle and open the biography of Isaac I downloaded. It takes me a short while to find the relevant chapter and section, but when I do, I gasp.

I *am* right.

Isaac's childhood home was in Wenlock Road, which I write down on a fresh piece of paper. Then, in the same capital letters, I write Aden Rowlock directly below it. It's so glaringly obvious written down I can't believe I didn't spot it sooner: Aden Rowlock is an anagram of Wenlock Road, the street in Jarrow where the Naylor boys grew up.

The reason Aden Rowlock's legal practice isn't listed anywhere online is because *he* doesn't exist – it's a fictitious name for a fictitious person. Toby's story about Aden being a family friend was a lie from beginning to end and I think the reason he booked into the hotel under the name is because he's the person who's been acting for the mystery songwriter all along.

My emotions ping-pong as I stare at the page. I'm thrilled to have solved the puzzle, but troubled I've uncovered another of

Toby's lies and the fact it now points to him being behind the attacks on me. Yet there's growing excitement too. I'm now certain Toby's been masquerading as Aden Rowlock – which means he also knows where Isaac is.

Chapter Forty-Nine

THURSDAY, 4TH

INVOICE 2372

WORD FOR WORD TRANSCRIPTION SERVICES

CLIENT: NATALIE GLASS

SUBJECT: FULL TRANSCRIPT OF INTERVIEW WITH DERRICK
CORDINGLY (HEREAFTER DC) CONDUCTED BY NATALIE GLASS
(HEREAFTER NG)

SUBMITTED: 2 JULY, 12:33PM. TURNAROUND TIME THREE HOURS
AND 14 MINUTES

AUDIO LENGTH: 108 MINUTES VERBATIM, ALL HESITATIONS AND
PAUSES EDITED OUT

FEE: £1 PER AUDIO MINUTE

NG: Thank you for agreeing to see me at short notice. After
I saw you at Bronwyn's funeral I meant to call Alice but I

had stuff to deal with. Then yesterday I reached what you'd call a tipping point in my research where I realised I couldn't continue without your input on the events of December 2011 and what happened afterwards.

DC: You were lucky my morning meeting was cancelled. More coffee?

NG: No thanks. I'd like to start now, if I may.

DC: Go on.

NG: Can you talk me through the immediate aftermath of what happened in Glasgow? I've been looking through old articles and it doesn't look as though you've ever talked publicly about the two weeks between Isaac skipping bail and him committing suicide. What was that period like for the band?

DC: Hell. Pure hell. The boys and me, we were beside ourselves with worry. Despite the awful thing Isaac had done we still loved him and wanted him to be OK. Every time my phone rang I'd pray it was him wanting me to pick him up from wherever he'd run off to.

NG: Where do you think he went in those two weeks?

DC: Haven't the foggiest. We did suggest some places to the police but they checked them out and he wasn't there.

NG: From what I've read, the police presumed he must've been holed up somewhere in Devon the entire time, close to the beach where his belongings were found. But do you think someone could've been sheltering him elsewhere, before he travelled there?

DC: The only place Isaac might possibly have been was in Jarrow, within the community he grew up in. He once told me the people there are as thick as thieves and they'd lay down their lives for one of their own. But the police went through the town with a fine-tooth comb and found no trace of him having been anywhere near it. You know, it's the hope that kills you. For two weeks we clung to the belief that Isaac would do the right thing and turn himself in, so when we got the call saying he'd drowned it was devastating. I actually threw up I was that upset. I just wish he'd reached out to me first. I'm not saying I could've saved him – certainly I couldn't, nor wouldn't, have stopped him standing trial for his involvement in Emily's death – but I wish he'd have let me try.

NG: If he had turned himself in, it would've been disastrous for the band, though, wouldn't it? He would most likely have been charged and there was a good chance of a conviction, and the band's reputation might never have recovered from the scandal. Isaac taking his life meant The Ospreys could continue, and prosper. Some might say he even did you a favour.

DC: Bloody hell, Natalie, that's a bit harsh. You think we wanted him to die to save the band? No, absolutely not. We would've stood by him whatever the ramifications.

NG: But the others publicly stated they had been planning to sack him and had already involved lawyers.

DC: A lot of things were said afterwards that were twisted in the press. What the boys actually said was there had been times when they didn't know if Isaac could continue being in the band. It got blown up into this big thing where they were going to sack him but it wasn't the case. The stuff about the lawyers simply isn't true.

NG: The band's lawyers hadn't drawn up papers for Isaac to sign agreeing to quit?

DC: No. Any suggestion they did is bollocks.

NG: I did read one interview with Danny saying he, Renner and Archie wanted to break up after Isaac was gone. He said they thought disbanding was the right thing to do, but you persuaded them not to. Is that true?

DC: I didn't want them to make a decision in haste, while they were grieving, that they might come to regret. I know it might sound daft, but I don't think Isaac would've wanted them to split. Despite the public's understandable revulsion at what happened to Emily, no one blamed the other three. Everyone knew it was him who'd caused all the trouble. I thought the fans and the public would give them a second chance and I was right and then Jem came along and was the perfect fit. It was the best outcome.

NG: Going back to those two weeks when Isaac went missing, where were you all?

DC: You mean where were we staying? Well, for the first few days we were all still in Scotland, because the police needed to interview us all. But after Isaac was bailed and we got the OK to leave, we came back to London and I got the lads to come and stay at mine. The media attention was ferocious and

I thought it was better if we stuck together behind the same closed doors. Every other day Isaac had to report to our local police station as part of his bail conditions though. Usually I went with him but this one afternoon, about two weeks after Emily's death, he asked to go alone. Said he needed some space. But he didn't come back to the house and then he went missing. The rest of the lads continued to stay with me while everyone searched for him. It was an extremely anxious time, but I think it helped being together. We could lean on one another for support, although my job was obviously to sort out everything, like cancelling the remainder of the tour, so I was really busy too.

NG: What about Isaac's brother, Toby. Did he travel back to London with you?

DC: No, he didn't. Toby stayed on in Scotland for a bit. The poor lad was in pieces about Isaac's arrest and I think he thought he could get to the bottom of what happened himself. It was pointless though, because by then it was a police matter. I did think he might come to London after Isaac absconded, but he went back to Jarrow instead, presumably in case Isaac showed up there. But as I said, the police checked all of Isaac's old haunts and had no luck.

NG: I listened to the *Downbeat* podcast when Renner said he regretted that none of you spoke to Toby these days. Why did you lose touch?

DC: I don't know, we just did.

NG: Do you regret not keeping an eye out for him more?

DC: I haven't given it much thought to be honest. Look, I have to ask, why all the interest in Toby?

NG: I plan to cover what happened to all the main players in the aftermath of Glasgow, and that includes him.

DC: OK. I see. I guess things just drifted between us. He was very, very angry about the press coverage and he blamed me in particular for not being able to stop what was being written. He couldn't come to terms with what his brother had done. There was no big row though; he just stopped returning our calls.

NG: What would you say if I told you Toby claims Isaac actually went to bed in his hotel room that night, but that someone drugged him and put him back in his own suite alongside Emily's dead body?

DC: I'd say he was wrong. Seriously, did he actually say that? I know he wanted to believe Isaac didn't harm Emily, but that's crazy.

NG: Toby says he told the police, but they wouldn't listen. I'm trying to confirm with the officers who originally investigated the case if he did give a statement saying it.

DC: They didn't listen because it wasn't true. I don't blame Toby for not wanting to think the worst of his brother, but Isaac was the only person with Emily in his suite. We saw them go in together.

NG: We?

DC: A member of Isaac's security team and myself.

NG: Can you give me that person's name?

DC: It was Kenny something. I don't remember his surname, it was a long time ago and he stopped working for us soon after. I remember he took Emily's death very badly – he blamed himself for standing aside to let her into Isaac's room. I might still have his name on file somewhere; I can ask Alice to look it up if you like.

NG: That would be helpful, thank you.

DC: For the record I had no idea how young Emily was. She told us she was twenty-one. Not that it's any excuse, but had I realised how young she was I wouldn't have stood aside either, no bloody way.

NG: But there was a culture among the band of sleeping with young fans, wasn't there? I heard they even had a nickname for their groupies – the Little Birdies.

DC: I've heard that nickname, but I promise you it wasn't the boys using it. It must've been something the road crew came up with it. I won't deny the lads had their fun – they were young, good-looking, had the world at their feet – but I don't think they behaved inappropriately with their fans. Certainly no worse than any other band in their position, put it that way.

NG: Do you remember one fan in particular called Pippa?

DC: Doesn't ring any bells. Why do you ask?

NG: Just wondering if you knew her. OK, next question,

did the band have any connection to Nepal at the time? Ever toured there?

DC: Nepal? No, they never went there.

NG: Right. So, going back to Toby. You said it's sad you lost touch: does that mean you would consider reaching out to him?

DC: I haven't thought about it. But I've got no way of getting in touch with him as he changed his number years ago, I told you that at the funeral. Can I ask you something now?

NG: Sure.

DC: Have you spoken to Toby for your article? Is that why you keep asking me about him?

NG: I'm just trying to establish what happened to all the main players in the aftermath, that's all.

DC: That doesn't answer my question, Natalie. What's with the obsession with Toby Naylor?

Chapter Fifty

FRIDAY, 5TH

Is it ever possible to win an argument when the person you're arguing with is shouting their side of it and not letting you get a word in edgeways? I consider this as the woman whose door I knocked on moments ago continues to bellow at me at a decibel level that's almost glass-shattering. On and on she rants, all because I asked if she knows, or knew, Toby Naylor. Concluding she's not going to listen to whatever else I have to say, I start to back away.

'That's it, you crawl back under your stone, you tabloid scum,' the woman hollers triumphantly, before slamming her front door shut in my face. The vibration rocks me on my heels a fraction.

She is the fifth resident in a row of Wenlock Road to tell me to bugger off in no uncertain terms. The closing of ranks has been quite spectacular. By the time I'd finished explaining to the first neighbour whose door I'd knocked on who I was and why I've come to Jarrow and what I'm hoping to find out, the rest of the street was aware of my presence and number five was already yelling before she opened the door. I heard her coming down the hallway proclaiming what a bloody cheek it was for reporters to think they'd give them dirt on the Naylors and I could fuck right off if I thought she'd be the one to cave. She didn't pause for breath even as she opened the door; she just carried on shouting, face puce from the release of letting rip.

I retreat back to the edge of the pavement. I could try the other side of the road but I'm pretty sure the response will be the same. The first neighbour I spoke to said most of them lived here when the Naylor boys suffered the loss of their mother and none of them would take kindly to me dredging up the past. I should've heeded that warning but I didn't, which is why I'm now standing in the middle of an empty street acutely aware I'm being watched from behind twitching net curtains.

With a sigh, I hitch my holdall onto my shoulder and make my way up the road, towards the bus stop I disembarked at only half an hour ago. The bag has everything I need for a couple of nights' stay and the weight of it makes the strap dig into my shoulder. I've got a room booked at a budget chain back in Newcastle, which is half an hour away by train. Check-in wasn't until three, so I came straight here after my train from King's Cross arrived on time at one-thirty.

My decision to travel to Jarrow is not the impulsive move it might seem. It was after unravelling the anagram of Aden Rowlock and Wenlock Road that I rescheduled my interview with Derrick Cordingly in the hope he could shed some light on where Toby might be. He was clueless in that regard, but during the course of our chat he mentioned Isaac once told him the people of Jarrow would always shelter its own, which made me consider Toby had in fact returned to the north-east after he checked out of the York & Albany hotel. He no longer owns the mansion left to him by Isaac or his old family home in Wenlock Road, but he could still be somewhere local. It's only now I'm here and I can see for myself how fiercely protective the community is, and how unlikely people are to help me, that I realise it's been a wasted journey and one I can ill-afford.

Yet solving the anagram of Aden Rowlock and Wenlock Road has given me renewed zeal to pursue the story – I am more certain than ever that Isaac is alive and Toby knows where he is. However, I need to confirm the facts of the story as quickly as possible now, because I fear I raised Derrick's suspicions by quizzing him a bit too relentlessly about Toby and I'm concerned he might try to contact him himself and the truth will inauspiciously tumble out that way. I will kick myself if that happens now, after everything I've endured in its pursuit.

The next bus is a fifteen-minute wait. I while away the time flicking through the apps on my phone until the sensation of being watched crawls across my skin, like a spider has scurried over the back of my hand. I look up to see a man standing a few metres away glance over at me. He has lank, collar-length, dirty blond hair that's tucked behind his ears and he's wearing dark blue trousers and a matching T-shirt with a logo for a plumbing firm printed on the front. I pretend to concentrate on my phone again, but from the corner of my eye I see him continue to glance my way and he's doing it furtively enough to make me anxious. I'm living on my nerves as it is, still looking over my shoulder for the man who attacked me at the awards to rear his ugly shaved head again. I look up at the same time the plumber glances round again and this time our eyes lock. Squirming, I quickly look away but it's too late: he's coming over.

'All right,' he says.

I don't reply but give the briefest of nods to politely acknowledge his presence. He, however, takes that as an invitation to keep talking.

'You're not from round these parts.'

Again I stay tight-lipped.

'You've been asking about Toby Naylor.'

This makes me look up. 'Yes I have. Do you know him?'

'You could say that.'

Sensing a breakthrough, I get to my feet. 'I'm Natalie Glass. I'm a writer.'

'I know who you are. I heard you talking to me mam on the doorstep.'

I wonder which of the women who told me to bugger off he's related to, then decide it doesn't matter. Unlike the hostile reaction I received knocking on their doors, this man is neither unfriendly nor threatening.

'So you know Toby?' I ask. Close up, I'd put him in the same age bracket. 'Were you friends when he and Isaac lived on Wenlock Road?'

Slowly he nods. 'But I was closer to Isaac. We were best mates from the crib, born only a couple of weeks apart.' He stares at me beadily. 'My mam says I shouldn't talk to journalists, but fuck it.'

'I can interview you?' I ask excitedly.

'Yeah, you can. Someone needs to remind the world what an arsehole Isaac Naylor was.'

His name is Jimmy Trewin and apparently he is co-founder of The Ospreys.

He tells me this as the two of us travel to Newcastle in his work van, his plumbing tools rattling in the back of the estate vehicle each time we round a corner. I had suggested we find a cafe close to Wenlock Road for a cup of tea as we chat but Jimmy's eyes had widened with fright at that and he said someone was bound to see us and tell his mam and she'd skin him alive for fraternising with the press. He asked where I was staying and when I said in the centre of Newcastle he offered to drive me back, save me getting the bus, and we could talk on the way. Not the most ideal interview setting but I didn't want to put him off by saying no.

'We weren't called The Ospreys when Isaac and me put the band together,' he reveals, once we're in the van and on our way. 'I came up with the name The Jarrow Heads, after where we come from. Still don't know why Isaac didn't keep it.'

I have a pretty good idea but keep my opinion to myself.

'How old were you when the band started?'

'Thirteen. We were a pile of shite at first but we practised every day in my dad's lock-up and got pretty good. I was bass guitar. I still play.'

'What happened to make you leave?'

He shoots me a scathing sidelong look. 'I didn't leave,' he says huffily. 'I got replaced.'

'How come?'

'When we did our GCSEs I picked different subjects to Isaac, so we weren't in the same classes any more and that's when he got friendly with Danny Albright. Danny played bass and Isaac reckoned he was better than me, so that was that.'

'That must've hurt,' I venture, 'if you and Isaac were best mates.'

'Aye, it did, but not as much as when he said no to giving us what I was owed from the band.'

'Sorry?'

Jimmy grimaces and grips the steering wheel tightly, baring knuckles that have turned white. 'When they got famous I asked Isaac for my share. He said no, because I hadn't written any of their songs, because when I was in the band we just did covers. But starting the band in the first place was my idea and that should've counted for something. I kept asking, even threatened getting the law on him and the like, but Isaac wouldn't budge. That's why I call him an arsehole even though he's dead. I'm no hypocrite though: I'd say it to his face if he weren't.'

I don't have the heart to point out that Isaac was legally correct in his refusal: The Ospreys didn't owe Jimmy a penny for being the co-founding member of a different line-up with a different name. Only a verified contribution to the songs The Ospreys subsequently recorded and performed would have earned him a payday.

'So you fell out after The Ospreys made it big?'

'Aye. But I stayed friends with Toby.'

I was leading up to asking about Toby but as Jimmy's saved me the bother I dive straight in.

'Are you still friends now?'

'Well, I'd call us friends, like, but Toby's not been in Jarrow for about two years now.'

'He's not here at the moment?'

'No, like I said, he's not been back. I'd have got word if he had.'

My mood deflates. I'm certain Jimmy isn't lying to protect Toby and that he would tell me if he knew where he was. Which means Toby isn't here in the north-east and this trip has been for nothing.

'I did read he'd sold the house he inherited from Isaac but I thought he might have bought another one locally.'

'No, he's cut all ties with the place. The way he left was well weird if you ask me,' Jimmy muses.

'In what way?'

'Toby used to take off a lot on holiday. Not in posh hotels and the like, but backpacking and staying in hostels. He'd take off for a couple of months at a time and when he did I had a key for his place and I'd go round to keep an eye on it and water his plants. Then one trip he goes on I don't hear from him for ages, which is not like him, and then it gets to ten weeks, then twelve weeks, and I start to worry. He's not answering any texts or emails. I goes round to his place to water the plants again and I decide to have a poke around to see if I can work out where he might've ended up this time and track him down that way.'

'Didn't you know where he was going?' I say, surprised.

'He never stayed in one place. He'd always start in Goa, fly there first, and then he'd go on from there.'

I feel a flutter of excitement at the mention of Goa. It's on the coast of India, a country that neighbours Nepal, and is another starting point on the Hippie Trail that backpackers can follow into Kathmandu, Nepal's capital. What if Toby's backpacking excursions were really a cover for him to visit Isaac in hiding?

'Only I couldn't get into the house,' says Jimmy.

'How come?'

'The locks had been changed.'

'Toby had them changed while he was abroad? Why would he do that?'

Jimmy shrugs as he flicks the indicator to turn right at the approaching junction. 'I wish I knew, but that wasn't the only thing wrong – the house had been cleared out. I looked through the window when I couldn't open the door and all of Toby's stuff, furniture, everything, was gone. The place had been emptied.'

'He sold the house while he was away and didn't tell the friend meant to be looking after it? That *is* weird.'

'I don't mind he didn't tell me, it was his business, but not bothering to get in touch again to say thanks for keeping an eye on the place did piss me off,' says Jimmy gruffly. 'Turns out he could be a selfish prick just like his brother.'

I twist in the passenger seat to face him directly. 'Let me get this straight: Toby sold up while he was on a trip abroad, didn't tell you and you never saw or heard from him again?'

'That's right. It's not like we had cross words or anything, before you ask. The last message I got was Toby wishing me a happy birthday and telling me he looked forward to us having a belated pint when he was home. Even though he lived in that big fancy house he was still a Jarrow lad at heart and still my mate.'

I shift back round in my seat and stare out of the windscreen, my mind fizzing. Why would Toby not bother to tell Jimmy, the childhood friend he'd entrusted to safeguard his house while he was away, that he was selling up? To never get in touch with him ever again? It doesn't make sense . . . unless something, or someone, stopped Toby making contact.

Chapter Fifty-One

I don't stay overnight in Newcastle in the end, even though it means losing what I'd already forked out for a hotel room and also having to pay through the nose for a single train ticket back to London on the 19.30 train that's triple the price of the one I pre-booked. Within seconds of the payment being processed on my credit card I receive a text message from the bank saying I am now within £150 of breaching the card's limit, which already runs into five figures. But while the text's contents make me break out in a sweat, I can't worry about it now. I have to get back to London and intensify my efforts to track down Toby. He's the key to all this. Spending the night in Newcastle isn't going to get me closer to locating him.

The train is hurtling through the Nottinghamshire country-side when Daniel calls me to say goodnight. My mood lifts instantly on hearing his voice. We talk about school for a little while then he suddenly blurts out a question that leaves me stunned.

'Mummy, are you going to die like Bronwyn?'

'What on earth's made you think that?'

'Maya said you're not very nice and someone will stab you too.'

I am enraged. First throwing stones at cars, now this. I need to have strong words with Spencer about that girl's influence on Daniel. If she and her mother are going to be in his life, stuff like this can't keep happening.

'Will you Mummy? Will you be stabbed as well?'

I can hear the tremble in his voice and I feel sick, because I want to say no, it won't happen to me, but how can I be so sure? What if Bronwyn wasn't meant to die that night, if it was only meant to be a warning, until she fought back and her assailant unwittingly knifed her in the struggle? It still doesn't change the fact she died. However, I mustn't let Daniel know I'm worried.

'Nothing bad is going to happen to me,' I reassure him.

'Do you promise?'

I hesitate as a flashback of being attacked at Alexandra Palace fills my mind. I don't want to promise something I can't guarantee. 'Nothing bad is going to happen, sweetheart,' I say again.

Then I hear a voice in the background, a female one. It's Jo, telling Daniel his bath is ready. 'Hurry and say goodbye,' she adds. Hearing her speak makes me bristle. How dare she tell my son to hang up on me! I should be the one getting him ready for bed, not her. Before I can stop myself, I break my cardinal rule of keeping Daniel out of our custody wrangles by telling him his dad and me have agreed he can come to live with me half of the time.

'Really?' Daniel's voice lifts in excitement. 'When?'

I can't bring myself to say not until after the house is sold, not with Jo lingering in the background ready to scoop him up when he gets upset that I've got his hopes up and then dashed them, because for a nine-year-old 'after the house is sold' might as well be sometime in the next century.

'Really soon,' I say.

'Will I have my own bedroom?'

261

'Of course you will. And you can paint it whatever colour you like.'

As he launches into a stream of chatter about how he wants to decorate the bedroom – a Minecraft mural will feature large, apparently – I try to ignore the gnawing panic that I need to deliver on this now.

'Only Josh is going to be allowed to see my room, because he's my best friend now,' Daniel goes on, referring to one of his classmates. 'He told me a secret the other day but I can't tell you what, because best friends don't tell.'

I frown. 'Well, it really depends on the secret, honey. If it's something Josh has done and doesn't want people to find out, that's one thing, but if the secret is about something that's been done to him and he's upset and needs help, it's OK to tell a grown up. In fact, you really should tell.'

'It's not that. He did something naughty. But I can't tell you what because best friends don't tell and if I told I'd be in trouble.'

The latter part of Daniel's comment makes me sit up. 'Say that again,' I instruct him. 'The last bit.'

'I said if I told I'd be in trouble. Josh would be cross with me for telling his secret.'

My mind begins to whir and excitement rises in me. *If I told I'd be in trouble.*

That's it, that's how I force Toby out of hiding – and hopefully Isaac with him.

Chapter Fifty-Two

It's only as I ring the doorbell that I question the wisdom of my coming here so late at night and how I'm risking my safety by doing so. It was gone ten by the time my train pulled into King's Cross station and then I had to wait for a bus to bring me here and I was so het up about what I was planning to do that the lateness of the hour never occurred to me. But now I'm trembling with apprehension, because everything awful that's happened began on this very spot, and what if me being here ends in more violence? What about Daniel? Then I see a figure coming along the hallway towards the door to open it and it's too late to back out.

Bibek is discernibly surprised to find me on the doorstep. 'Why are you here?' he asks.

'I'd like you to call Toby for me so I can speak to him. If I try to call him he won't answer and it's imperative I speak to him now.' I brace myself for a burst of hostility or anger, but this time Bibek reacts with a nervousness that matches mine.

'Toby who? I don't know any Toby.'

I swallow my nerves down.

'Bibek, I don't know you and I might be completely wrong about this, but I think you are a terrible liar. I know you know who Toby is and that he's been pretending to be Aden

263

Rowlock, because Aden Rowlock doesn't exist. There is no lawyer called Aden Rowlock operating from this house,' I jab my finger towards the upstairs windows for emphasis, 'but I know that you've been falsely representing yourself as his legal associate.'

I watch Bibek's expression keenly as my words sink in, looking for telltale signs that might confirm his complicity. I don't have to look hard. First his forehead creases into a frown as he digests what I've said, then a look of panic swamps his entire face as the ramifications hit home.

'Well?' I prompt him.

Bibek shakes his head. 'I don't know any Toby.'

'Again, that was a terrible attempt at lying.' I tilt my head to one side as I stare up at him. 'Why are you so willing to protect Toby? Is it because he pays you to? Or is it because you feel protective of him because you were friends with Isaac and one of the people who helped him illegally flee the country and evade justice?' I invoke Daniel's line. 'Are you covering for the Naylor brothers because if you told you'd be in trouble yourself?'

'I don't know what you're talking about,' Bibek stammers, clearly terrified, and for a moment he has my sympathy. If he did help Isaac, I imagine he did so out of loyalty and belief that his friend wasn't guilty of killing Emily Jenkins. But smuggling someone out of the country after they've skipped police bail is aiding and abetting and perverting the course of justice at a minimum. Judging by his expression, Bibek knows that too.

'Look, I'm not interested in you or what you did or didn't do to help Isaac. I just need to speak to Toby and you're the only person who can help me, because I think you're the only person who knows where he is. Will you help me?'

He shakes his head.

'Does that mean you won't help me or don't know where he is?'

'I know where he is but I made a promise not to tell anyone. Toby begged me.'

'Please Bibek. I need to speak to him.'

He swivels round and stares furtively up at the imposing house, as though it's silently listening to our conversation and casting judgement. Apart from the illuminated window at the top right, the rest of the house sits in darkness.

'We cannot talk here. Please, we walk?'

There are two main roads straddling each end of Rushton Avenue, meaning lots of traffic and passing footfall, so while I don't entirely trust him, I figure I'll be safe either way. 'OK,' I nod.

He pulls the door quietly closed behind him and we hit the pavement, our step in unison. We're halfway along the street when he suddenly utters: 'I am the lawyer.'

'What?'

'I did my advocate training at university in Nepal before coming to England and I did a conversion course when I arrived. When Toby asked for my help with his contracts I was happy to be of service.'

'Contracts to sell Isaac's songs to producers.'

'Yes.'

There it is – confirmation Isaac *is* the mystery songwriter. I feel vindicated but there's no time to revel in it, because I have other questions I need to ask and I can't be sure Bibek's not going to make a run for it once we're near the main road.

'How did you and Toby meet?'

'Isaac and I were friends and he introduced us.'

'How did you meet Isaac?'

More confirmation: Bibek tells me their paths first crossed at Camden Market, just as I suspected. Isaac liked to browse the stalls where Bibek's housemates worked and one day Bibek was there too and he and Isaac got talking. Isaac was interested in hearing more about Nepali culture and music so Bibek and his housemates invited him back to the house. After that he became a regular visitor.

'He said that being with us was the only time he felt normal,' Bibek explains. 'With us he was Isaac our friend, not Isaac the rock star.'

'Where's Isaac now, Bibek?' I ask.

He stares at me. 'He's dead.'

'No he's not. His suicide was faked and I'm pretty certain you were involved in setting it up. Where is he now?'

But Bibek ignores the question and returns to the subject of Toby.

'It was Toby's idea to use the name Aden Rowlock. I tried to dissuade him but he was not to be convinced. But while the name was made up, the content of each contract we drew up was 100 per cent accurate,' he states proudly. 'I signed them myself as associate.'

'Who's named as the songwriter on the contracts – wouldn't you have had to state who they were?'

'I cannot discuss the details for reasons of client confidentiality,' Bibek replies primly.

He's got me there. Undeterred, though, I plough on.

'What I don't understand is why Toby, in the guise of Aden, wants to harm me. I was attacked backstage at an awards show, had funeral flowers sent for my son and I've also been followed and each time it's been to warn me off pursuing the story that Isaac is still alive. It's been terrifying.' There's a genuine tremor of fear in my voice as I say it, because if I cannot convince Bibek to help me and he tells Toby about this conversation, there's no knowing what might happen next. 'I also think that Toby was behind the murder of my friend, Bronwyn. She gave me your address and then a few days after I came round that first time she was stabbed.'

Bibek is aghast. 'Murder? No, no, you are wrong.'

Then it hits me. 'It was you, wasn't it? You wrote the legal letter to the studio after Bronwyn sourced your address. You scared her and then Toby had her killed!' I exclaim, my voice rising in anger.

'No, that was not Toby's doing. He wouldn't do that.'

'Wouldn't he? What about the man who smashed my face in?' I furnish Bibek with a description of my assailant but he shakes his head.

'I do not know of this man you talk of. Toby has never mentioned him.'

I don't believe him and say so. 'The easiest way for us to clear this up is for me to talk to Toby,' I add. 'Can you call him for me?' We've reached the main road and across the street I spy a pub that's now shut for the night, but there are benches outside. 'We could sit down there while you do it.'

Bibek looks unconvinced.

'Please, I need to talk to him.'

'It's not that. I don't know where he is. He's not answering his phone.'

Again, I don't believe him. Frustrated, I decide to fight fire with fire.

'How did you do it, Bibek? How did you manage to smuggle Isaac out of the country when the police were looking for him?'

He stares at me and I don't need to be a mind reader to tell he's deeply troubled by what I'm saying.

'I could go to the police with everything I know and yours will be the first door they knock on. But I'm not going to do that yet, at least not until I've spoken to Toby. Where is he? I know he's not in London and he's not back home in Jarrow.'

'I cannot tell you.'

His stubbornness infuriates me. 'There's a police station not far from here,' I say. 'I am prepared to go there right now and tell them what you did to help Isaac escape unless you tell me where Toby is.'

Bibek looks stricken but I swallow down the guilt it prompts. He has no one to blame for this situation but himself.

'One visit to a police station, that's all it will take to bring this crashing down on your head. Are you really prepared to go to prison for the Naylors?'

The mention of prison has a domino effect on Bibek and his confession comes tumbling out. 'I was just trying to help my friend! Isaac swore to me that he never hurt Emily and Toby said they could prove it. I wouldn't have helped him get to Nepal if I thought he hurt her.' He exhales shakily. 'But her family, it hurt them when he disappeared, and I am very sorry for that.'

'Now is your chance to put things right with them,' I say. 'I can help, if you tell me where Toby is.'

There's a prolonged pause and I'm about to lose what little patience I have left when Bibek quietly says: 'Toby's in Devon.'

Devon. Of course. Holing up in a place that holds such significance makes perfect sense. If anyone worked out who he was, Toby could easily explain away his presence as wanting to be close to where his brother killed himself. The last place anyone would think to look for Isaac again . . .

'Is Isaac with him?' I gasp.

I'd assumed Isaac was sending his songs to Aden Rowlock from wherever he was hiding abroad. It hasn't occurred to me until now that he might have somehow smuggled himself back into the UK. Yet Bibek's expression tells me all I need to know.

'I want the address,' I say.

Bibek retrieves his phone from his back pocket and reads out an address for a cottage that, he tells me, is three miles inland from Beesands, a small coastal village.

'The cottage is quite remote,' he adds.

'Don't worry, I'll find it.' I'm about to walk away, when something else occurs to me. 'If you warn Toby I'm coming to find him I will go straight to the police and tell them everything. I don't want him to know beforehand.'

Bibek gives me a look I can't quite decipher, hovering somewhere between despair and annoyance.

'I won't tell him, but you are wrong about everything, Natalie,' he says solemnly. 'You think you know, but you are still far from the truth. Nothing is as you think it is.'

Chapter Fifty-Three

Taryn here. You won't believe it, but I've managed to get my hands on the transcript of Isaac's second interview while in custody. It's from a good source of mine so I know it's legit. Present were Detective Sergeant Bill Monroe (BM) and Detective Constable Samantha Deacon (SD) from Glasgow's Major Investigation Team and Perry Humphries (PH), Mr Naylor's legal representative. IN denotes Isaac Naylor, duh. It's so obvious they had an agenda from the get-go. He kept telling them he didn't do it but they wouldn't listen! #neverforget, Ospreyers!

SD: Did you manage to get some sleep? [pause] For the purposes of the tape the witness is nodding.

BM: I bet our cell was a change from the kind of fancy hotels you're used to staying in, Mr Naylor. How much does it cost for a night at the Regency?

IN: I don't know. I didn't book the room myself.

BM: Ah, you're too important for that, aren't you?

PH: Is there a purpose to this line of questioning?

BM: I'm getting to it. You see, Mr Naylor, I'm getting to thinking that you're so big and important you don't appreciate the consequences of the trouble you're in, because you're not showing us much remorse.

IN: I've got nothing to be sorry about. I didn't touch that girl.

SD: You're not sorry she's dead?

IN: Of course I am, that's not what I meant.

SD: The fact remains her body was found in your bed.

IN: I told you, I don't know how she got there. I went to sleep in my brother's room because I wasn't feeling well and there was a party in another room on my floor and it was keeping me awake. Ask Toby.

BM: We have and he's spinning us the same story you are.

IN: It's not a story. It's the truth.

SD: We have witnesses that saw you going into your room with Emily Jenkins after you arrived back at the hotel following the gig.

IN: They're lying. They didn't see me going into the room with her because I wasn't there!

BM: Please lower your voice, Mr Naylor. I don't take too kindly to being shouted at.

IN: You people need to listen to what I'm saying.

SD: You people? What's that supposed to mean?

BM: I think I can answer that, DS Deacon. Mr Naylor here thinks he's above us and that he can order us about. But it doesn't work like that, not in here. Your millions and your prestige won't get you anywhere.

IN: I'm sorry. I didn't mean to come across as rude. It's just so . . . so, frustrating. You interviewed me for hours yesterday and I told you over and over that I didn't hurt that girl and I don't know how she got into my bed, or how I even got there because I fell asleep in Toby's, I know I did, but you won't listen and you keep asking me the same question over and over. Why won't you believe me?

BM: It's our job to question your version of events, especially in the light of the witness statements.

IN: It's them you should be questioning again, because I tell you they're making it up. The last time I saw that girl she was in the back of the SUV. I didn't go into my room with her and I didn't take drugs with her and I wasn't there when she died. Anyone who says otherwise is a barefaced liar.

BM: That's not quite true about the drugs though, is it? You've tested positive for traces of ketamine. That's quite the party drug, I'm told.

IN: I've told you, I didn't take it. I was drugged. That's the only way I could've been moved between the rooms.

SD: Why would the witnesses lie, though?

272

IN: To make it look as though it's my fault. Give me their names. Let me talk to them and I bet I can get them to admit they didn't see me. They're probably making it up to get in the papers.

PH: Isaac, you can't talk to anyone.

BM: Listen to your solicitor, Mr Naylor, because you really don't want to add witness tampering to your charge sheet.

IN: I'm being charged?

BM: Not yet.

SD: Did you talk to Toby about what to say to us?

IN: Of course not.

SD: Are you sure? He was with you at the hotel when you were arrested – there was plenty of time for you to get your stories straight before you were brought here.

IN: No, no, I didn't say anything to him because I didn't need to. Toby knows I didn't have anything to do with that girl dying.

BM: How does he know? Are you covering for him? Are we looking at the wrong Naylor?

IN: Are you fucking insane? My brother's not a killer.

SD: But can he say the same about you, Mr Naylor?

Chapter Fifty-Four

SATURDAY, 29TH

I rule out a midnight dash to Devon on the grounds I'm too tired to drive safely after the lengthy train journey back from Newcastle and also because on my way back to Maida Vale from Kentish Town I realise there is a rather major stumbling block to me getting there: no money. I wincingly check my bank account and it's worse than I feared. I have about thirty quid to my name and I daren't put anything else on my credit cards.

After a fitful night's sleep I awake knowing I'm going to have to swallow my pride and ask someone for a loan. I don't want to ask my parents because of the conditions they'll attach and while I could call Spencer and he'd probably help, I don't want to relinquish any of the advantage I have over him presently and my asking to borrow money will do that.

So, with reluctance, I decide to take up the offer from my godmother Gayle to lend me some money, just to cover the train fare. If I can just get to Devon and track down Toby it will be worth the toe-curling embarrassment of having to ask. Her reaction when I call her in Kenya, where she's still on holiday with Andrew, is as I expected however: she agrees instantly to lend me the money when I tell her it's so I can travel for a significant story I'm working on and within five minutes I receive a text from her to confirm the money's been transferred. But when I check my account I'm thrown by the amount listed and call her straight back.

'You've made a mistake,' I say. 'I only asked to borrow two hundred, enough to cover a train fare to Devon, but this says three thousand.'

'That's right. It won't make a dent in what you owe, but it will keep you afloat for a while longer,' she says. 'It's not a loan either – it's a gift. Call it an advance on your inheritance.'

I am teary-eyed with gratitude. 'Gayle, I don't know what to say—'

'Then say nothing. Take the money and get to work. I'll see you when I'm back.' The line clicks dead.

I am so grateful I could cry. I log out of my online account and look up train times to Devon. My search tells me I'll have to travel to one of the mainline stations such as Torquay and Paignton and then either hire a car or take a multitude of buses. Or I can simply hire a car in London and drive the entire way, which should work out cheaper. I might have a bit of money in the bank now but I am determined not to squander it.

I find a rental place close by and reserve a small hatchback to pick up in an hour's time. It doesn't give me long to get ready but I have a quick shower, throw fresh clothes into my holdall and set off. Toby Naylor is in Devon, perhaps Isaac too, and I have to factor in the possibility that Bibek will have gone back on his word and tipped Toby off that I'm coming. The sooner I hit the road the better.

Two and a bit hours later I'm reminded how much I hate the monotony of motorway driving and also the abject terror of being overtaken by huge juggernauts that could squash my little hire car with one swerve of the steering wheel. Unused to driving – living in London I've never felt it was worth owning a car, so haven't – I stick to the slow lane and keep my speed at a steady seventy.

I manage to make it all the way to Exeter before I need to break my journey to use the toilet. The services I stop at, on the M5, are a bustling mini village of shops and restaurants thronging with holidaymakers and commuters grateful to leave their vehicles to stretch their legs. I queue for the toilet then buy a coffee and sit outside at one of the picnic tables to make the most of the sunshine. I raise my face to the sun, enjoying the sting of it burning against my skin. It's the perfect weather for an escape from the city, even though the purpose of my trip is not exactly leisure.

Lowering my chin, white spots of light dance across my eyes and I have to blink hard before I'm able to focus properly on people walking from the car park towards the entrance of the services. But as my eyesight sharpens I double take, because coming towards me is Bronwyn. She's wearing three-quarter length Capri trousers with a billowy white blouse tucked in at the front only and ballerina flats, her bobbed hair straight and shiny. She is with someone, a man, and she's smiling and laughing and my heart catches in my throat as she walks closer, and I half rise in my seat, ready to call out, until I blink again and my eyesight adjusts and I see that it's not Bronwyn, of course it's not. It's someone who just looks a lot like she did.

The anguish I feel on registering it's not my friend is so intense I have to grip the edge of the table to steady myself. With so much else going on, and perhaps as an act of self-preservation, I haven't thought about Bronwyn that much during the past couple of days, apart from when Daniel brought up me being stabbed like her, and since her death I shamefully haven't taken time to remember her in the way she deserves to be. I should be thinking of her constantly, not pushing her to the back of my mind like she doesn't matter.

The woman who resembles her passes my table and I have to turn away as she does. I am so angry she's not Bronwyn that I want to scream. Instead, I gather up my things and stalk back to my car, an indescribable feeling of loss propelling me forward. Yet I'm furious too. I can't bring Bronwyn back but I can make sure her death wasn't in vain. Like Emily Jenkins, Bronwyn deserves justice and this time both Naylor brothers are going to answer for what they've done.

Chapter Fifty-Five

It takes being stuck for twenty minutes behind a car pulling a powerboat at a tortoise pace on the approach road into south Devon to calm me down. I decide against driving straight to the cottage and instead head into Beesands first to find a public toilet and grab another coffee to gather myself. How I wish I wasn't driving and that it could be a glass of wine for Dutch courage though, because now I am in the vicinity of where Toby is staying I am fast becoming more nervous than angry. I know what he's capable of now and it will pay me to be wary.

Beesands isn't where Isaac staged his suicide – that particular beach is almost seven miles from here. I park on the seafront and spend a few moments after climbing out of the car breathing in the invigorating sea air. I can't remember the last time I came to a British coastal resort – holidays with Spencer and Daniel were usually spent abroad in Spain or on one of the Greek islands, somewhere with a decent pool because I loathe swimming in the sea and avoid it wherever possible. Now, standing here, listening to the gentle lap of waves against the sea wall, I wish we'd stayed closer to home sometimes, so Daniel could have experienced a proper bucket-and-spade holiday with us. I resolve that when I'm able to afford it I'll take him on one.

Beesands is a lovely little fishing village devoid of the

attractions that typically denote a seaside resort. No pier, no amusement arcade, no kiosk selling inflatable beach toys. The beach itself is shingle. Yet its simplicity is what makes it so utterly charming and as I walk along the front, passing fishermen sitting on the sea wall, their buckets full of crab, I feel my mood lift. Eventually I stop outside a place called The Britannia-at-the-Beach. From the exterior it looks like a cafe but I can see it's also a fishmonger, store and takeaway too. There's an outside seating area with enviable views over the bay and my mouth waters reading the specials board beside it, so I give myself permission to linger so I can have something to eat as well as a coffee. It's been a long journey and while I'm keen to find Toby I know I'll feel better confronting him on a full stomach. I also feel safer here, outside, with other people around me.

I treat myself to a doorstop crab sandwich and a coffee and luxuriate in the view as I eat. To the casual observer it must look as though I'm relaxing on holiday as I sun myself on the shoreline, not chasing down a story that caused me an enormous amount of stress and endangered my life and likely cost my best friend hers. Had I known what it would set in motion, I would never have sent Bronwyn the screen-grab of the blind item. I'd have filed it away as some great gossip and left it at that. But I didn't and now I must finish what I started. I cannot let Toby get away with everything he's done while he's been pretending to be Aden Rowlock.

I send a text to Daniel to say I hope he has a lovely time at football practice after school with his friends and that I'll call him later. A shiver runs through me as the question of whether I'll be able to rears its ugly head, but I bat the thought to one side: if I've learned anything about Toby in these past couple of weeks it's that he likes other people to do his dirty work for him. Then, lunch over, I rise to my feet with a sigh, wishing I could stay and be that tourist, but knowing I can't delay what's coming next.

I left my sunglasses in the hire car and as I hurry along the sea-front to where it's parked I am walking into direct sunlight and can barely see a thing. I raise my hand to shield my eyes from the glare and as I do I can make out someone sitting on the sea wall right next to it, their legs dangling over the drop. They are staring out to sea but as I come closer they turn towards me and I let out a gasp when I realise who it is.

'Hi Natalie,' says Toby. 'How was the journey?'

The surprise of seeing him makes me forget the speech I had prepared for when I saw him again.

'How did you kn— oh, right, Bibek told you I was coming,' I surmise angrily, and Toby nods affirmatively. Of course Bibek told him, I was naive to think he wouldn't. His loyalty will always be to the Naylor brothers. 'But how did you know I'd stop in Beesands?'

'Lucky guess. Most people stop off here. I've been hanging around all day waiting for you to show.'

'Where's Isaac? He's here, isn't he? He's been hiding in Devon with you.'

Toby swings his legs back over the wall and stands up. 'Let's go back to the cottage.'

'No, I don't trust you,' I glare at him. 'You've been lying to me from day one.'

'I'm not going to hurt you, Natalie. I'm going to tell you the truth.'

'How can I be sure of that?'

He stares at me. 'You can't, you'll just have to take my word for it. So it's up to you – do you want to hear the full story or not?'

Chapter Fifty-Six

Bibek was right when he said the cottage was in a remote spot. I follow Toby's car, a beaten-up saloon that looks like it would never pass an MOT, along a series of back lanes that become more impassable the further we are from Beesands, overhung by hedgerows and branches that make me wince as they scrape the side of the hire car. The summer months have left the roads dried out and smooth and I would hate to think what they'd be like in wet, wintry weather. I doubt you could drive on them at all, which may well be why the Naylor brothers have chosen to hide out here. Such an inhospitable spot isn't going to attract unexpected visitors.

I follow Toby in parking directly outside the small, low-slung bungalow that was probably painted white once but is now a dirty, yellowing approximation of the colour. The windows are so filthy you can't see in or out of them, which I presume is the point. At face value it is a perfect secluded hiding place for a disgraced former rock star who doesn't want to be found.

Yet within seconds of stepping inside at Toby's invitation, I realise Isaac's not here. I can tell because the interior of the cottage pokily amounts to one room. There is a lounge area to the left, with two armchairs angled to face a TV, a kitchenette in the middle of the room, virtually opposite the front door where we've come in, and to the right is what appears to be a curtained-off sleeping area. Through the gap in the curtain I can make out one bed.

'You're both staying here?' I ask Toby, surprised.

'I'll make some tea,' is all he answers.

I thought I would be nervous in his company – certainly on the drive down from London I felt anxious enough as my mind played over how I would confront him – but now I'm here any concern has oddly dissipated. I do not think Toby will hurt me. However, that doesn't mean I am going to let my guard down, nor am I going to let him off the hook in any regard about Aden Rowlock and the thug-for-hire sent after me at the awards and in Camden Market, and for what he did to Bronwyn.

'Bibek told me everything about Aden Rowlock,' I say.

Toby has his back to me while he brews two mugs of tea in the kitchenette. He stills briefly, then proceeds with removing the teabags and adding the milk.

'I know. He told me.'

'You're answering his calls now? He said he hadn't been able to get hold of you for days.'

He flashes a wry grin at me over his shoulder. 'When he texted to say you'd forced the address out of him I figured I should call him back.'

'Forced? I'd hardly call it that. I just made him aware that the police might frown upon his colluding to help Isaac escape justice.'

'Bibek is a good person,' says Toby, handing me a mug of tea and gesturing towards the armchairs. I lower myself into one of them and he takes the other. 'Everything Bibek has done been with the right intention.'

I scoff. 'Next you'll be telling me that thug you sent to warn me off is lovely too.'

'Who?'

'The man who attacked me at the Motif awards and who came after me again in Camden Market.'

'The one you thought Aden had arranged to hurt you? I told you when I was at your flat I knew nothing about that.'

'No, you said it wasn't anything to do with Aden. There's a difference.'

'Is there?'

'Yes, because Aden doesn't exist. Nice anagram, by the way. It took me a while to work it out.'

Toby flushes.

'You lied to me about Aden, about him being an old family friend,' I say hotly. 'But that's not the worst of it. What you did to Bronwyn, for helping me with Aden's address—' I am suddenly overcome with distress. 'You didn't have to have her killed. I know it was you.'

Toby lurches forward in his chair, shaking his head wildly. 'Natalie, I did no such thing. How could you think that? I didn't do any of what you're accusing me of. Yes, I have been using the name Aden Rowlock and Bibek did send a letter to The Soundbank after you told him that's where you got your information from, but that's all we did. I didn't send anyone after you or your friend. You have to believe that.'

'I don't know what to believe.' It's only now, facing Toby, I realise how upset I am with him for misleading me.

'Natalie, look at me.' Reluctantly I do, and his gaze bores into mine. 'I swear on my life I'm not responsible for the attacks on you, or for the death of your friend. Nor is Bibek.' He hesitates. 'And nor is Isaac.'

I glance warily at the curtain separating the living space from the bedroom. 'Where is he?'

Toby's about to answer but then thinks better of it. 'What is it you want, Natalie?' he asks. 'Why have you come here?'

I feel torn. I wanted him to admit his wrongdoing and yet I

find myself swayed when he says he wasn't responsible. Then I realise what I really want is for him to admit everything, starting with Isaac faking his suicide.

I set the mug of tea down on the floor by my feet and from my bag I retrieve my voice recorder and my notebook. I place the device decisively on the arm of his chair. He stares down at it, frowning.

'I want the interview you agreed to give me and I want the truth about where your brother is,' I tell him. 'I'm not leaving here until I have both.'

Chapter Fifty-Seven

Toby sits quietly for a moment, staring at the voice recorder. The wait for him to speak serves to highlight exactly how remote our surroundings are: I cannot hear a thing beyond the walls of this cottage and I'm not sure I've ever experienced silence like it. It's like a blanket of noiselessness has settled over us and it has me straining for the slightest sound, and yet I hear nothing, not a peep. To describe it as unnerving would be to understate it hugely.

'I will give you your interview,' says Toby eventually, prompting me to release the breath I didn't realise I was holding in, 'but I can't help you about Isaac. I wish I could, but I can't. My brother is dead, that's all I know.'

I am crestfallen Toby is continuing to play the oblivious card but I do my best to hide it. I shall play along for now and concentrate on asking the right questions to poke holes in his pretence.

'But I can confirm he is the mystery songwriter.'

My shock at hearing him say this I cannot hide. I was not expecting Toby to admit it so freely.

'But not in the way you think,' he adds.

I manage to collect myself. 'May I?' I reach over and turn the voice recorder on. 'Can you repeat what you just said, please?'

'Isaac Naylor is the mystery songwriter you have been investigating. But not in the way you think.' Toby settles back in the armchair. He looks surprisingly relaxed for someone who is about to spill his guts to a journalist. 'When I moved into the house in Jarrow I was going through Isaac's stuff and came across some lyrics he'd written. They weren't tracks for The Ospreys though and I didn't know they existed until I found them, he hadn't said a word to me about writing them.'

The same songs, I assume, Isaac played to Gregory Robertson on the morning Emily Jenkins died. I nod at Toby to continue.

'I know enough about the music industry to know that the songs were good. Better than good, in fact – they were the best he'd ever written. Although I didn't know for sure, I guessed Isaac had intended to offer them to other artists, so I decided to hold on to them until it felt like the right time to get them out there as he intended.' He looks sad for a moment. 'I thought I could remind people how great he was by releasing the songs and give him the legacy he deserved.'

'Why not sell them under his own name then?'

'Producers would've run a mile. It wouldn't have mattered how great the songs were: Isaac's reputation was too damaged. That's when I came up with the idea of creating Aden Rowlock to act for me and I asked Bibek to help because I knew he'd done the conversion course that could allow him to practise law here. When the time was right I was going to reveal Isaac was behind them.'

'Except the blind item did that for you,' I concede.

'Yes.'

'Any clue as to who tipped off the website?'

'No. It could've been anyone working at one of the studios or alongside a producer or even an artist curious about the provenance of the songs they were recording.'

'Then I started ferreting around.'

'That's one way of describing it,' Toby says with a half-smile. 'Look, I'm sorry I stormed off like I did. It threw me, you saying you believed Isaac was alive.'

'I'm sorry I blurted it out the way I did. I meant to wait until I had more proof.'

'Have you found any?'

I stare at him curiously. Bibek admitted to me yesterday that he helped Isaac flee the country, yet Toby is still maintaining the line that his brother's dead. Could he really not know his brother was spirited out of the country to Nepal? How could Bibek not have told him? I think of Jimmy Trewin, Toby's friend back in Jarrow, and what he said about him going off backpacking for weeks at a time and I know I mustn't accept what Toby says as fact because so far he's shown himself to be an accomplished liar.

'I've gathered a lot of detail that, when stacked together, does point to your brother being alive,' I say carefully.

Toby shakes his head. 'Isaac went into the sea and never came out, Natalie. He's never coming back.'

His voice breaks with emotion that appears genuine. Is he faking it or could he really not know? I decide to wait a while longer before I put Bibek's confession to him. I don't want him walking out of the interview again.

I wait for him to compose himself.

'To be clear, you are happy for me to include in my piece what you've just told me about you finding the songs and Isaac being the mystery songwriter?'

'I am.'

We spend the next two hours going over what Toby previously told me about the events of that night in Glasgow and how Isaac had gone to bed in Toby's room feeling ill but woke up in the morning in his own suite with Emily dead next to him, not knowing how he'd got there or what had happened. He barely stops for breath as he recalls his immense panic as the police swarmed the hotel and Isaac was arrested. Then he details how Isaac had returned to London with Derrick and the others, but he stayed in Scotland. Then Danny contacted him to say they didn't know where Isaac was and it slowly dawned on them all that he'd skipped bail. Toby kept ringing Isaac's phone, leaving message after message begging him to come back from wherever he'd gone, but the phone remained switched off and on day six Isaac's voicemail was full and no longer accepting messages. That's when Toby began to fear the worst.

I let him talk with as little interruption as possible, but all the while I'm formulating follow-up questions in my head and on the pages of my notebook. When there is finally a lull in his narration, I ask him if the absence of a body made it harder for him to grieve, just to see how he'll react. His answer is so convincing that again I start to doubt what is a lie and what isn't.

'It really did and I was dreading the funeral because of it, knowing that the coffin would be empty. It didn't feel right,' he says. 'But then Danny and Renner had the idea we should fill the coffin with Isaac's guitar collection, so that it was weighted down. Mad, I know. But the band and me were the pallbearers and it made it easier for all of us thinking he was in there. A few people thought we were mad though, because the guitars were probably worth a few hundred thousand and they would've been mine to inherit.'

The mention of inheritance pertinently segues into asking him about the house Isaac left him.

'Why did you sell the house in Jarrow?'

'Would you believe me if I told you I needed the money?' he says sheepishly. 'I frittered away most of what Isaac left me and I needed the cash.'

'But Isaac was worth millions,' I exclaim.

'He was, but nowhere near as much as was reported. It turns out he also owed millions in unpaid taxes. It all had to be settled from his estate.'

'Were you aware he was in financial trouble?'

'I knew he was crap at keeping tabs on his spending but not to that extent. He spent money like it was going out of fashion according to his accounts.'

Isaac's chronic and years-lasting drug habit wouldn't have come cheap, I think to myself, but there still should've been plenty for Toby to live comfortably off for years, especially with no partner and no dependents to account for. Where did the money really go? To Nepal, to cover Isaac's living expenses there? He'd have needed to get his hands on money somehow.

Toby clambers to his feet. 'Do you fancy a drink? I've got some wine.'

I check the time and am taken aback to see it's nearly seven. 'I better not, I'm driving.'

'I'll have to drink for two then,' he says with a grin and gets up to fetch a bottle of red from the kitchenette. 'Would you like a glass of water?' he calls over to me.

'Yes please.'

We continue talking for another hour, this time going over his and Isaac's childhood. I ask him about Jimmy Trewin and his claim he co-founded the band and Toby gets quite irate as he defends Isaac's decision to ditch their friend and I register that his increasing volatility correlates with the wine disappearing from the bottle. So I'm mindful to tread carefully when I ask my next question.

'But you stayed friends until you sold the house, didn't you?'

Toby frowns. 'I couldn't stand the fucker after all the aggro he caused about starting the band.'

'Really? He told me he kept an eye on the place every time you went off on your trips abroad.'

'He what? Oh, yeah. He did. I forgot.' Flustered, Toby gets to his feet again. 'Excuse me, I need the loo.' He disappears behind the curtained-off area and I hear a door open. Then, a minute or so later, a toilet flushes. Yet he doesn't return as I'd expect him to and when five more minutes pass and he still doesn't come back I go to look for him.

The bedroom area is very small, but it's neat and functional, with a queen-sized double bed pushed under the window and next to it a small chest of drawers. An exposed clothes rail with only a few items hanging from it has been squeezed in at the end of the bed.

'Toby?' I call out, passing the bed and going through the doorway I presume is the way to the bathroom but actually spills out into a tiny corridor. Just along it there's a door to the left that's for the bathroom while a second one directly ahead leads outside. I check the bathroom first but Toby's not there. Then I see the door to outside has been left open a crack.

'Toby?'

But there's no sign of him in the garden, although it's hard to see what exactly constitutes it, because there is no rear boundary from what I can see and the lawn simply bleeds into the downs behind it. I look from left to right but can't see any other properties nearby. Apprehensively I call his name again but am met again by silence. It's still fairly light out, the sun not due to set for another hour at least, but the combination of quietude and vast, uninhabited space is both creepy and unsettling.

Then I hear footsteps on the gravel path that runs along the side of the cottage. I turn, expecting to see Toby, then let out a cry of shock. It's the man who attacked me at Alexandra Palace. He must've been outside the entire time and Toby must've called him when he went to the bathroom. I can't believe I have been so stupid to believe Toby when he swore blind he didn't know him.

I try to make a run for it, but the thug's size belies his speed and agility and I scream as he grabs me by the shoulder and wrenches me round to face him.

'You were told to back off, you stupid cow,' he snarls. His fingers are already coiled into fists and while I see the punch coming this time, he doesn't hold back like he did before. The shattering blow lands on the side of my head and I'm sent spinning across the grass and by the time I hit the floor I'm already blacking out.

Chapter Fifty-Eight

I'm not sure which brings me round first: the sensation of cold, hard tiles against my left cheek where I'm lying on the kitchenette floor, or the discomfort caused by my ankles being bound and my hands tied behind my back. Or maybe it's the splitting headache I have from being hit again. Groggily I try to move, but then I hear my assailant telling me not to move an inch.

'Why are you doing this?' I rasp at him.

His face looms into view beside mine. 'Just do as I say and you won't get hurt any more,' he snaps.

'Where's Toby? I want to speak to him.'

The bastard knucklehead smirks and shrugs, so I cry out. 'Toby, tell him to let me go.'

'He's not listening,' he sneers.

I can't believe Toby's going this far to shut me up. The horror of what might happen next brings tears to my eyes. 'I want to sit up,' I tell the man.

'Go on then.'

'I can't do it alone, I'm trussed up like a turkey.'

Laughing, he rolls me onto my side and by bringing my knees up I manage to awkwardly sit up, then shuffle my bum backwards until I'm leaning against the oven door for support. It's only when I'm uncomfortably settled into position – my shoulders are already strained from my arms being unnaturally tethered behind my back – that I realise I was not alone in being bound hand and foot on the floor.

'Toby?' I gasp.

He's laying a few metres away but is barely recognisable – his face has been beaten to a bloody, messy pulp, his nose grotesquely misshapen and his eyes sealed closed and swollen. Like me, he is bound hand and foot. My attacker follows my gaze to where Toby lies and makes a show of flexing his fingers and wincing as though he's done himself an injury and I see his knuckles are stained red. There are splashes of crimson on his face too.

'You sick bastard,' I yell at him, unable to stop myself. This man, this thug, has brutalised me and threatened me and now he's beaten Toby half to death. 'Why did you do that to him? Who are you?'

He leans over Toby and puts his hand on his chest. To my relief I can see it's rhythmically rising and falling.

'It's not as bad as it looks,' he grins at me.

My distress has robbed me of the ability to come up with a better insult. 'You sick bastard,' I say again.

'I'm just following orders, love,' he shrugs.

'Whose orders? What the hell is going on? I thought you worked for Toby.'

Then a familiar voice rings out from across the room. 'Shall we tell her?'

Startled, I shuffle and scoot forward on the tiles and manage to get a clear view of the living area just in time to see Derrick Cordingly rise from one of the armchairs.

'I don't understand,' I stammer. 'What on earth are you doing here?'

Derrick doesn't look at me and instead pulls his shirt collar away from his neck with his finger.

'Is it me or is it really stuffy in here? Kenny, can you open a window?'

Kenny. The name clangs a bell.

'You're Isaac's former security guard,' I exclaim. Kenny grunts at me in acknowledgement. 'But hang on,' I say to Derrick, 'you said he was torn apart by what happened and had to quit afterwards—'

'You really shouldn't believe everything you're told Natalie,' Derrick replies. He glances at Toby. 'You hit him too hard, Kenny,' he reprimands.

'He was following your orders,' I say, my voice hoarse from shock. 'You're behind all this? Why?'

Derrick comes into the kitchenette area. I scoot backwards, turning my head from side to side looking for an escape, but there is none. I am tied up and at his and Kenny's mercy.

'Natalie, you were warned time and time again to let the story drop but you wouldn't. So all this,' Derrick makes a sweeping gesture that takes in both me and Toby, 'is technically your fault.'

'You've been making all the threats?'

Derrick adjusts his cuffs, as though this is a tedious boardroom discussion he's being forced to participate in. 'Here's something you need to know about me, Natalie. I will do whatever it takes to protect my interests and I haven't worked this hard and for this long to have you fuck it all up. You told me you were working on a piece about the band surviving the tragedy of Isaac's suicide when all along you've been trying to prove that he's still alive. I'm sorry, but I can't have that.'

'I haven't been able to prove it though,' I flounder.

'Yes you have.'

'I haven't,' I say desperately. 'I'm no closer to confirming Isaac's alive now than I was when I started looking into it.'

'Oh but that's not true. You know all about Aden Rowlock,

his friend Bibek, Nepal. You're just missing the final piece of the puzzle.'

'What's that?'

He leans down. I flinch at him coming near me, but force myself to meet his gaze.

'Isaac himself,' he says softly.

My mouth falls open. 'Isaac's here? I was right all along?'

There's a pause, then Derrick shakes his head, bemused. 'You really haven't worked it out, have you?' he says. 'You still don't know.'

'Know what?'

He turns to Kenny. 'I think it's time our old friend joined the party.'

'Yes sir.'

I expect Kenny to go outside to bring Isaac in, but instead he walks over to the sink and I watch, transfixed, as he fills an empty glass vase that was on the side with water. Why is he doing that? To my surprise he then empties the vase onto Toby's face. Toby immediately begins to splutter and groan as he comes to and as the water washes the blood away I can see with relief that Kenny wasn't lying: his injuries aren't as severe as they first appeared, the blood was making them look worse.

'Toby,' I call out, 'try not to move or they might hurt you again. They've got Isaac!'

'I honestly thought you'd figured it out and were just biding your time to publish your story,' says Derrick wonderingly. 'Well, allow me to make the introduction.' He crouches down beside Toby and roughly grabs his chin so Toby's forced to look straight at me.

'Natalie Glass, meet Isaac Naylor.'

Chapter Fifty-Nine

My reaction is to swear, then laugh incredulously. 'That's not Isaac.'

'Look again, Natalie. Same height, same features, just a lot fatter, so it's harder to be sure it's him. But it is,' says Derrick. 'I'd know Isaac anywhere.'

I stare down at Toby. It can't be true. He can't really be Isaac. I would've known . . . Then it comes to me, like a lightening bolt. 'The tip of Toby's finger was burned off as a kid,' I cry out. 'Look, you can see it right there. That's Toby's injury.'

'I'll let Isaac explain how he did it,' Derrick retorts, then nods to Kenny again, who refills the jug and throws water over Toby a second time. He splutters and coughs again and his eyes flicker open as much as they're able to, given how swollen they are—

Suddenly I remember something else I know about Isaac. His eyes.

'It's not just his finger,' I say triumphantly. 'Isaac had blue eyes. Toby's are brown, see? He can't be Isaac.'

Derrick leans down and roughly opens Toby's left eye with his fingers. 'So they are.'

Toby cries out in pain. 'Get off me,' he yelps. It's a relief to hear him speak. Derrick lets go of him and he slumps back against the tiles.

'It was Cicely, the stylist I hired to come up with the band's look, who suggested Isaac wear bright blue contacts, to make his eyes stand out against all the black he wore,' Derrick tells me. 'She said it would make him look remarkable and she was right. Those blue eyes of his became a trademark. He hated wearing the lenses though. As soon as he got home he'd rip them out.'

Shock ripples through me. What he's saying is plausible, but I still don't believe it. Even taking into account their similarities, how can I have been in such close proximity to Toby and not noticed he was really his brother? It's not possible.

Derrick orders Kenny to help Toby into a sitting position. When he's finally upright, Toby turns his swollen face in my direction.

'I'm sorry I lied to you, Natalie.'

I gasp. 'You really are Isaac?'

'I am. I wanted to tell you, but I was scared. I didn't know if I could trust you.'

I am lost for words. I stare at him and try to imagine him standing next to his old self on the *Rolling Stone* cover in Derrick's office. It can't be the same person, and yet . . . As I slowly rake my gaze over him, drinking in every inch of his features, I begin to realise just how he's evaded attention all this time – by transforming himself into his brother. He's packed on at least three stone in weight to achieve Toby's stockier build, grown his hair longer and darker – and mostly hides it under that red baseball cap anyway – let his eyes revert to their natural colour and somehow has butchered his finger to replicate Toby's childhood injury. He appears nothing of his former self. Only someone who knew him really well would be able to ascertain he's Isaac, which is presumably why he hasn't been anywhere near Jarrow and old friends like Jimmy, and why Derrick and Kenny recognise him now. For someone like me who never met Isaac in person, the injury to his finger and the different eye colour alone are enough to distract from the person he really is.

'Where's Toby?' I ask. 'If you're being him now, where is he?'

Isaac swallows hard. 'He's dead.'

I glare up at Derrick. 'Was that your doing?'

'Of course it wasn't.'

'You had Bronwyn killed though, didn't you,' I snarl at him, my anger peaking. 'All because she helped me.'

Derrick looks genuinely horrified. 'Jesus Natalie, what do you take me for? That was a mugging that went wrong; that had nothing to do with me. I liked Bronwyn and I'm sad she's dead.' He shakes his head. 'I can't believe you thought I'd rob those kids of their mum. Shame on you.'

This makes me scoff. 'Can you blame me for thinking that when you had your goon here attack me at Alexandra Palace and now this?' I nod in the direction of Isaac, whose breathing is becoming worryingly laboured.

'Those things I'll admit to, but no way did I arrange for Bronwyn to be hurt. Nor did I have Toby killed. I didn't even know he was dead until Isaac just said.'

'Nobody knows,' says Isaac.

'What happened to him?' asks Derrick. He sounds as though he actually cares and it makes me feel sick to my stomach.

'It was a motorbike accident. After I got settled in Nepal, Toby would come out to visit me. The last time was two years ago and while he was there we decided to take a road trip to India on motorbikes. There was a cliff-top road along the route, Toby took a corner too tightly and went over the edge. He didn't stand a chance.'

'That's awful,' I say. 'I'm so sorry.' I pause. 'So you were in Nepal then? I was right about that?'

Isaac nods. 'It was for Toby that I ended up there.' He takes a deep, shuddering breath. 'I really was close to ending it after what happened in Glasgow. I couldn't see a way out; I thought I was going to prison. It devastated me, knowing I didn't do anything wrong, that I didn't hurt poor Emily, and, well, suicide really did seem the answer. Toby guessed what I was thinking though and he begged me to change my mind. He was beside himself at the thought of losing me – I was all he had, with our mam and dad gone. It was his idea for me to go abroad and lie low and he came up with staging the suicide on the beach.'

'He always was the smartest kid,' remarks Derrick, and the sadness with which he says it inflames me.

'How can you sit there pretending to be sorry for his loss when you've got us tied up like this!' I shout at him.

Kenny advances on me but Derrick holds him back. 'It's OK, she has every right to be upset.'

'If you're so concerned, you could untie us. We're not exactly going to run off with him looming over us. Or at least let us sit on a chair.' I no longer feel scared, just furious, and I want answers from all of them. 'You owe me more of an explanation,' I add.

Derrick nods to Kenny. 'Put them in the armchairs. But keep the binds on them.'

It takes a few minutes to get us settled because Kenny has to untie our arms from behind us and retie them in front so we can sit down properly. As he unties my wrists, my loose hand brushes against something in the chair and I realise it's my voice recorder: it must've slipped off the arm and fallen down the side of the cushion. While Kenny's distracted sorting out a fresh cable tie, I grope with my fingers and press what I hope is the button on the front that activates the recording. Then Kenny orders me to put my hands out to retie my wrists in front of me and the voice recorder thankfully stays hidden squashed between the seat and my thigh. I have no idea whether it will

299

pick anything up but at least I've tried.

Once Kenny's done the same to Isaac, Derrick stands in front of the pair of us, his expression set and hands clasped behind his back like a teacher about to tick off an unruly class.

'I never wanted any of this to happen,' he begins, prompting me to glance sideways at Isaac, but it's hard to read what he's thinking because his face is too puffy to tell if he's grimacing or smiling. 'But you should've quit The Ospreys when we asked you to, Isaac.'

'Whether I left or not wasn't your decision to make,' Isaac seethes through gritted teeth and swollen lips. 'I wasn't going to let you force me out of my own band. If I was going to leave, it was going to be on my terms.'

'But I heard you wanted to quit,' I interrupt. 'You'd had enough of the limelight and wanted to write songs for others.'

'I had, that's true. But The Ospreys were my band. I put us together, not him,' he says, shooting an unmistakeable look of pure loathing at Derrick. 'I wasn't going to let him dictate the timing or way in which I left.'

'Why did you want Isaac out?' I ask Derrick. 'He was the one the fans adored the most, the one who wrote all the songs, the one whose name was known to everyone. It makes no sense.'

Derrick crosses his arms. 'True, but he was also a fucking liability and we'd had enough. Do you know what it's like having to deal with someone who is off his head the entire time? It's exhausting. When Isaac was high he'd be manic and it was like dealing with a toddler having an all-day tantrum every day of the week with no let-up. This had gone on for years and the record company were starting to make noises about dropping us. They were done with the aggro and the constant appearances in the tabloids and it was starting to affect us financially. Our insurance premiums for touring were through the roof because the underwriters expected him to OD at some point.

We had to pay hundreds of thousands out in compensation for every gig missed or cancelled. Everything revolved around keeping an eye on Isaac and it was too much. So we asked him to quit after the tour.'

'You told me the stories about the others wanting Isaac to leave were rubbish,' I put to Derrick.

'No, I said the stories about them drawing up legal papers were wrong. We hadn't quite reached that point yet. We were still hoping Isaac would step aside gracefully without a fuss.'

'But I wouldn't go quietly,' says Isaac. 'I wasn't going to let them take away everything I'd worked so hard for.'

'You worked hard?' Derrick jeers. 'Don't make me laugh. I was the one who put all the graft in to get you your first deal, to make The Ospreys who they were. You just turned up and played and sang and by the end you weren't even doing that.'

'That's not true,' I say. 'He'd got sober in rehab.'

'Do you want to tell her?' he directs at Isaac.

'I wasn't entirely on the wagon,' he says sheepishly. 'I was still drinking, I just managed to hide it better than the drugs.'

I think of all the alcohol Isaac's drunk in my company, him passing out on my sofa, and realise he still hasn't conquered his demons.

'But the band and I were aware and we knew it was only a matter of time before he relapsed into taking drugs again. For Isaac the booze and the smack always went hand in hand, so the boys and I agreed we wanted him gone before that happened. A fresh start.'

'With Jem,' Isaac snipes. 'The most boring man in rock.'

'He was a safe bet,' says Derrick.

'But Jem didn't come on the scene for another two years,' I say. 'Until after the hiatus.'

'That's what he wanted everyone to think,' says Isaac. 'Jem wasn't backstage crew who suddenly got discovered by the others, that was all PR spin. Derrick had been grooming Jem all along to take over when the time was right.'

'Is that true? Was Jem waiting in the wings all that time?'

To my surprise Derrick nods. 'I wasn't going to let The Ospreys crash and burn because of Isaac. I believed they still had a future without him; it just needed to be handled carefully. Jem had sent me a demo of some solo stuff he'd recorded and as soon as I heard it I knew he'd be a good fit. So he became my plan B. It was just good business, making sure we had options.'

'What about Emily Jenkins? Was she good business too?'

My question hits home and Derrick shifts uncomfortably on the spot. But before he can speak, Isaac leaps in.

'I didn't inject her, I swear,' he says to me. 'What I told you about me going to sleep in Toby's room and waking up in mine not knowing how I'd got there, that was all true. Everything else I told you, about how Toby coped afterwards, that was true too. We went over it a lot when he came to Nepal, so nothing I told you was a lie. It was just his side of the story, not mine.'

That would explain why he seemed such an accomplished liar. Technically he was telling me the truth, only it was Toby's truth.

'I felt so sick that night I pretty much passed out and I know I must've been drugged. How else could they have got me back to my suite?'

'I believe you. I don't think you did it. Because it was you who set Isaac up, wasn't it?' I say to Derrick. 'Isaac wasn't going to leave the band without an almighty legal wrangle but if he got into serious trouble, got arrested even, you'd have grounds to force him out. So you drugged him and put him in the bed with Emily.'

'She wasn't meant to die,' Derrick says weakly.

'What was the plan then?' I ask scathingly. 'Get her jacked up on heroin and send her home to her mum?'

'No. It was just meant to be some pictures of her in bed as though she'd been partying with Isaac and I was going to slip them to the tabloids. The presence of drugs and her age would've finished Isaac off as far as the record company and insurers were concerned. That was all it was meant to be.'

'Did Emily know she was a pawn in your sick game?'

'I was told she was in on it. There was a girl who hung out with the band, who used to do me favours, she said she'd squared it with her—'

'Pippa Mirren,' I state.

'That's the one. She told me Emily was willing to pose in Isaac's bed to make it look as though she'd been taking drugs with him – we didn't know she would end up doing it for real though. Pippa told me afterwards that Emily wanted to know what it was like, as though it would make her closer to Isaac, who she idolised.'

Something doesn't add up.

'If she was that much of a fan, why would she agree to setting him up?'

Derrick snaps and his voice rises. 'For god's sake, I don't know. Pippa arranged it. If I'd known what was going to happen, I'd have stopped it there and then,' he insists. 'We didn't need Emily to take the smack for the pictures to be effective.'

'But she did and she died and that's all on you. Which of you put her in Isaac's bed and helped her inject?' I demand to know. 'Who left her there to overdose? Was she already dead when you put Isaac in the bed with her? Were the rest of the band in on it?' Angry tears fill my eyes as I think about how Emily was nothing more than a commodity to them, a means to an end.

'The boys had nothing to do with it,' Derrick protests.

'He's telling the truth Natalie. I know my friends and no way would they have gone along with anything like that,' says Isaac.

'They might've wanted me out of the band, but they wouldn't have set me up and exploited Emily like that.'

'She was just a kid and you used her,' I shout at Derrick. 'Her mum and dad deserve to know what you did and Isaac deserves to have his name cleared. You let everyone think he caused her death. I'm going to tell the police what you did and then I'm going to tell the world. Everyone will read my story of how you framed Isaac.'

Derrick slowly shakes head. 'No they won't. I'm sorry Natalie, but you won't be writing a word. Your story ends here, tonight.'

Chapter Sixty

My voice catches in my throat. 'What do you mean?'

'Shall I bring the car up the lane now?' Kenny asks.

'No, it's too early still. We need to leave it a few more hours.'

'What do you mean?' I repeat, more forcefully this time.

'I'm sorry Natalie, really I am,' says Derrick. 'But I can't let you tell anyone what you know and I can't let Isaac make the big comeback he wants.'

Isaac flares up. 'You're not going to get away with this. You are not fucking my life over for a second time.' He tries clambering to his feet, unsteady and patently in pain; Kenny pushes him back into the chair with the minimum of effort.

'You framed me,' Isaac shouts at Derrick.

'You gave me no choice,' Derrick hurls back. 'You were out of control, destroying everything I'd worked for.' He is shouting as well now and it is chilling to witness his loss of control when he's usually so composed. 'Without me you'd have been nothing, you fucking waste of space. I took a so-so band with a so-so sound and I turned you into megastars.' He jabs himself hard in the chest with his index finger. 'Me. I did that. Slogging away to get you deals and gigs while you sat on your arse getting drunk and high and taking the fucking piss.'

'You think you made us a success because you got us to sign

on a few dotted lines?' Isaac scoffs. 'We were a success because we were brilliant. Our songs were brilliant. Our fans loved us. Our fans loved *me*.' He raises his bound hands to his mouth and wipes blood from his lips with all eight fingertips. 'You should've had more faith in me. Actually, you should've given me a fucking break. I worked for six years straight with barely a day off. It was barbaric.'

'What, you thought it would be an easy ride at the top?' says Derrick. 'You were one of the biggest bands in the world, but to stay that way you needed to put in the graft.'

Isaac shakes his head. 'We could've been the biggest full stop if you'd given me the time and space to heal.'

Derrick's expression wavers. Isaac suddenly turns to me. 'Do you want to finish our interview?'

'Yes, of course, but it's a bit tricky right now,' I say, raising my hands to show they are tethered together at the wrists. 'I can't exactly take notes.'

'Why don't I give you the background in lieu of doing it properly? If there's time?' he asks Derrick pointedly.

'Knock yourselves out,' says Derrick. 'It makes no odds to me, because whatever you say won't go any further than this room anyway. You won't be making any comeback, Isaac, and Natalie most definitely won't be getting her exclusive by-line.'

Kenny, who has remained almost statue-like throughout the entire confrontation, his expression void of emotion, grunts a smile. My hatred for him boils over.

'You're an animal!' I scream at him.

His smile spreads even wider.

Chapter Sixty-One

'The fact is,' Isaac begins, 'that night in Glasgow I experienced the best high of my life.'

I am stunned. 'So you did relapse like everyone said?'

'No, you've misunderstood me. The high was from performing sober. I wanted the opening night to go well so I didn't drink before the gig and when I got out on stage I realised I couldn't remember the last time I'd stood in front of an audience without being wasted on booze or high on drugs. I was terrified at first, I didn't think I could do it, but once the crowd reacted to the first song, that was it. I was soaring on that stage; the feeling was incredible. I never wanted it to end – and that's when I knew I was in trouble.'

'In what way?' I ask.

'I knew I was at risk from myself. I feared the temptation to keep the high going would overwhelm me and I'd end up scoring drugs and partying all night. I didn't want to undo all the work I'd put in at rehab, so when we got back to the hotel I asked Toby if I could crash in his room. It was one floor down from where the others were partying so I thought I'd be safe.'

'You met Emily in the car going back though, didn't you?' I ask.

'Honestly? I barely remember her. She was in the back with

Derrick and Danny and I sat in the front, with Kenny driving. He was my lead security then and all the way back we talked about how amazing the gig was. I was buzzing.'

For the first time I see a twinge of emotion imprint itself on Kenny's poker face, a fleeting pang of what could either be read as regret or embarrassment. His betrayal of his boss is evidently something he hasn't forgotten about entirely.

'By the time I got to Toby's room I felt terrible, dizzy and nauseous like I was going to pass out. I thought it was from performing sober but I've had a lot of time to think about that night in the past eight years and I remember Kenny giving me a bottle of water to drink on the way back in the car and I think it was laced with something.'

Isaac looks squarely at Kenny, who ducks his face from scrutiny.

'Yeah, I thought as much,' says Isaac bitterly. 'The next thing I remember is coming to in my suite with Emily in my bed next to me. I panicked and called reception to ask for an ambulance. Then I called these two.' He nods at Derrick and Kenny. 'They checked Emily and said she was definitely dead. I was so naive. I thought they were helping me, but instead they made sure I incriminated myself. Derrick took charge, saying we had to make it look like an accident or I'd be in trouble because she was in my room and he told me to see if I could pull the needle out of her arm. I couldn't bring myself to do it and he got annoyed with me. It was only afterwards I remembered Kenny was wearing gloves when he came into the room. They already knew Emily was there and they were being careful. So even though my fingerprints weren't found on the syringe, no one else's were either, so it made it easier for the police to blame me because it was my room and she was in my bed.'

I glance over at Derrick and his expression is blank.

'Why did you skip bail?' I want to know. 'The lack of

fingerprints could have worked in your favour, not to mention Toby's testimony that you had gone to his room. You could've mounted a defence.'

'Oh I wanted to, I intended to. But he stuck the boot in,' says Isaac bitterly, jerking his head towards Derrick. 'He told everyone I was the last person to be seen with Emily and that he and Kenny had watched us go into my room together and within twenty-four hours I was the most hated man in Britain. Derrick kept assuring me it would blow over, but I knew it wouldn't.' His voice quivers. 'I don't know if I'd have gone through with drowning myself, but I hated myself so much that I couldn't see any other way out. It was Toby who talked me round and suggested I ask Bibek for help.'

Isaac describes how he secretly met up with Bibek in London and over the next couple of days they hatched the plan that saw the two of them drive to the port of Hull – Isaac laid across the back seat under a blanket – where he was smuggled onto a fishing boat that took him across the Channel to Rotterdam, at a cost of tens of thousands of pounds in cash in exchange for no questions asked.

'You never went anywhere near Devon?' I exclaim.

'No. Toby took my belongings and left them on the beach. He took care of setting all that up.'

'Why wasn't Bibek questioned by the police at the time if he was a known associate of yours?'

'He wasn't known, certainly not to anyone to do with the band. I really cherished the friendship I had with him because it was something I had just for me, that had nothing to do with The Ospreys. Only Toby knew I'd been hanging out with Bibek at his house, but even he had never met him.'

'Wasn't Bibek's number on your phone?' I ask.

Isaac winces. 'I was a rock star. Do you know how many

phones I had? Multiple. One for band stuff, one for family and friends, one for my dealers, one for girlfriends.'

'OK, so you got to Rotterdam, then what?' I ask.

'I gave Bibek the money to buy a cheap transit van and we drove across country to Slovakia and from there caught a flight to Nepal. I had a fake passport by then, arranged in Rotterdam, so it was easier than you think to cross the borders.'

'You were the most famous rock star in the world on the run – how the hell were you not spotted?'

'I took my lenses out and wore a long dark wig and a fake moustache.' Isaac chuckled. 'I looked like a member of Deep Purple circa 1972.'

'Why stage the suicide though? Why not disappear to let the dust settle but give yourself an out to return?'

'Two things, I suppose, ego being one of them.'

'Meaning?'

'I was Isaac Naylor, one of the biggest stars on the planet. If I was bowing out, I wanted to have an ending that would ensure my place in the history books.' He grimaces. 'God I was an arrogant prick back then even when I was sober.'

'You said there were two things. What was the second?'

'I was scared. I didn't want to go to prison for a crime I didn't commit. I felt terrible – I still feel terrible – that Emily's parents must've suffered so much more because of my running away. But when I got to Nepal, it was easier to pretend that I was someone else and that Emily's death had nothing to do with me. And I *was* someone else – Jack, who worked part-time in a bar and taught local kids how to play guitar.' He stares at me beseechingly. 'You have no idea what it was like to be able to walk down the street again and not have everyone stare at me, to be able to go into a shop without being mobbed. It was the kind of freedom I'd be dreaming of for years.'

'You should've stayed and put things right for Emily's parents' sake,' I say quietly.

'I didn't know how to undo the damage.'

The room falls silent for a moment. Then Kenny pipes up. 'Is it time yet?'

'No,' Derrick snaps at him. 'It needs to be later.'

'What does?' I ask.

Derrick wavers for a moment then squares his shoulders. 'I meant what I said. I can't have you writing about this or Isaac reclaiming the spotlight. That's why I wrote the blind item in the first place, to flush him out and put a stop to it.'

'*You* posted it?' I gasp.

He nods grimly. 'It was a stupid, kneejerk reaction to hearing from a producer mate of mine about this songwriter who was making a name for themselves, but no one knew who it was. Straight away I knew. Call it instinct, call it whatever, but I never thought Isaac was dead. I'd always suspected it was a set-up. So I put the blind item up thinking it might scare him back into hiding but then Bronwyn rang me after you sent her the screen-grab and I panicked and had it taken down. I should've known better than to write it, because all it did was get you poking your nose in.'

I sit back, my mind whirring as I replay everything that's happened since I read that bloody gossip. Then a thought occurs. 'At the awards, the note that was delivered to my table for Bronwyn, it wasn't for me, was it? She wrote that to you. I thought it was weird, her doing that.'

'She was worried about the legal letter that was sent to the studio after you stuck your nose in and wanted my advice, so she had the note slipped to my table, so I'd meet her outside the venue. That's when I realised I'd been such a fool in posting the blind item and that I had to stop you following it up. So I re-used the note.'

I feel sick to my stomach. Emily wasn't the only pawn in his sick scheme; Bronwyn was another.

'But what I don't get,' I say, trying to ignore the bile burning my gullet, 'is why Isaac's return would be such a problem for you. He still couldn't prove that he didn't hurt Emily and when people found out he'd faked his suicide, no amount of good songs were going to sway public opinion in his favour. His comeback wasn't assured.'

'I couldn't be sure he didn't have proof, though. For all I knew that's why he was resurfacing now, because he had evidence to show he was wrongly implicated.' Derrick glances towards the window, where the sunshine of earlier has been replaced by nightfall's inky sky. 'It's academic now anyway. As soon as it's dark enough we're going back to the beach where Isaac didn't die the first time. This time, though, there will be two unfortunate souls going into the sea never to be seen again: the mystery songwriter and the journalist he had to silence to keep his secret safe.'

Chapter Sixty-Two

SUNDAY, 30TH

We are made to wait in silence and I am overwhelmed with despair. Two questions loop continuously through my mind: will drowning hurt and how will Daniel react to my death? The thought of both makes me weep copiously and Isaac tries to comfort me by pressing his arm against mine as the pair of us sit on the floor again with our backs to the kitchen cupboards, where we have been unceremoniously made to stay as the minutes tick by.

I have no idea of the exact time though, other than it's past midnight. Kenny's napping in one of the armchairs while Derrick is outside having another cigarette. I think of Daniel tucked up in bed and begin to weep again. Isaac whispers that it's going to be OK, he won't let anything bad happen.

'How are you going to do that?' I whisper back. 'You're as tied up as I am.'

'I'll think of something.' He pauses. 'I'm sorry for not being honest with you.'

I could vent at him, but what's the point? 'It wouldn't have made a difference if you had,' I say. 'We'd have just ended up here sooner, that's all. Derrick was never going to let you make

313

a comeback. There is something I want to ask you though.'

'Go on.'

'How did you damage your finger to make it look like Toby's?'

'I seared it off on a hot plate. Never known hurt like it.'

That makes me wince, and also reminds me of the fate we're facing. 'Do you think drowning hurts?'

'I won't let it get that far,' he hisses fiercely. 'You have to trust me.'

I want to, but I don't know if I can.

'They're going to have to untie us before we go into the sea, otherwise the police will be able to tell we didn't do it willingly,' he adds in a hushed voice. 'If our bodies are found tied up there will be a murder investigation and it won't take long for the trail to lead right back to Derrick's door.'

I hope that's true. I can see it now, Derrick standing in front of the media pretending to be sad about our deaths and spinning lie after lie to make himself look good.

'It's our chance to escape,' says Isaac.

'What about Kenny? The man's a monster.'

'Leave him to me,' says Isaac, and I want to laugh despite my distress, because with the best will in the world an overweight, out-of-shape former rock star with an already bashed-in face is going to be no match for a 6 foot 6 inch muscle-packed knucklehead like Kenny.

'If we do end up in the water,' he adds, 'don't struggle to swim. The tide will be too strong and you'll end up exhausting yourself. Just lie on your back with your arms out and float until help comes.'

I stare at him with naked scepticism.

'I read it somewhere,' he whispers.

'I don't want to die,' I sob.

'It's not going to come to that,' Isaac repeats, and presses his arm against mine as I cry. Then, a few minutes later, as my eyes begin to dry, I ask him what happened after Toby died in Nepal.

'What happened to his body? I'm surprised his death didn't make the news here,' I add, my voice hushed again.

'It wouldn't have done. He's buried in Nepal under a different name.'

'What name?'

'Jack Minton, the name I used while I was living there.'

'Is that when you switched identities and started being Toby? How did you convince the authorities he was you and vice versa?'

'I didn't have to. The crash took care of that. He didn't resemble much of anything after falling into the ravine,' says Isaac wretchedly.

'I'm so sorry. That must've been awful.'

'It was. But his death did mean I could come home, and I think Toby would've liked that. We talked about it a lot, me returning one day.'

'Why not keep your house in Jarrow so you had somewhere to return to, though? Why sell it?'

'I wasn't lying when I said Toby had frittered my money away. He would get involved in people's hair-brained business schemes and in the process lost millions. He always was a soft touch. That's partly why I decided to start selling my songs – I needed the money.'

'Do you really want to be famous again?'

He shakes his head emphatically. 'God, no. I don't want to be Isaac as I was. My years living anonymously in Nepal have confirmed that. But I love music and I still want to write and obviously I want to clear my name.'

There's a snort from the armchair as Kenny shifts position. I lower my voice even further.

'I know you're still drinking because I've seen you. What about drugs?'

Isaac looks shamefaced. 'No drugs, I swear. The whole time I was in Nepal I didn't drink a drop either. Then I came back to England and the stress of being back meant I couldn't help myself—'

He abruptly stops as Derrick returns; he ignores us and goes across to shake Kenny awake.

'It's time,' he says.

Rubbing sleep from his eyes, Kenny comes over and hauls us to our feet, lifting me with the same ease of a child picking up a teddy bear. Once again I despair at how we're going to survive this.

We haven't got a hope in hell.

Chapter Sixty-Three

The drive to the beach takes less than twenty minutes from the cottage in the blacked-out SUV Derrick and Kenny travelled to Devon in. I don't know what time it is, but my tiredness suggests somewhere in the early hours. We don't see another soul on the way, on foot or in a vehicle.

Isaac and I have been seated together on the back seat like a pair of truculent siblings, our hands behind our backs again and our ankles re-tethered after the binds were removed to allow us to walk outside to the car. Kenny used guy rope instead of cable ties to re-tether our legs once we were on the back seat – I realised with horror that Isaac was right and the rope will be easier to remove once we're on the beach and about to go into the sea.

He and Derrick have assumed the role of grown-ups in this dysfunctional outing, occupying the front seats, with him in the driver's seat. None of us speak but Derrick whistles a tune under his breath the entire way that I recognise as an Ospreys' hit. I want to scream at him to shut up but I don't want to aggravate him, or Kenny, any more than I can help. I want to survive this – I need to, for Daniel – and if that means playing the dutiful victim for now, that's what I'm prepared to do.

Isaac has other ideas though. He's pushed himself against the rear left door, directly behind Derrick, and I can tell he's trying to loosen his wrist restraints. I shake my head as a caution to stop, fearful of what might happen if he's caught, but Isaac just grins and sits back in his seat. My mouth drops open. Has he done it? Are his hands free? Hope zips through me.

The road takes a bumpy turn on the approach up to the cliff-top car park. It's no surprise to see that we are the only ones here at this ungodly hour, exactly how Derrick planned it. The car at a standstill, Kenny reaches into the rear foot-wells and loosens our ankle binds again. The cramped space and the lack of light makes it awkward for him so I take advantage by forcing my feet as far apart as I can to make the binds as loose as possible and when he yanks me from the vehicle and orders me to line up with Isaac I don't need to look down to know that my binds are pretty much slipping off my feet. If I run they'll fall off completely, but neither Kenny nor Derrick has noticed in the darkness. For the second time in a few minutes hope zips through me.

Kenny gets another length of guy rope from the boot of the car and I realise he means to string the two of us together for our walk down to the beach, then presumably release us one by one for our fatal walk into the waves. I frantically catch Isaac's eye: it's now or never. He returns the tiniest nod of acknowledgement to me.

Derrick leans against the bonnet of the SUV to watch the proceedings, his gaze intent and his frame silhouetted in the light glowing from the illuminated headlamps, another cigarette clamped between his lips. Kenny advances towards us with the rope and I say a silent prayer, knowing that should he tie me up first it will be far harder for us to escape. When he makes a beeline for Isaac, I sag with relief.

The punch comes from nowhere. With a bellow of rage, Isaac aims his freed fist squarely between Kenny's eyes. The impact of bone against bone makes a sickening crunch and as a stunned Kenny falls backwards I am propelled into action, wriggling my feet free of my ankle binds and aiming a kick at Kenny's groin. Kenny groans and grabs the front of my dress, and I scream, but Isaac rears up again and in his hands is a mug-sized rock he must've found on the floor. He swings his arm and catches Kenny on the temple and he crumples to the ground like a paper doll.

'Run Natalie!'

But I'm too late. Derrick is pelting towards us brandishing a tyre iron he's taken from the boot of the SUV. He slams it across the back of Isaac's shoulders, sending him flying face forward into the ground. I try to run, but Derrick swings the tyre iron at my face, missing it by millimetres.

'Don't!' I yell at him. I am rooted to the spot now, too scared to move. Isaac is trying to get up, but is in too much pain and collapses on his front again.

Derrick keeps the tyre iron raised, panting hard.

'Don't do this,' I plead with him. 'We can work something out. I won't write a word, I promise.' I'm sobbing now, the only noise louder being the crashing waves on the beach below. Yet Derrick is unmoved by my distress. If anything, it seems to embolden him.

'It's too late, Natalie. There's no going back.' He glances down at Isaac, injured and unable to move, and at Kenny, who is no use to him in his current unconscious state, blood trickling from his nostrils, a sign that Isaac's rock might have done him some serious damage. 'Looks like it's down to me then,' he says.

Brandishing the tyre iron, he grabs me by the upper arm, fingers digging in so hard that I cry out in pain. Then he starts to pull me away from the others in the direction of the cliff top. I try to resist and yank myself free, but he's too strong and my wrists are still tied and so I slip and slide across the car park and then we're going down the steep path to the beach and there's nothing I can do to stop him.

Chapter Sixty-Four

I've never liked swimming in the sea. Even the slightest tang of salt water on my lips makes me gag. Such was my loathing of it as a child that on holiday I would never venture further than the shallows, primed to run back up the beach the moment I feared the sea was getting too rough and might splash me. As an adult I never willingly go near it.

This I am reminded of as Derrick shoves me forward into the next breaking wave and it hits me full in the face. I retch as my mouth is doused and water reaches my throat. Coughing furiously to expel it, I battle between wanting to keep my lips tightly sealed and knowing I have to keep sucking down deep breaths for as long as I can, for as long as I remain above the surface.

The waves are at my waist now and the further we've waded from the shoreline the more urgent they've become. The rising current pulls at the folds of my dress while the trainers Derrick forbade me to discard on the beach now encase my feet like cement. Every step forward is a physical strain but he doesn't care – he is impatient and testy, pushing and shoving me onwards until dry land is far beyond my reach.

We shuffle onwards until the water laps my shoulders. It's here he finally unties my wrists. I beg him to let me go back, to think about what he's doing, but he's much taller than me so he's not out of his depth yet, and because of that he wants to keep going. I'm shivering with terror as much as from cold and I'm trying desperately not to cry, knowing I need to pre-serve every ounce of energy I have left if I'm going to survive this. And I need to survive for Daniel. I want to howl when I think about how I've let my son down. I could've stopped all this after what happened at the awards. I should've heeded the warning. But I didn't, I kept going in my pursuit of the story and this is where it has brought me, up to my neck in freezing cold sea off the Devon coast, about to be drowned.

I take another step forward but this time my foot doesn't connect with the bottom. It's a shelf break and the sudden drop knocks the wind out of me as I plunge below the surface. I want to scream that I'm not ready, that I haven't taken a big enough breath, but the water has already closed over my head and then I feel Derrick's hand upon my crown, pushing me deeper still. I claw at his skin, raking it with my nails so sharply I must be drawing blood, but he has a fistful of my hair now and I'm writhing back and forth but it's not getting me anywhere, so I grab his wrist with both hands and pull as hard as I can so he loses his footing and plunges beneath the waves with me and it works, he's loosened his grip.

But I can't fathom which way is up now. The current is pulling me back and forth like I'm a rag doll and I'm trying to kick, I'm trying to get back to the surface, to fresh air . . .

Come on, Natalie, kick.

I break the surface, gasping, but the next wave pummels into me and I'm under again. I keep trying to swim upwards but I'm so tired already and my eyes are stinging and I know I can't scream or call for help because I mustn't let any water in.

Kick, Natalie, kick.

Then he's next to me. I can't see him in the murky darkness

but I know he's there. He's grabbing at me and I'm trying to swim away but he's too strong . . .

OhmygodallIwanttodoisbreathein.

My lungs are burning now and I feel dizzy and sick and my arms are heavy and everything hurts, everything really hurts . . .

Kick Natalie, kick.

I'msinking . . .

lungsburning . . .

thepain . . .

Kick, Natalie, kick.

needair . . .

haveto . . .

breathein . . .

So I do.

Chapter Sixty-Five

The next thing I know someone is pushing down hard on my chest, so hard I think I'm going to throw up. I turn my head to the right and vomit up a stomachful of seawater and the pressure on my chest is relinquished, but now I'm coughing uncontrollably, my lungs burning as I do. Then I gasp, as finally some air reaches them and I'm breathing again.

OhthankgodI'mbreathing.

'Natalie, it's OK, you're safe.'

Toby's face hovers over mine. No, not Toby, I suddenly remember. Isaac. He's Isaac. I found him.

He helps me to sit up. I feel as weak as a kitten and I'm shivering from both the cold and trauma of almost being drowned.

'But you were both injured. Your back, he hit you so hard,' I stutter.

'He did, and I couldn't move at first, but when I realised he was taking you down to the beach and was going ahead with it I couldn't just lie there. I couldn't let him drown you, not because of me.'

'You saved my life,' I say tearfully.

'I couldn't save you both though.'

'Both?'

Isaac shifts position so I can see past him. Derrick is lying flat

324

on his back on the shingle and I don't have to move closer to tell there's no life in his body.

'He drowned. I couldn't save him or Kenny,' Isaac tells me. 'They went too far out.'

'Kenny? I thought he was out for the count.'

'So did I, but he came to and followed me down to the shore. He went in after Derrick but got into difficulty himself.'

'He's dead as well?'

'He must be. I've been back in a few times after pulling Derrick's body out but I can't see him.'

Isaac looks distressed but I cannot bring myself to feel sad for a man who systematically terrorised me. The loss of Kenny is no loss at all.

'I didn't want Derrick to die,' says Isaac, crying now. 'Even after what he did to me.'

'It's his fault he drowned, not yours. Not mine. He did this,' I say, and I pull him into a hug.

A noise above the beach, at the cliff-top edge, makes us look up. I can hear voices and the crackle of radio transmissions and then, in the beams thrown from their torches, the outline of uniforms, of shiny buttons and epaulets.

'Who called the police?' I croak.

'Kenny did, when he realised Derrick had gone under. He called them and then waded in to get him.'

Help is coming. I give way to tears then, the enormity of what just happened finally hitting me.

But rather than comfort me, Isaac grabs me by the shoulders. He looks terrified. 'What am I going to do? They're never going to believe this was an accident. I can't prove what Derrick did to me in Glasgow. They're going to think I'm a liar and arrest me again.'

The air around us is filling with the sound of boots crunching against pebbles as the officers come further down the beach.

Soon we'll be separated to give our statements about what happened here and what led up to it.

'I might have something that proves it,' I say, thinking back to the voice recorder I left at the cottage, and I pray it's not garbled from being stuck down the side of the cushion.

'You'll help me?' he asks.

'I'm going to try,' I reply hurriedly, 'but I have one condition.'

'What's that?'

'You promise to help me too.'

Chapter Sixty-Six

NME.COM

BREAKING NEWS: F*&!"@* HELL, ISAAC NAYLOR IS ALIVE!

By Lizzie Hendricks

UPLOADED 10:33 AM MONDAY, 1 JULY

In what surely ranks as the mother of all comebacks, police in Devon have this morning confirmed Isaac Naylor has been found alive. The 37-year-old former lead singer of The Ospreys is currently being treated in a Plymouth hospital for a head injury after an incident on the same stretch of beach where he was presumed to have committed suicide in 2012. It's understood that a woman, named on Twitter as music journalist Natalie Glass, is also in hospital and is being treated for shock and the effects of water inhalation. A second man apparently drowned in the incident while a third is missing. Police say they won't be releasing any further details until next of kin have been informed.

To say the news is a shock is the understatement of the century. While there has been plenty of conspiracy theorising over the years that Naylor might have staged his suicide to cover his tracks, there has never been any concrete evidence of him doing so. At the time of his 'death', he was being investigated by police in Scotland for his involvement in the death of 17-year-old Emily Jenkins, whose body was found in Naylor's hotel suite after she'd overdosed on heroin. Suspicion fell upon Naylor because he was the last person to be seen with her, entering his room together, and because his prolific drug use made him the obvious candidate to administer the injection that killed her.

Needless to say, the police confirmation that Naylor is inexplicably and astoundingly alive has prompted an outpouring of shock and delight from Ospreys' fans, who are taking to social media in their millions to celebrate and debate Naylor's return, with #TheSecondComing trending alongside #Isaacisalive and #Wherewashehiding.

Sherry Caputo, The Ospreys' spokesperson, released a brief statement this morning saying the band were shocked beyond belief by the news and needed more information before they could comment further, adding that there were lots of questions that needed answering in the meantime.

Heather and Richard Jenkins, parents of Emily, have also said they won't be making a comment at this time. As the law stands, Naylor, whose own parents passed away when he was younger and who was 'survived' by his brother Toby, could be re-arrested over their daughter's death.

So far there's no word on where Naylor's been all this time, how he's managed to stay hidden or why he ended up back on the same beach – but we predict it's going to be one hell of a story. We'll update as soon as we have more details.

Chapter Sixty-Seven

FOUR MONTHS LATER

Another cottage in a remote destination, another precarious approach up a narrow road crowded by overhanging hedge-rows. This time, however, Isaac and I are travelling up the lane together in a different hire car, me behind the wheel and him in the passenger seat. The radio is on low but neither of us is listening to it. Instead we are talking about what is waiting for us at our journey's end. Both of us are riddled with nerves.

It has taken many phone calls and some delicate negotiation to get here. The request came out of the blue and was forward-ed to me first, the belief being that I was the right person to facilitate it. Isaac took some persuading however, knowing what emotions it might throw up and also because he has struggled enormously since his return to the spotlight. There have been times in the past few months when I feared he might be having a breakdown. It's of little surprise: he's re-emerged in an era where everyone with a keyboard or a Smartphone has an opin-ion and for every Ospreys' fan who tweets how overjoyed they are to discover he's not dead after all, there is a critic or a troll who thinks what he did in faking his own suicide was the height of immorality and he should be punished in a court of law.

That, though, is up to the police. Their investigation into Isaac's flit to Nepal is ongoing and while there is talk of him being charged with fraud, failing to surrender to bail and falsely obtaining a passport, Isaac's solicitor seems to think a prosecution may not happen because of the very mitigating circumstances – namely that Isaac has finally been exonerated for Emily Jenkins' death and everyone now knows what Derrick Cordingly did.

It wasn't my voice recorder that proved Isaac's innocence in the end. The chair cushion muffled the conversation to the extent that not even the skills of audio forensic experts could manage to isolate any of the dialogue. Nor was it my testimony, compelling though it was, that swayed the police into releasing a statement confirming Isaac had been set up to take the blame for Emily overdosing. It wasn't even Isaac's version of events that convinced them either.

It was Kenny's.

It transpired Isaac and I weren't the only ones who survived that night on the beach. After he went into the sea to help Derrick, the current swept Kenny almost three hundred metres further along the shore in the pitch black. He told the police he feared he was on the verge of drowning too, but he managed to summon the brute strength to heave himself towards the beach where he crawled onto the shingle and collapsed and was found by the same officers who came to our rescue. Maybe it was the near-death experience that prompted his change of heart, but while recovering in hospital Kenny gave the police chapter and verse about what happened in Glasgow in December 2011. He's maintaining Derrick's line it was Pippa Mirren who recruited Emily into their nefarious plan and that Emily taking the drugs was down to her, and I feel awful for Belinda Mirren that her daughter's name has been dragged into it. Every time I call her she puts the phone down on me.

'I think it's the next turning on the right, then continue for another two miles,' says Isaac, peering closely at the map that's unfolded on his lap. Our destination is so remote that there's no phone signal and we've had to instigate old school methodology to get here. I'm glad I'm driving because I can't tell one end of a map from another.

'How are you feeling?' I ask him.

Isaac grins. 'That's the fifth time you've asked me that.'

'Sorry. I'm just concerned.'

'You're not my mam,' he says, but not unkindly.

He knows I've been worried about what we have planned for today, because when he's nervous he drinks even more than usual and I didn't want him to have a hangover. I feared the enormity of it was going to prompt him to get utterly legless last night, but true to his word he didn't touch a drop during our dinner at the hotel and even asked for the mini bar in his room to be cleared out so he wasn't tempted. He's painfully aware of how important this meeting is and how much work went into making it happen, and he doesn't want to mess it up.

I don't know if Isaac will ever stop drinking but at least since rejoining society he's remained clean of drugs. I'm pretty confident that even if he were to be offered any he'd still turn them down – he associates them now with losing eight years of his life, not to mention the needless death of a young girl at his expense.

'Did you get any more work done on the book last night?' he asks.

It was Neil Caffrey who negotiated the deal for us, as I didn't have a clue where to start. Offers were flying in thick and fast from publishers all over the world for Isaac to write his memoir and the one condition he had was that I be the person to write it. It was what we agreed on the beach as the police approached, when he asked for my help. In return for me telling them everything to clear his name, he would finish the exclusive interview we started, which was serialised in *The Times* over three days. The book deal is the by-product of those articles and the film rights have already been sold to a Hollywood-based production company. Suffice to say, my debts are no longer an issue and I now rent a house round the corner from Spencer's, meaning Daniel has less than a two-minute walk between his two homes. He was a bit bewildered at first by all the attention that came with his mum being involved in the return of the long-lost rock star, but now he revels in it. Isaac and I are spending a lot of time together while writing the book and he and Daniel have become firm friends. I think Daniel secretly hopes Isaac might become my boyfriend, especially now Spencer's got engaged to Jo, but I remind him we're just friends and that's OK.

'I did a bit before I went to bed, but I'm finding it hard writing about Derrick's death.' I cast a sideways glance at him. 'Do you ever have nightmares about that night?'

'I haven't, no. Mine tend to focus on Glasgow and waking up with Emily. Sometimes she's not dead and she's yelling at me for letting her overdose and I wake up properly drenched in sweat. Why, do you?'

'The occasional one.'

That's a lie. I'm having them every night. Only it's not just me in the sea with Derrick, it's Daniel too and I'm trying to save him from drowning as well as saving myself and I can't manage it and I wake up crying. I had hoped writing about what happened might release the trauma of what I went through, but it hasn't so far.

'Have you spoken to Bibek this week?' I say, eager to change the subject. So far, we've been able to keep Bibek's name out of things and he's now safely back living in Nepal. He didn't deserve to be prosecuted for helping a friend in need and Isaac's using the Ospreys' royalties he's now in receipt of once more to help fund Bibek opening his own law firm in Kathmandu.

'No, but Renner called me again last night. He's as bad as you are for checking up on me.'

Isaac's reunion with his band-mates was held privately, without anyone else there, including me. Afterwards Isaac told me there were angry, tearful recriminations for the grief he put them through 'which I took on the chin, because of course they have every right to be furious with me. But once they got that off their chest it was like we'd never been apart. I hadn't realised how much I'd missed them until we were in the same room again.'

There will be no reunion on stage, though. Isaac has no intention of rejoining The Ospreys, however much the band's millions of fans worldwide want it to happen. 'It's Jem's band now,' Isaac told me. 'I don't want to perform again; I'm past that. But I am going to carry on writing songs and Danny and I have even been kicking a few ideas around for some tracks for their new album. I might even produce a couple of them.'

Isaac's talk of becoming a producer made me think of Bronwyn working at The Soundbank. I miss her desperately. Kenny confirmed neither he nor Derrick had anything to do with the mugging that killed her – it was a tragic, opportunistic knife crime for which no one has been arrested yet. Lucy and the boys are coping okay, all things considered. The trust fund Derrick organised for them was his last good deed.

The revelation that Isaac was the mystery songwriter sent shockwaves through the music industry and quite a bit of consternation when it emerged which songs of his artists had claimed as their own. Suffice to say, Derrick's death and the story behind it has been picked over endlessly in the media and within the industry and I think Neil spoke for many when he told me Derrick got what he deserved.

'Slow down,' Isaac suddenly orders me. 'I think it's the next on the left. Sidwell Lane.'

I take the turning and the road disappears from beneath us and in its place a muddy track appears. I'm grateful that our hire car of choice is a Land Rover – in this part of the Highlands, it's requisite. We continue for another thirty metres until the cottage looms into view. It couldn't be more different from the one Isaac rented in Devon, with flint-brick exterior walls and a prettily painted bright blue front door. It's been booked via a holiday lets website under an assumed name. I wonder what the owners would think if they knew exactly who was staying here and why. But they shan't ever find out, because that was the deal that was struck: a secret venue far from prying eyes for a secret meeting. Word won't get out unless both parties decide they're happy for it to.

I bring the car to a stop and turn off the engine. Then I turn to Isaac. 'Ready?'

'No. Yes. I don't know,' he says, and I can hear the panic in his voice.

'They just want to meet you. Nothing bad will happen.'

He nods and we climb out of the car. I take his hand as we walk towards the front door and his palm is sweaty against mine. We're still a few steps away when it swings open and Heather Jenkins appears on the threshold, her husband Richard behind her. Their faces are taut with tension and I can see Heather is trembling. Isaac grips my hand even tighter, a gesture that tells me how scared he is to meet Emily's parents in person for the first time.

But he needn't be, because Heather's expression suddenly cracks and she smiles through the tears now wetting her cheeks.

'We're so glad you're here, Isaac,' she says, her voice breaking. 'What happened was as much a tragedy for you as it was for us. It wasn't your fault Emily died.'

I turn to look at Isaac and see instantly the effect of her words. He's shaking and crying with relief. Emily's parents truly believe his innocence; hearing them say it is all that's mattered to him these past few months.

Heather and Richard step forward to hug him and that's my cue to step back. I'm not going to sit in on their conversation; what's said will be between the three of them. I'm going to wait out here in the car, as agreed.

My work here is done.

Acknowledgements

I started this novel before the first lockdown and finished it during the second, so I really must begin by thanking my partner, Rory, and our daughter, Sophie, for supporting me through the writing process when we were grappling with home schooling and everything else that goes with living through a pandemic. This is one novel I won't forget writing in a hurry, and I couldn't have completed it without their love and understanding.

Equally I owe a debt of gratitude to my editor, Francesca Pathak, and my agent, Jane Gregory, for their regular pep talks and confidence boosting during the times I was struggling to string a sentence together. You both rock! They and the teams at Orion and David Higham Associates have been so supportive and I'm in awe at how they've kept the publishing process running so smoothly when they've all been working remotely. Similarly, I want to thank my fellow crime writers for making me laugh and keeping me sane during the low moments, you are all ace, and Jo Jhanji and Alison Bailey for taking the time and care to give me such excellent feedback on the early drafts. Mum and Dad, thank you for always being there for me, even when you physically couldn't be because of lockdown.

This book mostly draws on my experience as a freelance

journalist but a special shout-out goes to Phillip Bowen for giving me the idea of using Nepal as a setting. His insight into life there was invaluable and really turned the plot on its head. Finally, I want to thank you, my readers, for your enthusiasm for my characters and the worlds they inhabit. I love writing the stories I do and knowing that you love reading them makes it all worthwhile.

Credits

Michelle Davies and Orion Fiction would like to thank everyone at Orion who worked on the publication of *The Death of Me* in the UK.

Editorial
Francesca Pathak
Lucy Frederick

Copy editor
Francine Brody

Proof reader
Laetitia Grant

Audio
Paul Stark
Amber Bates

Contracts
Anne Goddard
Jake Alderson

Design
Debbie Holmes
Joanna Ridley
Nick May

Production
Ruth Sharvell

Editorial Management
Charlie Panayiotou
Jane Hughes

Finance
Jasdip Nandra
Afeera Ahmed
Elizabeth Beaumont
Sue Baker

Marketing

Folayemi Adebayo

Publicity

Alainna Hadjigeorgiou

Rights

Susan Howe
Krystyna Kujawinska
Jessica Purdue
Louise Henderson

Sales

Jen Wilson
Esther Waters
Victoria Laws
Frances Doyle
Georgina Cutler

Operations

Jo Jacobs
Sharon Willis
Lisa Pryde
Lucy Brem

Don't miss Michelle Davies' haunting debut thriller, *Shadow of a Doubt* . . .

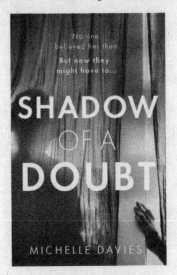

Twenty-six years ago,
my brother was murdered in my family home.
I was sent to a psychiatric unit for killing him.
The truth is, I didn't do it.

The whole world believed eight-year-old Cara killed her younger brother, though she blamed it on a paranormal entity. After two years of treatment in a psychiatric unit for delusional disorder, Cara was shunned by her remaining family.
Now she's being forced to return to the family home for the first time since her brother's death, but what if she's about to re-discover the evil that was lurking inside its walls?

'*Dark, spooky and brilliantly plotted, the perfect read for dark winter nights . . .*'
Harriet Tyce, author of *Blood Orange*